Darynda Jones has won several awards, including a 2009 Golden Hear[illegible]he Paranormal Category for *First Grave on the Right* and the 2012 [illegible] award for Best New Book.

Sh[illegible] in New Mexico with her husband of more than 25 years and tw[illegible]ns, the mighty, mighty Jones boys.

Visit Darynda Jones online:

www.daryndajones.com

www.facebook.com/darynda.jones.official

@Darynda

Praise for Darynda Jones:

'Hil[illegible]us and heart-felt, sexy and surprising, this paranormal has it all . . . [illegible]n absolute must read – I'm already begging for the next one!'
[illegible]. R. Ward, No.1 *New York Times* bestselling author

'Fro[illegible] unique premise to its wonderfully imaginative characters, Jon[illegible] award-winning Charley Davidson mystery series . . . will c[illegible]inue to attract and delight a broad spectrum of readers'
Booklist (starred review)

'Jones perfectly balances humor and suspense . . . will leave readers eager for the next instalment' *Publishers Weekly*

By Darynda Jones

First Grave on the Right
Second Grave on the Left
Third Grave Dead Ahead
Fourth Grave Beneath My Feet
Fifth Grave Past the Light
Sixth Grave on the Edge
Seventh Grave and No Body
Eighth Grave After Dark
The Dirt on Ninth Grave
The Curse of Tenth Grave
Eleventh Grave in Moonlight
The Trouble With Twelfth Grave

For the lovely Caitlin Dareff
because you always make me smile

Acknowledgments

I have a confession to make. I love writing Charley Davidson. I love her style and wit and irreverence. And I know what you may be thinking at this point, "Um, you're the writer. Aren't you complimenting yourself?"

The quick answer? Not so much.

See, when I write Charley, I channel her. I get to be this saucy badass with great hair and a comeback for any situation. I get to live on coffee and sarcasm. I get to catch bad guys and right the wrongs of the world.

When I'm Darynda, I'm doing good if I can string two sentences together without getting tongue-tied. My morning appearance could be better explained if I were a rock star. Or a binge drinker. And I rarely have a witty comeback in any situation, much to my chagrin.

But I have people. I have wonderful, wondrous people.

I have my very own Reyes who goes by the name of Mr. Jones. I have a couple of remarkable Beeps: Jerrdan and Casey. And even second-generation Beeps: Konner and Kodin. Combined, those five irascible males make up the Mighty, Mighty Jones Boys. A.k.a., my heart and soul.

My Cookie is fondly referred to as Netter Pot Pie and I adore her more than air. I also have a Dana who humbles me with her energy and enthusiasm and the fact that she doesn't hate me even though I slept through our last meeting. For three hours. And I have a Jowanna who makes me giggle and sends me the best memes.

One might think those are all the characters I need in my life, but wait! There's more!

There's Quentin and Luther and Crystal and Karen and Lacy and Ashlee and all my beautiful nieces and nephews from whom I draw endless inspiration. There's Nanoo and Dan Dan and Andrea and Robyn and all my Ruby Sisters and SMP siblings and LERA chapter mates. And there's my writerly friends who understand and support and commiserate.

But there are a few people to whom I owe a special gratitude. Some I blatantly stole lines from for this book and some I put through heck because of this book. Remember, according to Alexander Pope, to err is human, to forgive divine.

I'd like to thank, from the bottom of my right ventricle, Patricia Dechant, Trayce Lane, and Theresa Rogers for letting me . . . ahem . . . quote them.

I'd like to send a special shout-out to The Mercenaries: Mega, Moonie, Moji, Sketti, and Sully for not only naming my girls, but letting me pilfer our dinner conversation for the benefit of this book. Thank you, thank you, thank you.

Thank you to the insanely talented Lorelei King for breathing life into Charley's world and fire into our listener's hearts.

And thank you, dear reader, for sticking with Charley and the gang through thick and thin. I am beyond honored to be a part of your life.

But mostly I'd like to thank my incredible agent, Alexandra Machinist, my extraordinary editor, Jennifer Enderlin, and my super-savvy film agent, Josie Freedman. I would not be here without you. Thank you so very, very much.

The Trouble with Twelfth Grave

1

Coffee: A warm, delicious alternative to
hating everyone forever.

—TRUE FACT

Few things in life were more entertaining than haunted houses. The people living in said haunted houses, perhaps. Or the time-honored tradition of watching paint dry because, sadly, most haunted houses were not actually haunted. I sat on a hardwood floor next to a Mrs. Joyce Blomme, a woman who swore her house was inhabited by the dead—her words—and waited with bated breath for a ghost to appear. Egads!

Just kidding.

My breath rarely bated. Being the only grim reaper this side of eternity, I didn't scare easily, especially after getting an inquiry like the one I'd received from Mrs. Blomme. I got a crap ton of the things. People swearing their houses were haunted. Imploring me to cleanse the offending abode of the evil that lurked within. Assuring me I was their only hope.

What can I say? Word gets around.

Mrs. Blomme was everything one would expect a grandmother to be. She had salt-and-pepper hair in rollers, a floral housecoat, ragged slippers with threads poking out around the toes, and reading glasses dangling around her neck. Ink stained her fingers, probably from crosswords, and a pinch of white powder smudged her cheek and the tip of her nose. So, either Mrs. Blomme liked to bake or she was a cokehead. I leaned toward the former.

On any other day, I would have explained the situation more clearly to the elderly woman. Yes, I could see the departed. As the grim reaper, I ferried lost souls—those souls left behind after their initial offer of a one-way trip up—to the other side, when they were ready. Basically, that entailed me standing there while the departed stepped into my light, a light that could be seen by them from anywhere in the world, and crossed over.

So, yes, I could see them. I could also talk to them and arm-wrestle them and style their hair. But seeing the departed and convincing said departed to *go into the light* were two very different skill sets.

Yet there I sat—in the dark because Mrs. Blomme swore the dead were easier to see that way, and well past my bedtime because Mrs. Blomme said they mostly showed up late at night—listening to a fascinating tale of angels and demons. Of heavens and hells. Of gods and monsters!

Mostly because I was doing all the talking.

Mrs. Blomme, poor thing, was scared speechless. In her defense, and to her credit, the house was indeed haunted. But I was too busy soliloquizing the struggles of the past few days of my life to pay that fact much mind.

"And then," I said, raising my voice in preparation for the big finale, "he shoved me against the wall and disappeared into a swirling sea of smoke and lightning."

I moved my hands in a circular motion to demonstrate the aforementioned swirling mass, then turned to Mrs. Blomme to check her reaction. It'd been a hell of a tale.

To my delight, Mrs. Blomme's eyes were saucers. Her mouth hung open and her breaths came in tiny, sharp pants. Unfortunately, her state of absolute terror had little to do with my harrowing tale and more to do with the twiglike boy standing in the doorway, his mouth full of crackers.

We had already met. His name was Charlie, too, only spelled differently, and he liked riding his tricycle and painting the walls with his mother's markers. Her permanent markers, if the walls were any indication. Soap and water could only do so much.

"There!" Mrs. Blomme pointed toward him.

He was adorable, all dark hair and skinny limbs.

Mrs. Blomme didn't agree. She clawed at my arm and shrank in to my side, peering over my shoulder to look at the boy while using my body as a shield. Clearly, if the fecal matter hit the fan, I would be sacrificed.

She whispered into my ear, ever so slowly, enunciating every word. "Do you see him?"

The moonlight shone in his mischievous eyes as he cradled a plastic dinosaur in one arm and a silver gravy boat in the other. No idea. His fists held as many crackers as each could carry, and he had to carefully maneuver his load to stuff another orange square into his mouth. Then he smiled at me with orange-dusted lips.

I smiled back a microsecond before his mother appeared out of nowhere to scoop him up and carry him down the hall, disappearing into the darkness.

Mrs. Blomme squeaked and hid her face. That didn't surprise me. What did surprise me was her reaction—or lack thereof—to the little girl named Charisma sitting cross-legged in front of us, listening as I regaled the horrors of the past week.

Charisma blinked up at me, sipped the last of her juice through a cup with a twirly straw, then asked, "So, he's not your husband anymore?"

She was talking about Reyes. Reyes Alexander Farrow. My husband. Or, well, I hoped he was still my husband.

"I'm not sure," I admitted.

After bringing down a bloodthirsty cult a few days ago, then devouring a malevolent god—'cause apparently that's what I do—I'd succumbed to drowning my sorrows in a bottle of tequila named Jose. Three innocent people lost their lives that day, and there was nothing I could do about it. It was a bitter pill, one I was having a difficult time swallowing, so I'd been contemplating entering a hell dimension to save a handful of other innocent people who were trapped inside. Reyes convinced me to send him instead.

Just another day in the life of Charley Davidson.

That's me, by the way, Charley Davidson. PI. Grim reaper. Screwup extraordinaire. Oh, and let's not forget my newest designation: god. Not *the* God, but *a* deity nonetheless. A title I never imagined would be thrust upon me and one I never wanted.

Then again, so was my husband. A deity. A celestial being with the power to give life. To create worlds. To convince me that his plan was best when it was anything but.

Thus, I sent my one and only husband into a hell dimension via a pendant that housed a glittering stone called god glass. Probably because God, *the* God, made it.

I rested my head on the cool wall at my back and thought about that moment. The doubt that'd been roaring in my head. The doubt I should have paid heed. The doubt I ultimately ignored.

The workings of the god glass were quite simple considering its complex nature. It was, after all, a hell dimension of vast proportions set inside a stone set inside a pendant. Something so fragile that housed something so terrible.

To send someone to his doom, one simply placed a drop of the target's blood on the god glass then said his name.

The pendant, through the machinations of a howling tempest, would reach out and draw the person's soul inside, locking it there for all eternity. But with Reyes, the storm took every molecule of his being, not just his soul. I assumed it was because of his supernatural status, but now I wondered if there'd been more to it. At the time, however, that fact hadn't registered.

Reyes'd had a job. One simple job. He would jump in, get the lay of the land, then jump back out when I called his name. A process that was supposed to be easy according to a six-hundred-year-old rumor. It stated that to retrieve a soul from the god glass, the person who originally sent the soul inside need only reopen the pendant, say the target's name, and the soul would be freed.

Rumor was wrong. I know because that's exactly what I did.

I called. I screamed. I whispered. I begged. And still no husband.

Distraught and disoriented, I came up with a plan. I would go in after him. I would have Cookie, my best friend and confidante, send me inside.

I would have to trick her, of course. She would never willingly send me to hell. But I would leave her a note explaining how to get me back out. In theory, because I'd apparently stumbled upon a flaw in the process. But I figured go big or go home.

Just as I was about to put my plan into action, the storm erupting out of the pendant changed. It became darker. Smoke swirled around me, and heat saturated every pore, rushing over my skin. Electric. Almost painful.

Then the pendant became too hot for me to hold. I dropped it seconds before an earsplitting explosion rocked the apartment. It slammed me against a wall, causing my vision to darken around the edges and my lungs to burn from lack of oxygen. I fought to stay conscious but didn't dare move.

The storm shifted. Smoke, thick and black and alive, pooled around me. I'd looked up, tried to focus, but just as I was able to take in air, a dozen souls desperate for escape rushed through me, into my light and, in turn, heaven.

Their stories flashed before my eyes. The souls'. Innocent. Condemned for centuries by a madman.

A priest who'd somehow come into the possession of the pendant was using it for evil. He'd sent soul after soul inside. A widow who'd spurned his advances. A man who'd refused to sign over part of his land to the church. A young boy who'd seen the priest in a compromising position. And on and on. More than a dozen lives destroyed by one man.

The priest had been locked inside as well by a group of monks who took him to task for his evil deeds, but I didn't feel him cross. Then again, he would've gone to hell. This dimension's hell. Perhaps he already had.

After the souls crossed through me, all from the same time period, the 1400s, I waited. Three more beings were inside the god glass. A demon assassin named Kuur. A malevolent deity named Mae'eldeesahn. And my husband.

I would never forget the vision before me as I waited. The smoke had filled the room and churned like a supercell lit by occasional flashes of lightning.

And then Reyes walked out of it, the billowing smoke falling from his wide shoulders and settling at his feet.

Elation shot through me as I scrambled to my feet and started toward him. But I stopped short almost immediately. Something was wrong. The man before me was not my husband. Not entirely.

Smoke and lightning curled around him. It caressed him like a lover. Obeyed him like a slave. If he shifted, it shifted. If he breathed, it breathed. It flowed and ebbed at his will, the lightning flitting over his skin.

He wasn't in the storm. He was the storm.

I stood astounded as he walked toward me, taking five ground-eating steps.

I stumbled back, then caught myself before whispering his name. "Reyes?"

He narrowed his eyes as though he didn't recognize me.

I reached up to touch his face. It was the wrong thing to do.

He shoved me against the wall and held me there as his gaze ran down the length of my body. His hand curled around my throat, then my jaw, his fingers cruel.

I wrapped my hands around his and pushed, but he didn't budge. If anything, he squeezed tighter, so I relaxed. Or tried to.

When he spoke, his voice was low and husky and resolved. "Elle-Ryn-Ahleethia."

That was my celestial name. My godly one. Why would he use it here? Now?

He seemed surprised to find me there. Astonished. Then he gave me another once-over. His expression filled with a disturbing mix of lust and contempt.

It sparked a memory. Kuur, an evil supernatural assassin I'd banished into the very same hell dimension, told me that when Reyes had been a deity himself, he'd had only contempt for humans. The same humans his godly Brother—yes, *that* godly Brother—loved so much.

And I was human. At least a part of me was.

I studied Reyes as he studied me, wondering what came out of the god glass. It may have looked like my husband. It may have smelled like him and felt like him and sounded like him, but the sentient being standing in a pool of billowing black smoke in front of me was not the man I married.

Was I meeting the god Rey'azikeen at last?

And, more important, had I just unleashed hell on earth?

"Will he ever be your husband again?" Charisma asked, snapping me back to the present.

I released the air from my lungs slowly. "I wish I knew."

She sucked on the straw again, siphoning every last drop.

I did the same, upending my coffee cup and letting the last precious molecules slide onto my tongue.

Then I returned to her. "He's very powerful, and I don't know what that hell dimension did to him. How much of him is still my husband

and how much is 'angry god guy.' I mean, he could destroy the world if he put his mind to it. That would suck."

The girl's gaze slid past me, her mind clearly pondering everything I'd just told her. Good and evil. Dark and light. It was a lot to take in.

"I'm not allowed to say *hell*."

Or not.

"That's probably best. Stay as far away from that place as you can. Don't even think about it."

"Or *damn*."

A part of me did wonder if I should be telling such a young child about hell dimensions and demons and world-destroying gods. At least I didn't tell her about the little girl who was killed by one such god just the other day. Surely my omitting that part of the story would warrant a checkmark in the "pro" column.

"Or *butt crack*."

"I think I hear something," Mrs. Blomme said.

"So, anyway," I continued, "that was three days ago, and I haven't seen my husband since."

"He just disappeared?"

"Literally."

And he had. He'd kept one powerful hand locked around my throat and jaw, his other hand braced on the wall behind me, and the fire that perpetually consumed him licked over his skin when he stepped closer. When he pressed into me.

I lowered a hand to his rib cage, encouraging him to close the distance between us. Praying he'd remember.

"Reyes?" I whispered, testing.

Then he did close the distance. He bent his head, buried his face in my hair, and brushed his sensual mouth across my ear. When he spoke, his voice was thick and breathy. "Reyes has left the building," he said, a microsecond before shoving off me and vanishing into a sea of roiling smoke and crackling lightning.

And he was gone. Just like that.

I'd stood there for what seemed like hours until the sun came up, watching the smoke slowly clear from my apartment. And for the first time in a long time, I had absolutely no idea what to do. Until I did. Until I'd been given a new case.

Before receiving the summons from the frazzled Mrs. Blomme, I'd been hunting.

Charisma jumped to her feet. "I have to pee."

"Okay, have fun," I said to her back as she rushed out of the room.

I still wondered why Mrs. Blomme couldn't see her. Not for long. Maybe, like, seven seconds. I had too many other things on my plate to wonder overly long, but it did tickle the back of my brain.

"I told you," Mrs. Blomme said. She was still using my shoulder as a protective shield. "My house is haunted. You saw them, right? The woman and the boy?"

"I did. But, Mrs. Blomme—"

Before I could continue with the bad news, my phone dinged. I dug it out of my back pocket. My uncle Bob, a detective for the Albuquerque Police Department, had texted me about a case we were working together. I sometimes consulted for APD, mostly because my uncle knew what I could do, and solving cases was a thousand times easier when the murdered victim could tell the police whodunit. This case, however, was far more disturbing than I'd led my uncle to believe.

Two bodies had been found mutilated and burned. But mutilated in a very unusual way and scorched in random spots. The burns didn't kill them. Internal damage and blood loss from the mutilations did them in. It was as though they'd been beaten and clawed to death, but the ME said the attacks were not from an animal. He said they were human.

Or, I had to wonder in the back of my mind, perhaps they were made by a god inhabiting a human body. An angry god made of lightning and fire and all things combustible. His temper, for example.

A pang of anxiety caused my stomach to clench and my cheeks to warm.

Uncle Bob's text asked simply, "Any luck?"

I texted back. "Not yet."

It would not be the answer he wanted, but it was the only one I had to give. I'd been using all my resources on the case, and no one, dead or alive, knew anything about the murders.

I turned back to Mrs. Blomme. One of her curlers had worked loose and hung lackadaisically over an ear. "Mrs. Blomme," I said, softening my voice.

She glanced up at me from behind my shoulder.

"I'm so sorry to tell you this, but you're right. Your house is haunted."

She swallowed hard and nodded, taking the news well.

"But, hon, it's haunted by you."

Straightening a little, she leveled a curious stare on me. "I don't understand."

"You died thirty-eight years ago."

She blinked, and I gave her a moment before continuing. To absorb. To process.

After another couple of minutes where she stared at the floor, trying to remember, I said, "It took me a while to find your death certificate. Your husband found you unresponsive on the floor in your kitchen. Massive stroke. He was devastated. He died a year later, almost to the day."

"No. That's not right. I live here."

"You did, yes. I'm sorry."

She leaned back against the wall, sorrow consuming her.

My chest squeezed tight. I took her hand into mine. "But the mother and son you've been seeing?"

Without looking up, she nodded.

"That's your granddaughter and your great-grandson. See?" I pointed to a wall where Mrs. Blomme's picture hung, a faded color photo of her and her husband.

She stood slowly and walked to the massive mantel that displayed generations of Blommes and, now, Newells. They'd kept the house in the family. Updated it over the years. And allowed one branch of the Blommes' children's children to grow up here.

She turned back to me, her eyes wet with emotion. "I had no idea."

"I know." I stood and walked to her. "It happens more often than you think."

A soft laugh accompanied a melancholy smile.

"You can cross through me. I'm sure you have tons of family waiting for you, including your husband."

"He didn't remarry, did he? He was always threatening to marry Sally Danforth if I died first. He knew I detested that woman. She stole my pickle recipe and won a blue ribbon at the state fair with it."

"She didn't," I whispered, scandalized.

"I wouldn't lie about pickles, Miss Davidson. Serious business, that."

I grinned. "No, he didn't marry anyone else, Mrs. Blomme. He died miserable and alone."

"Oh, well, good. He deserved it. Man was horrible." She turned when emotion slipped through her lashes and slid down a weathered cheek.

"I'm sure he was wretched."

As her reality sank in, her physical state became an issue. She smoothed her housecoat and patted the curlers in her hair.

"Good heavens, I can't go nowhere looking like this."

"What do you mean? You're perfect."

"Nonsense," she said, smoothing her housecoat once more. But something captured her attention, and her gaze flitted back to the door leading to the hall.

I turned to see that Charlie was back. Arms full. Fists restocked.

Leaning over, I whispered in Mrs. Blomme's ear. "That's Charlie Newell, your great-grandson."

A hand flew to her mouth as a new moisture threatened to push past her lashes to follow the first. "My goodness, isn't he beautiful."

"He's gorgeous. And you have a great-granddaughter here, too. Charisma."

Mrs. Blomme found a chair and sank into it, and I knew I'd lost her. No way would she leave these children to their own devices. They needed order and discipline. But mostly they needed spoiling.

"Can I stay just a little while longer? Can I watch over them?"

I knelt beside her. "Of course you can."

I said my thanks to Mrs. Newell, a single mom with two inquisitive children on her hands.

"Did you, um, make contact?"

She was gracious enough to let me in to do my thing, an openness I found surprising, and I couldn't help but wonder if she wasn't a tad sensitive herself.

"I did. And you were right. It's your grandmother Blomme."

She smiled to herself in thought, wiping her hands absently on a dish towel.

"I just have one question," I continued. I gestured toward the hall. "What's with the gravy boat?"

She giggled and shrugged. "Some kids have security blankets; some kids have gravy boats."

I laughed with her. "That needs to be a T-shirt."

I still couldn't help but wonder why Mrs. Blomme could see her granddaughter and great-grandson but not her great-granddaughter.

Ah, well. A mystery for another day.

After explaining to Mrs. Newell that her grandmother was going to be hanging out for a while, a fact she took with no small amount of enthusiasm, I left. I had much to do, including solve a couple of murders and hunt down a recalcitrant deity. But first, I had a skip tracer to harass.

2

I don't want to look pretty.
I want to look otherworldly and vaguely threatening.
—MEME

Half the time I sat at the Newells' house, my stomach growled. I hadn't slept, not deeply, in three days, and I'd hardly eaten as well. Anxiety kept my stomach full.

But I had a long night ahead of me. I needed sustenance, so I drove through Macho Taco, ordered three taquitos with extra salsa and a Mexican latte with extra foam, because anything worth having was worth having extra, and started for an irascible skip tracer's house on the other side of town. Luckily, at this hour on a weeknight, the town was nearly deserted.

I headed east on Menaul and had barely managed a bite when I picked up a hitchhiker. A departed thirteen-year-old gangbanger named Angel, also irascible. Though I hadn't met him until a decade after his death, Angel and I had become fast friends. And now he was my top—not to mention only—investigator. He popped into the passenger's seat of Misery, my cherry-red Jeep Wrangler, in all his gangbanger brilliance. Red bandana low over his brows. Dirty A-line T-shirt. Gaping chest wound.

Angel popping in was not unusual. Angel pretty much popped in and out as he pleased, but this pop seemed direr than most.

The moment he appeared, he turned to look out the window, his shoulders hunched, his mouth oddly silent. Like, seriously, it emitted no sound whatsoever. He was only quiet when he was upset, hiding something, or secretly checking out a hot girl on the horizon. Since there were no hot girls around . . .

I knew this would take my full attention, so I pulled into the parking lot of a strip mall, one replete with a nail salon, a gym, a bizcochito bakery—where has that been all my life?—another gym, a burger joint, and a psychic, the only open shop on the strip. She must've known we'd pull in there. Eerie.

"Okay," I said between bites. "What has your panties in a twist?"

He didn't turn to look at me. He was upset. When he hid things, he tended to look me right in the eye, as though that would throw me off the scent. In his defense, he'd died young.

"I can't find him." Disappointment edged his voice.

"Angel, it's not your fault. I can't find him, either, hence my siccing you on his trail."

"You don't understand." He shifted in the seat but continued his vigil. "I can feel him, I just can't find him."

"What do you feel?" I asked, dread inching up my spine. If Angel was feeling what I'd been feeling for the past three days, we could all be in a world of hurt. All as in the entire human race.

"Anger," he said softly.

Yep. We were screwed. But none of this was Angel's fault. If anyone was at fault, it was my boneheaded husband. Cause I damned sure wasn't taking the blame.

He turned to me at last, his brown eyes shimmering in the low light, his peach fuzz darker because of it. "The question is, *mija*, what the hell are you going to do with him when you do find him?"

"You're right," I said between crunches. "That is the question."

"If you have a plan, now would be a good time to implement it."

I swallowed the salsa-drenched taquito, then gaped at him. "Dude, did you just use the word *implement*? In a sentence? Correctly?"

"For real?"

"That's a mighty big word there, buddy."

"*Ay, dios mio*." He looked back out the window, but I felt the weight on his shoulders lift, if only a little. "Are you gonna tell me what this is about?"

"Yes. Just, not yet."

"When?"

"I'm going to talk to Garrett. He'll know what to do. I'll summon you the minute I know something."

He nodded, seeming to accept my conditions. Without argument or endless negotiations involving me in a state of undress. Something was definitely off.

"Sweetheart, what's up?"

He shrugged and looked out the window again.

I rested a hand on his cool one, and without turning his gaze toward me, he turned up his palm and threaded his fingers into mine. That act, that one, simple gesture, terrified me. I knew Reyes could be a problem, what happened could change everything, but for it to affect Angel to such a degree was unexpected.

I set my jaw, preparing to hear something I didn't want to, and asked, "Bottom line, Angel: Could he kill? Do you believe him capable?"

He glanced down at our hands. "That's the problem, *corazón*. Could Reyes kill? Hell, yes, but only to protect you. Or Beep. Could Rey'azikeen kill?" He pulled his lower lip in through his teeth, turned once again to stare out the window, then spoke so softly I had to strain to hear him. "By the millions."

By the time I got to Garrett's house, the clock had struck one. Thirty-eight. Ish.

Garrett would be asleep, which was why I didn't go to him earlier that day when I realized I was in a tad over my head. I could ambush him. Tell him what happened with the god glass and the smoke and the angry deity, and he'd be too sleepy and disoriented to reprimand me. Win-win.

Garrett Swopes had been one of the more reluctant believers in my circle of friends, but since he'd come to terms with who I was and what I could do, he'd become an invaluable asset. He was also a top-notch researcher, which was weird. Before he began exploring old texts and ferreting out ancient prophecies in one form or another, I had no idea he could read.

I grabbed the cupcakes I'd stolen from Cookie's apartment, the one right across the hall to which I had a key, wound up Garrett's walk, took out another key labeled "Secret Key to Garrett's House, Shhh," and let myself in.

Since I'd had the key made without his knowledge or, more importantly, his consent, the last time I used the key, I told Garrett I'd picked the lock. The schmuck believed me. I could pick locks, just not in a super timely manner. Those things were harder than they looked.

I used the light on my phone to traverse the harsh landscape of Garrett's abode. Books, papers, and manly things lay strewn about along with a couple of empty beer bottles and a half-empty bottle of wine. Since when did Garrett drink wine?

I finally made my way back to his bedroom and things just got curiouser and curiouser. Garments of all shapes and sizes peppered the floor, and since I doubted Swopes was a double D, I had to assume he was with a woman.

Yep. He lay sleeping on his back, his torso bare except for the double D draped across him.

This was awkward.

I sat on a weight lifting bench he had in a corner, trying to figure out if I should wake him or not. My sitting there in the dark, staring at a couple post-coitus, could be considered creepy by the more conservative of the population. Then again, Garrett had a great torso. At least half of said population would totally understand.

Before I had a chance to wake him, Garrett stirred.

I started to say hey, but no sooner had I drawn breath than I found myself staring down the barrel of a .45. I dropped the cupcakes and raised my hands in surrender.

"It's me," I said, my voice a mere squeak. "I brought cupcakes."

"What the fuck?" He reached over, without taking his eyes or the barrel off me, and turned on a lamp. "What the fuck are you doing in my bedroom?"

"Bringing you cupcakes." Since the gun was still trained on me, I kept my hands raised.

The girl moaned and rolled off him, exposing more of his mocha-colored skin. His hard, muscular mocha-colored skin. I stole a quick gander for posterity's sake, then returned my attention to the matter at hand.

"Charles," he said in warning, his voice deep and sleepy and edged to a razor-sharp sheen.

I may have ovulated, but only a little. I was a married woman, damn it.

When he continued to glare, and point a gun at me, I caved. "Fine. Holy cow. You called me, remember?"

He finally lowered the gun and rubbed his eyes. "I called you three days ago."

"Right. Sorry about that. I've been busy." I gestured toward the woman now sprawled across the other side of the bed. "Who's the ho?"

He glanced at his bedmate, then back at me, his mouth agape. Like literally. "Are you kidding me? She's not a ho. I thought you of all people would understand that, considering your background."

"My what?"

"You should be the last person to judge someone for jumping into bed with a superhot bond agent with fantastic abs—"

He did have great abs.

"—who may or may not have had a shitty night so he went for a drink and met a wonderful young woman with whom he shared a mutual attraction and, since they were both consenting adults, decided to spend some quality time together. For you to call her a ho—"

"Dude," I said, interrupting him mid-rant, "her shirt says HO." I pointed to make my point pointier. It was right there on her shirt. The letters *H-O*.

He let out an annoyed sigh and scooted back against his headboard. "Hope, Charles. It says Hope, as in Hope Christian Academy."

That time I gaped. "You're sleeping with a high school student?"

"She's a teacher," he said through gritted teeth. It was funny.

"At a Christian academy? Isn't that kind of, well, unethical?"

"She's a teacher, not a nun."

"Point taken," I conceded even though his point wasn't nearly as pointy as mine had been. "Why are you in bed with someone who is not your baby mama?"

Garrett had had a baby with a lovely girl, and because she'd set him up to purposely become impregnated by him, as they had a similar remarkable heritage, he distrusted her. Go figure.

"Why are you here, Charles?"

"I need your help, but first, why'd you call?"

"I told you in my message."

"Yeah, I don't really do messages." I did, actually. Something about a children's book? But I'd been busy at the time chasing the ball and chain all over the world. Dude was fast.

He ground his teeth—I did that to people—then looked at the floor. "You really brought cupcakes?"

Fifteen minutes later, Garrett was a new man, all freshly washed and smelling like an Irish spring. Not that I'd ever been to Ireland in the spring. Or any other time of year, for that matter.

"I stumbled upon these by accident," he said, handing me a set of three children's books.

"You're finally learning to read? Good for you, Swopes."

He strode to the coffeepot and poured two cups. I didn't want to tell him that I'd already had twelve cups that day. Mostly because one could never have too much of the dark elixir I considered more of a lover than a beverage. But also because it had been a long day.

He brought the coffee back and tore into the cupcakes. "Who made these?" he asked.

"Maybe I did." I examined the books he'd given me. The covers were beautifully illustrated with sparkling stars over a colorful kingdom.

"No, really."

"Fine, Cook did. What are these?"

"That's the first one," he said, pointing to the book in my hands.

It was titled *The First Star* and was written and illustrated by a Pandu Yoso.

"This is the English translation. They were originally published in Indonesia and have been translated into thirty-five languages."

"Cool. They look awesome, but why are they so interesting to you?"

He finished his first cupcake, took a draft of coffee, then said, "Because they're about you."

I frowned in suspicion and studied him a long moment before I let out a soft laugh. "Seriously, Swopes."

"Seriously. I couldn't believe it either at first. Until I read them."

"Okay, so what? They were written by some ancient prophet and only recently found and published, becoming an overnight international sensation?"

"Right on all counts save one. An ancient prophet didn't write them. A seven-year-old one did, and he—I think it's a he—is deaf and blind and lives in Jakarta."

I put the book on the table and offered him my best impression of a Doubting Debbie.

"Read the bio. His parents believe he's a prophet. He signs the books to them, and they write the stories down."

"It says the author also illustrates them. If he's blind—"

"He does. All by himself."

I ran my fingers over the embossed cover. "But if he's never seen these things . . . I mean, has he always been blind?"

"Since birth. But you're missing the point, Charles. Read the back cover."

I turned the book over and began reading as Garrett got up for more coffee.

I read the blurb aloud. "A long time ago in a faraway land, there was a kingdom with only seven stars in its sky. Of the seven, none were more beloved than the First, for though she was the smallest, she was also the brightest and most caring. The other stars were jealous of her and angry with the people of the kingdom for loving her the most. They decided to punish the people. They caused earthquakes and floods and made volcanoes erupt. The First Star was heartbroken, but what can one tiny star do? Anything to save her people.

"Okay," I said, opening to the first chapter. "Intriguing, but I'm not sure I'm seeing the resemblance."

"Read it," he ordered. He sat back in his chair and waited.

So, I took the next few minutes to read the book. And the more I read, the more I realized Swopes might be onto something.

Told from the perspective of an omniscient seer, the gist of the book was in the blurb. Seven stars watched over an ancient kingdom, but none were more beloved than the First. The other six were jealous and teased her. They knew that the First Star, who loved her kingdom and her people so much, would do anything to protect them.

The six stars began creating mischief in the kingdom. They summoned earthquakes and storms and volcanoes. People in her kingdom were dying, and the stars were growing more malevolent by the day.

Then one day the First Star warned the other six never to harm her people again. They laughed and pushed her out of her orbit and caused even more disasters.

When the First Star fought her way back into her orbit, hundreds of thousands of her people had died. A great and terrible anger came over her. She threatened to kill them all, but they laughed at her.

"You cannot kill a star," they told her. "Stars cannot die."

"Watch me," she said. "I will eat you. I will swallow you as the ocean swallows the sea."

They didn't believe her, so she ate one of the stars.

The five remaining were stunned. They scattered to the farthest reaches of the universe, but the First Star was furious for all the lives they took. She hunted another one down. There was a great battle in the heavens, causing tides to swell and lands to buckle. In the end, she defeated it as well. In the end, she did as she'd promised. She swallowed it whole.

The other stars, hearing of this, decided to merge to become stronger so they could fight her. Four became two, but they feared they were still not strong enough, so two became one.

That time, they went after her, and the smallest star had to face the now gigantic one, four strong. But her anger could not be contained. They battled for forty days and forty nights until only one star was left standing: the First.

Seven stars strong, the First Star became known as the Star Eater. She still protects all life, bringing her light to those in need and her appetite to those who cross her.

I closed the book and took a moment to absorb all the metaphors. "I get it," I said. "It's similar, but this story is different enough from the original prophecy to make me think it could all be a coincidence."

Garrett nodded in thought. "True. The original prophecy states that the seven original stars, a.k.a. gods, merged over the course of millions of years until there were only two, your parents. Then they merged to create you, the thirteenth incarnation. The last and strongest god of your dimension."

"This is almost the exact opposite," I said, holding up the book.

"It is, but take the books and read the other two. I think you'll find them very interesting."

I picked up the second book. "*The Dark Star.*"

"Can you guess who comes into the story in that one?"

I glanced up at him, surprised. "Reyes?"

He nodded.

"And the third?" But the moment I laid eyes on it, I knew, and my breath caught in my chest.

"What do two stars make when they, um, crash into one another?"

"Stardust," I said, now completely enchanted. "Beep. He predicted Beep."

"He predicted Beep."

A woman's voice sounded from the door to Garrett's bedroom. "Oh, hi," she said, dropping a sock and turning in circles to look for her shoes. "Sorry, I didn't realize you had to get up early."

"I didn't," Garrett said. He stood and helped the girl with her things. "Zoe, this is my associate, Charley. Charley, this is Zoe."

I would've shaken one of her hands, but they were both full, so I just waved a greeting. "Nice to meet you, Zoe. Sorry about"—I gestured to her bedmate—"that. Better luck next time."

She let loose a nervous laugh, not quite sure how to take me.

"Ignore her," Garrett said. "She has mental issues."

"Hey, do you know what I called the last guy who said something like that to me?" When he only raised a noncommittal brow, I said, "An ambulance."

"Like I said, mental issues."

I threw the saltshaker at him.

He caught it with ease, then saw Zoe to her car as I perused the second book. As fascinating as the books were, I still had a big problem that needed solving PDQ.

The moment he stepped back into the house, I hit him with it.

"So I accidently-on-purpose sent Reyes into a hell dimension and then couldn't get him back out again but around an hour later he exploded out of the god glass that has a difference of anywhere from several years if not several hundreds of years to a single hour here on Earth but when he came back he wasn't so much Reyes anymore as an angry deity with the power to destroy the world with a single thought."

He sank into the chair across from me again and just kind of stared.

I did a quick analysis of my nails. Nibbled on a couple. Conducted a visual assessment of Garrett's kitchen. Contemplated raiding his cabinets for Oreos. Took another sip of coffee. Wondered if Marvel and DC could ever live in harmony. Shifted in my chair to adjust my underwire. Tapped out White Stripes' "Seven Nation Army" on the table with my fingertips. Checked my phone for messages.

When the silence dragged out to an uncomfortable level, I clarified. "That's my conundrum. In a nutshell. That's why I'm here. More coffee?" I stood and grabbed both of our cups, allowing Garrett more time to absorb. To compute. To process. Some things were harder to process than others. I got that.

I topped off our cups, then returned to the table.

Garrett was still staring. He could have had a stroke, but I didn't think so. Was the first sign a droopy face? He didn't look droopy.

"Son of a bitch, Charles," he said at last, the words clear and vibrant like his silvery-gray eyes.

Whew. No stroke that I could detect. I was no expert, but when both of his hands curled into fists on the table and his gaze remained steady on mine as though he were plotting my death, I took it as a good sign. No visible weakness in his extremities. Mental acuity sharp and sustainable. Any stroke-free day was a good day in my book.

"Hey," I said before he actually carried out his diabolical plot to clobber me, "it was his idea. I didn't want to send him into that hell dimension. I was going to go in myself. Check shit out. Come back no worse for the wear. But noooo. The man with the balls had to go in because he's manly with manly balls and a penis to guide him. And now he's all savage and wild, but he still has his balls. That's all that's important, by God. His man parts."

"He's feral?"

I gaped at him. "Farrow. Reyes Farrow? Are you even trying to keep up?"

"Your husband." He ground out each syllable from between clenched teeth. "Is he feral, or is he still conscious of who he is?"

I scrunched my mouth to one side in thought. "Well, if I had to guess, I'd say yes, he did seem to be very aware of who he was. If we're talking about the deity Rey'azikeen. Otherwise, we're screwed. There wasn't a whole lot of Reyes in there."

When he just sat there again, either deep in thought or seizing, I snapped my fingers in front of his face.

"Earth to the Swope-a-nator. We need a plan, Stan. We can't just sit here thinking about it. You're *plan guy*. Why do you think I came to you first?"

Actually, I'd gone to Garrett first because I was stunningly worried about how Osh, a former slave demon from Reyes's old stomping grounds, would react.

"What's he capable of?" Garrett asked.

I pressed my lips together, then said softly, "World annihilation."

He nodded and yet didn't seem particularly surprised by any of what I was saying. I told him as much.

"You don't seem particularly surprised by any of what I'm saying."

He lifted a shoulder. "I figured it was only a matter of time. He's a god, Charles. And from what I can tell, he's a violent one."

"Why do you say that?"

"You said that God, *our* God, Jehovah or Yahweh or Elohim or whatever you want to call Him, you said that He created the god glass for His brother, Rey'azikeen. Why else would God create a hell dimension, a prison, for his only living relative?"

He had a point. "Well, I'm a god, too. If anyone can trap him and knock some ever-lovin' sense into him, it's me, right?"

He clenched a fist again and conceded with a nod. Then his gaze darted back to mine. "Wait, you came to me first?"

"Yes. I told you, you're plan guy. Speaking of which, dude, you know this whole research and development gig? You're killing it." I figured a little positive reinforcement would go a long way right about now. "Killing it. When it comes to research, I don't kill it so much as pet it and set it free."

"But this happened three days ago."

"Yeah, I tried to fix the situation on my own."

"And how did that work out for you?"

"I'm here now, aren't I?"

"What did you have in mind?"

"First things first. We need to kidnap and torture Osh."

"I'm good with that."

"Do you have torture supplies?" I asked, hopeful.

"Not on me, but there's a twenty-four-hour Walmart nearby. Any particular reason we have to torture him?"

"Not especially. Torture just pairs really well with kidnapping. As you know, I don't like to do things halfway. Also, I'm worried he'll be a little too happy to oblige."

"Meaning?"

"Meaning, we need to come up with a plan *before* we invite a slave demon, and a former enemy of my husband's, into our secret club. I'm worried that once he realizes Reyes has gone to the dark side, he'll go off half-cocked. We need him standing with us. At full-cock. Proud and strong."

"You're such a freak."

"You'd be amazed at how often I hear that."

3

It's weird how you can be in love with someone one day,
and hunting them for sport the next.

—MEME

Garrett and I decided to wait until we gathered the troops to get too invested in a plan. Mostly because we had nothing. Absolutely nothing. How did one track and capture a god? And once said god was in one's possession, then what?

Since I had a couple of hours before we were to meet the Scooby Gang at the office, I went back to my apartment to try to get some sleep. It had been three days since I'd gotten any quality time with my sheets. Whenever I lay down, I tossed and turned, worried that the world would explode.

But I'd been having the strangest dreams. Before I met, officially, my would-be husband, I was having dreams of an erotic nature. My new dreams weren't so much erotic as, well, disturbingly everyday.

Reyes starred in all of them, but they weren't about much of anything. Even so, I woke up moments after closing my eyes feeling distraught. Feeling lost.

But not this time, baby. I was going to score some z's if it killed me. To that end, I did something I rarely do. I resorted to downing a nightcap. Surely that would help keep my harried thoughts at bay.

I readied for bed by washing my face and pulling the brown mess on my head into a hair band. Then I crawled between the cool, superhigh thread counts, closed my eyes, and waited for the nightcap, a.k.a. a healthy dose of Kentucky bourbon, to take effect. Before it had a chance, however, the dishwasher started making that noise again. A clanking noise with little squeaks in between.

No. Way. Was that thing kidding?

Huffing with all the drama queen I could muster, I threw off the sheets and marched to the kitchen. Reyes's kitchen. Reyes's chef's kitchen with industrial appliances and lots of shiny things that I had neither the knowledge nor the desire to work.

I kicked the clanking dishwasher, which looked straight out of the Stone Age. Did they have dishwashers in the Stone Age?

Then I turned to Reyes. He was leaning against a counter, watching me in only a pair of lounge pants. The kind with the drawstring waistband. They rode low on his hips, showing off his hard stomach and abs. His hands rested on either side of him, gripping the edge of the granite countertop at his back. He tightened his grip, and his muscles leaped to do his bidding. They contracted with the effort, the hills and valleys shifting under his wide shoulders.

I stepped closer, my fingertips craving the texture of his body. Just one taste. Just one pass over his rib cage or up across his chest.

"There's something wrong with Princess Penelope," I said as I eased closer. Power emanated out of him in hot, sensual waves. He was like a predator on the verge of attack, barely able to restrain himself. Strength and grace incarnate.

He studied me, his gaze shimmering underneath his impossibly long lashes. "Who's that?" he asked, his voice like warm water rushing to all my naughty parts.

"You don't know the name of your own dishwasher?" I teased. "Do you remember my name? Or is that asking too much?"

His gaze dropped to my mouth, and my lungs stopped working. "Is there a point to this?"

I recovered enough to nod and answer him. "Yes, something is wrong with Princess Penelope. I think it's her carburetor."

He reached out and pulled the drawstring at my own waist. "I was referring to the fact that your clothes are still on."

I jerked awake and bolted upright, blinking into the darkness. It was a dream. It was only a dream.

Once I'd oriented myself, I searched the room. No idea why. Naturally, he wasn't there. He'd reverted back to his old ways. Invading my sleep. Making me crave him.

I just couldn't figure out his endgame. Why not just come to me? The dreams from before were pure, no-holds-barred eroticism. These were erotic, but not overtly sexual.

They were, however, the reason I'd slept so little over the past three days. Every time I closed my eyes, strange little vignettes, as perplexing as they were sexy, played in my head. And in every one, I'd get close enough to almost touch my husband, only to be startled awake before I could manage it.

Maybe that *was* his endgame. Maybe that was the point. To dull my wits. To keep me exhausted and disoriented, but why? So I couldn't track him? Like I could, anyway.

After I woke up, which was about ten minutes after I'd lain down, it didn't take me long to realize sleep was going to be just as elusive this morning as it had been yesterday. And the day before. And the day before that.

Was he doing this on purpose? Was this some sort of strategy on his part? But to what end? If his plan was to keep me disoriented, what would he gain?

I gave up, mostly because my brain hurt, and got out of bed. I needed coffee. And a shower. Or a coffee shower.

Hey . . .

Since I'd had enough coffee over the last twenty-four hours to see noise, I chose the shower first. The problem with showers was that I never got to enjoy them alone. Even with Reyes gone, I endured interruption after interruption. And this morning was no different.

"Hey, gorgeous girl," I said to a departed Rottweiler named Artemis.

She joined me most mornings to chase streams of water as they splashed on the rock walls and tile floor. Sadly, every time she found a new source of entertainment, she'd almost knock me over to get to it. Walls, she could go through. Me, not so much. I'd hoped she would learn that someday, but it had been several months since she officially became my guardian, and the situation looked grim.

She licked the wall—or tried to—and did her darnedest to catch a thin stream of water in her mouth. She barked at it, stopped just long enough to let me scratch her ears, then went back to licking the tile floor. I could only hope George, the shower, would forgive us for violating him so.

But Artemis wasn't my only visitor. I heard a soft, lilting voice come from my living room.

"Aunt Charley?"

"I'm in the bathroom, hon." I turned George off—probably in more ways than one—and reached for a towel.

"I just have a couple of questions for you," Amber said from behind the closed door. Amber was Cookie's thirteen-and-three-quarters-year-old daughter. "Are you, um, busy?"

"Busy?" I asked, wrapping a towel around my head.

"Is Uncle Reyes in there with you?"

After almost choking on my own spit, I cleared my throat and said, "Not at the moment."

"Oh, good. I didn't want to interrupt anything."

"That's thoughtful of you." I put on a robe, made sure I looked presentable-ish, and said, "Come on in, pumpkin."

She walked in, chipper as ever, her long, dark hair pulled back in a messy bun, her huge blue eyes bright and crystal clear. She waved steam away, gave me a hug, then closed the toilet lid, a.k.a. Curly—the toilet, not the lid—and sat on it.

"What's up?"

"Well, I just wanted to ask you a couple of questions about what you do."

"Oh, cool. Are you writing a paper for school?"

"No. And I'm only admitting that because you can tell if I'm lying."

I perched a hip against the sink, crossed my arms, and faced her. "I appreciate your candor."

"Thanks. I think. So, if you had to solve a case where someone was stealing something, like, say, office supplies, what would you do first?"

"Okay, is this for a story you're writing?"

"Nope."

"What about just idle curiosity?"

"Not that, either."

"Care to tell me what this is about?"

She drew in a long, melodramatic breath. "You'll just tell me not to do it."

"How do you know? I might be totally encouraging."

"No, you won't."

"Amber Olivia Kowalski."

"Okay, Quentin and I are opening our own detective agency, and we are starting with a case at the School for the Deaf. Someone is stealing office supplies, and we're going to figure out who."

Quentin was an adorable sixteen-year-old with shoulder-length blond hair and a smile that rivaled the beauty of a New Mexican sunset. He was very sensitive to the supernatural world. He could see the departed and demons, and he was one of the few people alive who could see my light.

His gift was one in a million. Literally. Many people were sensitive in that they could see a clear smoke or a blur when a departed was around, or they could feel a cold spot or hear a moan. But Quentin could actually see the departed, body and soul. He would've been able to communicate with them more if he hadn't been born deaf.

He attended the New Mexico School for the Deaf in Santa Fe, and

Amber was hoping to join him next year if Cookie agreed and the school approved her application. It was hard to get a hearing student into NMSD without a blood relative enrolled, but they loved Amber, and she was on campus at least two or three times a week. She was becoming Deaf—capital *D*, as in culturally—more and more every day. And her mo—

Wait. Did she say *detective agency*?

I stood in shock for a solid minute before remembering I'd said I'd be encouraging. "Your own detective agency?"

"Yep."

"Wow. I'm not entirely certain, but I think I'm flattered."

"Really?" she asked, turning her frown upside down.

"Wait, let me think about it." I held up a finger as I pondered the situation. "Yeah, I'm pretty sure I am. But the answer is no."

Her shoulder deflated. "See? I told you."

I giggled, walked over to her, and kissed her head. "Just kidding."

She brightened again. Her moods were comparable to someone switching the sun on and off, she wore them so overtly.

"Aunt Charley." She pretended to reprimand me, but teasing her was kind of an aunt's job. "So, you'll help us?"

The thought of Amber and Quentin opening their own detective agency was both the cutest thing I'd ever heard and one of the scariest. Adorable? Yes. Dangerous? Considering my world, also yes.

"I'll help you help yourself."

"Um, okay. Can't you just go there, ask who did it, test the emotions of everyone you ask, and tell us who the thief is?"

"No." I went back to towel-drying my hair.

"Is this going to be one of those life-lesson things? 'Cause they don't really work when you're around. Nobody compares to you, so it's not fair."

I tossed my wet hair back and gave her my best impression of a dead pan. "Is this going to be one of those guilt trip things? 'Cause they don't really work when I'm around. I can sense insincerity, remember?"

She pinched her mouth together, then propped an elbow on a knee and her chin in her palm. "Mom is so much easier to con than you."

I stuck a toothbrush in my mouth and worked up a good lather. "Honey," I said through the foam, "everyone on planet Earth is easier to con than I am. You're fighting an impossible battle."

"Okay, then, what should we do? We can't figure it out. We've tried and tried and tried."

"Did you find out who has access to the supply room?"

"Well, no," she said, thoughtful.

"Okay, well, that's where I'd start. Find out who has access, then eliminate those people one by one by checking their alibis until you have a viable suspect."

"Yes. That's what we need. A viable suspect."

She braced her phone against a tissue box, hit RECORD, and began signing everything I'd just told her. She stopped and asked, "How do you say *viable*?"

With a giggle, I signed it for her. She finished her message and hit SEND.

"Quentin can find out some of that today at school. I wish I went there."

"I know, hon. Maybe next year."

She shrugged acceptance and hopped up. "Can I call you if I have more questions?"

"You know you can, but there's someone else in this building who's a pretty incredible investigator."

"Uncle Reyes?"

"No."

"My stepdad?"

My very own uncle Bob had married my BFF and became Amber's stepfather overnight, a role he cherished and Amber found safety in.

"Nope."

She skewed her face in thought. "Mrs. Medina, the elderly lady in 1B who swears she was a spy in the Cold War and that she once used peanut butter to create a bomb to distract her enemies so she and her Chihuahua, the Mighty Thor, could escape from that prison in Siberia?"

I pressed my lips together to keep from saying something sarcastic. Since Sarcastic was my middle name, restraint didn't come easy.

When I had a handle on my innermost nature, I said, "No, not Mrs. Medina."

She finally gave up with a curious shrug.

"Your mother, hon."

"Mom?" she asked, the doubt as visible on her pretty face as her nose.

I laughed softly. "Who do you think does all the behind-the-scenes work for me? Your mother's a badass."

She blinked, then seemed to warm to the idea. "My mom? A badass?"

"Abso-freaking-lutely."

"Sweet." She turned, beaming, and headed out the door. "Thanks, Aunt Charley."

"Not at all, sweet pea. Tell Quentin hey for me."

"Okay."

"Oh, wait," I said, leaning out the door. "What's your business's name?"

"Q&A Investigations."

She paused and waited for my reaction.

"I love it."

She twirled around and bounced out.

4

I once made a pot of coffee so strong,
it opened a jar for me.
—T-SHIRT

I finished dressing, made a pot of coffee, and downed half of it straight from the carafe. That could've been why I saw it again. The dark gray swish. Before I'd officially met Reyes, he kind of followed me around but kept his distance. All I'd see was a black blur, but this seemed different somehow. Colder. Grayer.

I walked into the living room, opened a closet where the swoosh appeared to vanish into, then gave up. If it were dangerous, I'd know soon enough. Denial was a wonderful thing.

After pouring an actual cup of coffee, I checked email, grew instantly bored, and decided to check the news instead.

I was doing exactly that when Cookie walked in.

"Hey, pumpkin," she said, but my face was glued to the screen.

I couldn't believe what I'd found. "Did you know Penn Jillette and his wife named their daughter Moxie CrimeFighter?"

She poured herself what was left of the coffee, then joined me. "I read that somewhere. How cute is that?"

"Cute? Cook, it's horrible. I mean, what if, when the poor girl grows up, she wants to be the villain?"

"That is a conundrum. Speaking of which, did you take my cupcakes?"

"Only four. I had to wake up Garrett in the middle of the night, and I needed an olive branch. With chocolate icing."

"I don't think Garrett would mind your waking him up no matter what time it was."

"He pulled a gun on me."

"But it never hurts to take that extra step."

"Why'd you make them? Is there a special occasion I don't know about? Birthday? Anniversary? Guilt over an illicit affair?"

"No, I made them for you. You've been . . . off lately. I thought cupcakes might make you feel better."

"Cook," I said, leaning toward her for a big fat hug.

She was wearing a crinkly sage-green outfit with a lime-green belt and scarf. Her black-with-a-hint-of-gray-striped hair was spiked in all directions as usual, but if it had been lighter, she would've looked a little like Elton John. His loss.

"Cupcakes make everyone feel better," I said, letting her go. "Well, maybe not diabetics."

"What are you up to these days?"

"What? Nothing. I had nothing to do with it," I said, sure she'd already discovered my traitorous involvement in the case of the missing office supplies and the start-up detective agency.

Cookie had been concerned Amber and Quentin were spending too much time together, and encouraging the elfin in this new endeavor would definitely give them an excuse to do exactly that.

In fact, I wouldn't put it past those two to have made up the whole mystery for that very reason. I mean, she had to know we'd be flattered that they wanted to follow in our footsteps.

"Okay, then." Cookie sat quietly after that, sipping her coffee, until she could contain it no longer. "What the hell, Charley?"

"I'm sorry." I bowed my head in shame. "I didn't mean to. She was just so cute, and you know damned well I can deny that child nothing. She used her charm on me. It's lethal. It should be registered on a weapons database somewhere."

"What is going on?" She stood and began pacing. "After all we've been through together, after all the secrets we've shared—granted, you have a few more than I—but still, if you and Reyes are having problems, you know you can come to me. Hell, you've slept on my couch more times than I can count."

"Like, three?" Clearly, she wasn't very good at counting.

"And now you're obviously having serious issues and—" She turned toward me. "What did you say?"

Uh-oh. My words just sank in.

"Nothing. I had my listening ears on."

She pursed her mouth. "What did she do?"

"Who?"

"My daughter."

"Nothing. I swear."

"Charlotte Jean Davidson."

Wow, that really worked. "Okay, I'll tell you, but don't say anything. She wants to come to you for guidance and structure. So when she tells you, act surprised."

Cook narrowed her eyes on me, her expression one of absolute disbelief. She was catching on so much faster these days.

I explained all about Amber and Quentin's new venture. Cookie took it better than I'd hoped. I think it was the part where I told her Amber wanted to come to her first, but she was worried Cookie would be upset about them spending even more time together—you know, beyond the whole every-waking-moment thing—so she came to seek my counsel because she thinks she's found her calling. She wants to do what her mother does.

That pretty much clinched it. Amber so owed me.

"And the rest," I said, rising to hunt down my boots, "I'll tell you at the office. I've invited the whole gang."

She'd started for the door, but she stopped and turned. "It's that bad?"

I wrested a boot out from under Sophie, my couch, and slipped it on. Without looking back at Cookie, I said, "Yes, sadly, it is."

We walked to the office together since it was only about fifty feet from the front door of our apartment building. But we walked in silence, she in thought and me in a state of panic. I didn't let it show, though. I'd essentially lost my husband, his body taken over by a deity I knew nothing about. Was he volatile? That much seemed a given, but was he cruel? Was he malevolent? Only time would tell, but time was not something we had a lot of. If he turned out to be everything we feared, we needed to capture him. Period.

Davidson Investigations, not to be confused with Q&A Investigations, sat on the second floor of a historic brick building on Central, right across from the beautiful campus of the University of New Mexico. The first floor housed Reyes's bar and grill, Calamity's. My dad, who'd owned the bar before Reyes bought it, had called it Calamity's after yours truly. No clue why. Chaos rarely followed me.

We put on a fresh pot of coffee, because coffee made everything okayer, and waited for our guests to arrive.

Which they all did. Like all at once. It was weird.

Garrett. Uncle Bob. Angel. Gemma. Osh.

Wait, Gemma?

"Uh, hey, Gem," I said, greeting everyone with a hug, including the man who once tried to invent a hug repellent spray thanks to me, my wonderful uncle Bob. And now he was married to my bestie. It's like we were really related now. Not Cookie and I. We became sisters the moment we met. But Uncle Bob was always iffy at best.

I stepped to Gemma and pulled her into a hug, too.

"Whatcha doin' here?" I asked into the suddenly very awkward silence.

"Spending time with my little sister. Can't a girl spend time with her little sister?"

"No."

She laughed and waved a dismissive hand.

"No, really, Gem."

Growing more serious, she lifted her chin and said, "I'm ready."

I strode to the coffeepot for a refill. I just couldn't seem to get enough of it lately. Probably because of the lack of a good siesta. "You're ready?"

She braced herself and nodded.

"For?"

"This." She gestured around her. "You. Whatever it is you do, I'm ready."

"I'm not sure you are."

Uncle Bob stepped closer as the others staked their claims in Cookie's office. "Gem, I think maybe—"

"No," she said, her mind set. "It's time I got more involved. You know, step up to the plate. Go for the touchdown. Turn the dial to eleven."

For someone with a genius IQ, she was really bad at metaphors.

"What the hell does any of that mean?" I asked.

She drew in a deep breath. "I'm here for the meeting."

"No."

"I want to become more involved in your life and what you do."

"No."

"Why does Uncle Bob get to be involved and not me?"

"No. And who told you we were having a meeting?"

Osh spoke up from his chair in the corner. "I think she should stay."

Osh may have looked nineteen, but he was centuries old if he was a day. His inky-black hair brushed his shoulders, and he wore his traditional black top hat and black duster, a look he pulled off with such charm and style, it was hard to put him in his place, but put him in his place I did.

"Just pretend this is your hometown. Daeva don't have a say."

He narrowed his bronze eyes on me. "That's low, sugar. Even for you."

"See?" Gemma said. "That's interesting. What's a Daeva?"

"A slave demon from hell," I said, hoping to scare her right off the bat.

"Oh." She thought about that a moment, then said, "Okay. Well, I've learned something already."

This was going to be a long morning.

We sat around Cookie's desk, Uncle Bob next to my best friend and associate-slash-receptionist. He took her hand in his, and I felt a small rush of pleasure erupt out of her.

Garrett stood back, pretending to be annoyed that I'd asked him if the ho had called. He was worried about Reyes. As was I.

Osh sat in the farthest corner, tipping his chair back like a kid in high school.

Angel popped in and hung back with Osh, probably because Osh was the only person in the room besides me who could see him.

Even Artemis showed up. She sat at Angel's feet, and he and Osh took turns rubbing her ears.

Gemma sat next to me. I'd commandeered Cookie's chair and sat behind her desk so I could see everyone as I explained the situation.

I cleared my throat, but Garrett motioned to me, lifting the rope he had in his hands.

"Oh, right." I looked at Osh. "Osh, we are going to have to tie you up and torture you. Sorry."

"Really?" He stood and removed his top hat, a broad grin splitting his perfect face. With the enthusiasm of a virgin at a brothel, he slapped his hands together and rubbed them in anticipation. "Where do you want me?"

"That chair will be fine. Just scoot it to the middle of the room."

Cookie's office wasn't huge, but it was big enough to tie Osh up and torture him.

Gemma's eyes rounded in concern when Osh sat down and Garrett began the bondage process. Was it wrong that I had a hankering for gay porn at that moment?

I walked over to them to make sure Garrett's knots were inescapable. But inescapable to a human and inescapable to a Daeva were two very different things. Osh could most likely get out of pretty much any sticky situation, but if it did nothing else, it would damned sure slow him down. Garrett's handiwork made certain of that.

Osh grinned up at me. "You gonna do the deed, sugar? You gonna hurt me?"

"I might."

He winked, and a microsecond later I realized I was flirting with my future son-in-law. I'd seen what would become Beep's army. Who would become Beep's army. Most of it, anyway. And Osh was most definitely spoken for in the future.

Angel sidled up to me. "I want to be tied up."

I turned to him and put my hand on his forever-boyish face. "I'm fairly certain the ropes would slide through you, *lindo*."

"We should check it out, just in case," he said.

But I barely heard him. The moment I laid my hand on his face, I felt a warmth at the back of my neck. A heat slide down my spine.

I spun around, hoping, but saw nothing. When I turned back to Osh, however, he was looking in the same direction the heat had come from.

"What?" I turned again. "What did you see?"

All traces of humor were gone. Everyone in the room followed Osh's line of sight to no avail. But Osh tilted his head, completely bound now, and leveled a serious stare on me.

"Why am I tied up?"

"Because we have to take certain precautions."

Kneeling next to him, I placed a hand on his bound arm, his muscles straining against the restraints. Garrett did a helluva job.

"Osh, I need you calm when I tell you what's happened."

He glanced behind me, then back again. "You think I don't already know?"

I looked again but saw nothing. "What? Did you see him?"

He bowed his head. "How did it happen?"

"Osh, what did you see?"

When he refocused on me, his face had paled. "Him. For a split second. Angry. Wild. Volatile." His expression turned incredulous. "You released him."

"What? No." I shook my head. "I don't know." I stood and walked to the door of my office for some other place to look. Anywhere other than his accusing stare. "It was an accident."

When I turned back to him, his head was bowed again, his jaw tight behind his dark hair.

"Osh, what are you thinking?"

"Do you have any idea how powerful he is? What he could do with the slightest thought?"

"What do you mean, I released him? Released him from where?"

"He's a god, sugar. He was always in there, lurking. Waiting for his chance to rise again."

"Osh, he's been a god for . . . well forever. But he's known he's a god for weeks now. And I . . . I sent him into the god glass."

He sucked in a sharp breath of air, astonished.

"Not for that reason. Not for . . . look, he was just supposed to go in and check the place out. There were innocent people trapped inside. I wanted to go, but he insisted I send him. I was supposed to wait sixty seconds and call him back out. I didn't even wait that long. I called his name not fifteen seconds later, but nothing happened."

"Keep going."

"I tried everything. Nothing worked. Nothing . . ." I'd begun to panic. Osh's reaction made me realize even more how bad things were. "And then about an hour later, the glass exploded, and he came out as well as all the innocent people who'd been trapped inside."

The astonishment on his face turned to something akin to terror. "He opened the gates of a hell dimension on this plane?"

"I don't know. I guess."

"When?"

"Three days ago. I'm sorry I didn't tell you guys the minute it happened."

I scanned the room to assess reactions. So far, everyone seemed more confused than worried, though Cookie was leaning toward the latter. The only exception was Angel. My beautiful boy.

"I should've told you. I was just so taken aback. I thought I could find him and fix it."

"What are we talking about?" Garrett asked him. "What needs to be done?"

Uncle Bob spoke then, his patience quickly waning. "Pumpkin, you need to let the rest of us in on what's at stake here."

I offered him my best apologetic expression, then returned to Osh. "He's still Reyes."

"Untie me."

"No," I said, jumping forward. I knelt before him again. "He's still Reyes, Osh."

He nailed me with an expression I'd never seen from him. Pity. "He stopped being Reyes the moment he entered that hell dimension, love. Untie me."

"We need a plan."

"We need to get the fuck off this plane."

"Osh, not everyone here can do that."

One corner of his full mouth tilted up. "Not my problem."

His statement shocked me. I wouldn't have been more stunned if he'd slapped me upside the head. "You're going to leave us?"

He held my gaze a long moment before having mercy on me. "No, sweetheart. I just wanted you to feel betrayed."

I eased back onto my heels. "Why?"

"Because you need to get used to it. He'll kill you, sugar, and everything you love, starting with the people in this room."

Cookie gasped.

Gemma popped out of her chair.

Garrett turned to look out the window.

I shook my head. "No," I said, standing my ground. "He's still Reyes. Somewhere inside, he's still Reyes."

The ropes that held Osh fell off him like paper ribbons. Garrett tensed, readying for a battle. A battle he would've ultimately lost, but he would've put up one hell of a fight.

Osh clamped both hands onto my arms, then stood and pulled me up with him. We locked gazes, his teeth clenched like he wanted to shake some sense into me.

"I'm not budging on this, Osh."

"You're the god eater. You can take care of this right here and now."

I pushed away from him.

Uncle Bob stepped between us, glared at Osh a second, then turned to me. "What's he talking about?"

"Some stupid prophecy."

"It's not a prophecy," Garrett said. "You've done it here, on this plane."

"Once, and I didn't even know what I was doing."

When the men started to argue about the logistics of my devouring my own husband, which screamed cannibal in my humble opinion, my temper soared. Just a little. Just enough to cause a tiny quake to shake the room around us.

All conversations ceased.

"The answer is no. I would never resort to such a tactic with my husband, so the argument is moot. We need a plan. Not conjectures and innuendoes. A solid plan."

"We need two plans, actually," Osh said.

Garrett sank onto the love seat by the window. "What do you mean?"

"The problem is twofold. Even if we could somehow capture a volatile deity—and then, what, stuff him in a bottle?—you have another issue that even an act of God couldn't fix."

I frowned. What else could there be? "What are you talking about?"

"The god glass. The hell dimension. You said the gates were opened."

"They were pretty much destroyed," I said with a nod.

"Then you have created a dimension within a dimension. An anomaly. A singularity."

"What? Like a black hole?"

"In a sense. The new dimension will grow, slowly at first, then faster and faster as it feeds off this dimension. As it gains mass. Eventually, it'll take over."

I walked to Garrett and sat beside him. "So, yeah, that's bad."

"Sounds bad," Angel said.

Osh shook his head. "That's not the bad part."

"It gets worse?" I asked.

"To be blunt, the demons residing within said dimension will inherit the Earth."

"There are demons?" Cookie asked. "No one mentioned demons."

Uncle Bob raised his hands and patted the air to slow things down a bit. "Okay, okay, a singularity, but first things first. Let's deal with Reyes, try to bring him back or capture him or whatever we have to do. Then we can worry about the Earth-devouring hell dimension, which, believe you me, is not something I ever thought I'd hear myself say."

"I agree," Garrett said. "We need to concentrate on Reyes."

"That's easy enough. He's jealous," Osh said. "As most gods are. When you touched Angel's face—which, who wouldn't?—you got a reaction out of him."

"So, he's watching?" Angel asked.

"More like monitoring, and he's probably focused purely on Charley."

"Why do you say that?" Gemma asked, chiming into the conversation at last.

"Because she's the only one in the entire universe who can eat him should she get hungry enough."

Gemma looked from me to Osh, then back again. "But won't he know what we're doing?"

Osh shrugged. "That's always a possibility, but we can't let that stop us from trying."

"What do you suggest?" Garrett asked.

"I suggest running, but since no one else is in—"

"Drugs," Garrett said.

Osh nodded. "That might work. We can all do drugs. Then we won't care when the world is either destroyed by a volatile god or overtaken by a demon-infested hell dimension." He grinned at Garrett. "Good thinking."

"No, drugs. Charles was drugged just the other day. They worked on her despite her being a god."

I shook my head. "Too many complications, and we don't even know if they'd work on him. Before, yes, but now that he's full blown god? Who knows what effect they'd have?"

"They worked on you," he argued. When I continued to shake my head, he gave up. "Okay, fine. You're a god. How would you track and capture yourself?"

"I'd lure me in with coffee, then keep the cups coming. Trust me, I wouldn't go anywhere. I doubt that would work on him, though. Not all gods enjoy java as much as I do."

Gemma, who wasn't caught up on the latest Charley facts, began making her way to the front door. "Oh, my," she said, glancing at her watch. "It's getting late and I'm supposed to meet Wyatt for breakfast." Wyatt was a cop and a former patient she'd broken all professional codes of conduct to date. I was so proud of her. "Great meeting, guys. Same time tomorrow?"

"Gemma," I began, but she was out the door before I could get another word in. The only thing we heard was her footsteps as she practically fell down the outside stairs.

"Poor thing," Uncle Bob said. He offered me condolences with an encouraging pat on the head. "She always had blinders on when it came to your abilities."

"Can you blame her?"

"Not in the least. Remind me to check on her later."

"I think Swopes is onto something," Osh said.

I stood and began pacing the floor. "I'm telling you, it won't work."

"Why not?" Swopes asked. "It worked on you when that evil cult drugged you and threw you into that trunk."

"Actually, they threw me into the trunk and then drugged me."

"Seriously?"

"And there's a fatal flaw in your plan, Swopes. Reyes isn't exactly coming home for dinner. How am I supposed to drug him?"

"We lure him," Cookie said.

The room turned its attention to my delectable neighbor.

"Great idea, hon, but with what?"

When her gaze landed on Garrett and she grinned possibly the most mischievous grin I'd ever seen her wear, I knew I wasn't going to like this plan.

5

If I manage to survive the rest of the week,
I would like my straightjacket hot pink and my helmet sparkly.

—TRUE FACT

We had a plan. So that happened. Didn't matter that it would never work in a hundred thousand years, we had a plan. Mazel tov. I warmed up my coffee as the rest of the wild bunch planned my death. Reyes was going to kill me if he hadn't decided to do that already.

I leaned against the wall that separated my office from Cookie's. It hadn't been that long ago when Reyes appeared to me in this very room, pressed me into that very wall, ran his mouth along my neck and over my cheek.

As I thought back to that day, he walked up to me, wearing a white button-down with the sleeves folded up to his elbows, exposing his sinuous forearms. I always loved that shirt. He knew it.

His mouth tipped up at one corner into a sultry grin. The kind that made women drop their panties. The kind that turned my legs into a plate of spaghetti.

"What are you drinking?" he asked as he strode forward. He looked like an animal, sleek and powerful and sensuous.

"Battery acid," I teased, pretending my heart wasn't pounding a little faster.

He didn't stop his advance until we were almost touching, and then he braced a hand against the wall behind me near my head and the other on the opposite side at my waist. Locking me in. Begging me to make the first move.

"I want my tongue in your mouth." His voice caused a rush of heat that washed over my skin and settled in my abdomen.

"Then, by all means, put it there."

His gaze dropped to the object currently under discussion. "You won't bite?"

"Only a little."

He dipped a finger in my cup, then ran the scalding liquid over my lips. I reached out with my tongue, to taste him, to draw him in so I could suckle him, but the moment I made contact, I jerked awake, spilling coffee down my sweater and jeans.

"Damn it," I said aloud as everyone turned to look.

Then I realized it had happened again. But I was wide awake this time. What the holy fuck?

"Did you see him?" I asked Osh, scanning the room for any sign of my husband. "Was he here?"

Osh's brows slid together in concern, but he shook his head. "What's going on?"

"Nothing." I headed toward the restroom to clean up. "Other than the fact that I'm losing my mind."

When I got back to the office, realizing I'd simply have to change, Uncle Bob was on the phone, his tone aggressive. Almost angry.

"What happened?" I asked when he hung up.

"We got another one," he said, staring at me pointedly.

"Another body?"

He nodded.

"Like the others?"

He nodded again, kissed his wife, then headed out the door.

"I'll text when I know more, Cook," I said as Garrett and I followed him. "Meet us there?" I said to Angel.

He nodded, then disappeared.

Osh followed us out the door after giving Cook a quick wave goodbye. "I want to know what just happened," he said.

"You and me both."

Garrett, Osh, and I met Uncle Bob at a gas station near Fourth and Chavez. A woman had borrowed the key for the restroom and never returned it, so a female employee went to check on her and found her dead.

I covered my mouth and nose as we walked up, the smell hitting me about two blocks back. Ubie, who was apparently immune to such horrors, said I was imagining it. I didn't think so. There was nothing, absolutely nothing, worse than the odor of a dead body. Especially one that had been singed.

I took a quick look at the victim and crime scene, then ducked out before I puked. The woman had been killed in exactly the same manner as the previous two.

Her body was covered in superficial scratches and deeper gashes. Bruises covered her face and torso. Half her dress had been ripped off, but like the others, the attack had not been sexual in nature. At least not overtly. The attacker may have gotten off on it, but there'd been no sexual contact during the attack.

The odd part, however, were the burns. Just like the first two, this woman, a Patricia Yeager, had random burn marks on her skin and clothes. Many at her feet and along her backside. Since she was lying on her back and didn't appear to have been turned over, how did the burn marks get there? If the attacker was busy, well, attacking, when did he have time to burn his victim?

"Oh, it gets better," Uncle Bob said. He led us to a tiny office in the back of the store. They had one security camera angled on the pumps, and it just happened to catch the doors to the bathroom.

He scrolled through until we saw Ms. Yeager go inside. We watched as he fast-forwarded the recording to the point where the employee opened the door with a master key. The woman could be seen backing away from the restroom, her hands covering her mouth in horror. I was right there with her.

"But here's the kicker," Ubie said. "No one else entered. No one else left."

"And when we watched the rest of the video," an Officer Robb said, "no one entered or exited after the attack either."

"So," Ubie said, looking at me, "how did the perp get inside, kill Ms. Yeager, then leave completely undetected by passersby and security cameras?"

Ubie dismissed the young officer and closed the door. "This has to be something supernatural, right?"

Osh and Garrett nodded. I continued to stare at the screen. I'd learned that I could see supernatural entities even on digital recordings, but nothing ever showed up.

"Did you catch anything, Osh?" I asked the only other supernatural being there as Angel was off scouring the area for clues.

Osh shook his head. "Nothing."

"This can't be a demon. Not with the sun out, right?"

"Well, the sun wasn't getting into that bathroom. One could have found its way inside, I guess."

Garrett opened an app on his phone and read from it. "The first victim, Indigo Russell, was killed late afternoon two days ago."

"Right," I said. "Before Captain Eckert gave the case to you, Uncle Bob."

A grave smile spread across his face. "Yeah, I get all the weird ones thanks to you."

"Sorry about that."

"Not at all. But you're right, Garrett, the first one was killed while watering trees in her backyard. It had been late afternoon, but the sun had been out."

I turned to Osh. "Can a demon somehow slide along the shadows of, say, a fence or a house and kill from there?"

He shrugged. "Even if they could, why would they? I mean, demons don't really kill people. They possess them. To be totally honest, I'm not sure they *can* kill someone on this plane. They use other humans to do their dirty work."

"You can," I said, lifting one brow.

"Yeah, well, I'm special. And part human, so . . ."

"This does beg the question," Garrett began, but I stopped him before he got any further.

"No, it doesn't."

"Charles—"

"No. I just . . . no. Reyes is not doing this." But even as I said the words, doubt sprang inside me.

"It's just something we need to consider."

I bowed my head, mortified at what was happening. I had to tell them everything. That this could all be my fault.

Uncle Bob put a hand on my shoulder. "What is it, pumpkin?"

After a long, thoughtful moment, I said, "Reyes came out of that hell dimension, as well as all those innocent souls. But I know of at least three other beings that were trapped inside."

"How do you know?" he asked.

"Because I put them there. Well, two of them, at least. One was a kind of supernatural assassin named Kuur, and one was a malevolent god named Mae'eldeesahn."

Osh nodded. "Holy shit, I forgot about that. You didn't feel either one come out?"

"No. I only felt the victims of the priest. And according to legend, the priest was in there, too. He didn't cross through me, though. I'm pretty sure he went straight down. But I just don't know what happened to the other two, and they are supernatural beings more than powerful enough to do something like this."

I wasn't so love smitten that I refused to consider the possibility Reyes was behind the deaths. We needed to consider all angles. It just hurt my heart too much to consider it for very long.

"Have you found any kind of connection to the victims?" I asked Uncle Bob.

"None at all. We have an accountant, a recording artist, and Mrs. Yeager, a clerk at district court. No familial connections. Nothing in their backgrounds that would even suggest they knew each other."

"So, the killings are either completely random, which scares the crap out of me, or there is a connection we aren't seeing."

"Exactly." Uncle Bob took a copy of the recording and dropped it into an evidence bag.

If the murders were completely random, there would be no way to track the killer's next move. If there was a connection, we had to find it. We had to get ahead of this.

Just then, a woman's screams could be heard outside. We glanced at each other, then shot out of the tiny office and through a set of glass double doors to find a distraught woman trying to push her way past the officers.

Uncle Bob and I hurried over as an officer tried to subdue a young brunette, her expression full of terror and her emotions drowning in anguish.

"You need to leave the area, ma'am," the hapless officer said.

"No! That's my wife's car! They said the woman who owned that car had been killed in the restroom!"

I had to stand back as another officer joined his colleague in trying to subdue the poor woman. Her agony was so strong it wrapped around my chest in a viselike grip, squeezing the air out of my lungs. I put my hands on my knees and fought to refill them as a wave of dizziness washed over me.

The cops finally wrestled the woman back with Uncle Bob's help, even though a cameraman who was recording the entire altercation caused them to trip.

"Get back," the officer said, his voice like a razor, but it did nothing to stop the intrepid reporter and her stalwart cameraman.

"Keep recording," she said, her gaze glistening with the fodder she'd have for the evening news.

And the poor woman whose wife lay dead on a convenience store's restroom floor fought blindly, begging the officers to let her pass.

As nonchalantly as I could, I walked over to them, put a hand on her shoulder, and let a soothing energy flow from me and into her. She calmed almost instantly, collapsing against her captors, but her face was still flushed and her saucerlike eyes still wild.

"What's your name?" I asked her when the officers forced her to sit on the back of an ambulance.

The EMT checked her pulse and blood pressure and slipped an oxygen mask over her face.

"Maya," she said, trying to catch her breath.

Uncle Bob sent an officer after a bottle of water, then stood beside me.

She lowered the mask. "Is it her?" she asked, her voice pleading. "Is it Patricia?"

"We believe so," he said to her, and she broke down, sobbing and shaking her head.

"No. That's not possible. I just saw her."

Another woman came rushing up then and threw her arms around Maya. They looked too much alike not to be sisters. They cried together while Ubie questioned a couple more potential witnesses. But I needed to know why this woman was attacked. If it were human and random, that was one thing. But supernatural and random was a completely different situation.

After a while, Maya had calmed down enough for me to talk to her. She was still crying, and a big part of her was still in denial—she wanted to see the body to make sure—but at least she was more coherent.

"Maya?" I asked, easing closer. "Can I ask you a couple of questions?"

She sniffed as her sister handed her a cup of water.

Maya had brown hair cropped short and a tattoo of SpongeBob SquarePants on her arm. She also wore strings of leather around her wrist with different charms. One had her wife's name engraved on it.

"Did Patricia seem anxious lately? Worried? Maybe someone was harassing her or calling and hanging up?"

Maya shook her head. "No." She looked at the water in her hands. "Everyone loved Patty. She was just that kind of girl, you know?"

The sister agreed with a nod before squeezing Maya to her.

"Why would someone do this?," Maya continued. "She's been through so much, but she just picked herself back up and shook it off. She was so special. She was so . . . unique. It's like killing a mermaid or a unicorn. Why would someone do that?"

I found it interesting that she used mythical creatures to describe her wife.

"She was just so special," she repeated, her breath hitching. "You have no idea."

After that, Maya broke down again and crumpled into her sister's arms. They both sobbed, and when the ME finished with the scene and brought out the body in a body bag, it took another team of officers to keep her back. She would be able to see her, just not until after the autopsy.

6

I always carry a knife in my purse . . .
you know, in case of cheesecake or something.
—T-SHIRT

Uncle Bob and Angel stayed behind to continue the investigation, but Osh, Garrett, and I left the gas station feeling even more frustrated than when we'd gotten there. Reyes had gone feral, the world was being devoured by an alternate hell dimension, and a supernatural entity was killing humans on this plane.

We pulled behind Calamity's in Garrett's truck.

"I need food," Osh said. "And a shower."

"Late night?" I asked.

"Very."

"You aren't winning souls at the card tables again, are you?"

"What?" He winked at me, then opened the door and stepped out so I could vacate the premises. Garrett was going to give him a ride home.

"Are you going to be okay?" Garrett asked, his voice soft with concern.

Osh scoffed. "You know she can kill you with her pinkie, right?"

"I'll be fine," I said, ignoring him. "Let me know if you find out anything new."

"Will do, if you'll return the favor."

"Of course." I started to scoot out, but he put a hand on my arm.

"Charles," he said, his voice edged with warning, "that's the deal. We share info, right?"

I narrowed my lids. "Right."

"And I don't mean three days after the fact."

Ah. He was still bent about that. "So, the same day. Gotcha."

I gave him two thumbs-ups, then scooted across the seat and out the door. Osh offered me an encouraging grin before he climbed back in.

"Do we need to move this up?" Garrett asked.

We'd planned on luring Reyes into a trap the next day. Garrett had to get a few supplies first.

"No. We'll stick with the plan and meet up tomorrow morning."

"You got it," he said.

The truck roared away, as trucks are wont to do, and I headed around front to the outside stairs. I was just about to take said stairs, my mouth watering at the thought of a hot cup of java juice, when my friend Pari called.

I pushed a nifty button on my phone. "Hey, Pari, what's up?"

"Hey, Chuck. I've been meaning to call. See how you were. See if you've managed to destroy any small countries."

"Hey, I've only destroyed parts of small countries. Never a whole one."

"Yeah, whatever helps you sleep at night, babe." She was pretending to be okay. I could hear a slight tremble in her voice. Pari was not exactly the trembling sort.

"Pari, what's going on?"

"Oh, not much. The usual. Could you drop by sometime today? There was a detective here."

Alarm shot through me. Pari had a habit of hacking government facilities. "A detective? What happened? Are you okay? Did you hack the Pentagon again?"

"I'm fine. And no. He just had a couple of questions. You know, the usual stuff. Where were you on the night of the fifteenth between the hours of 9:00 P.M. and 4:00 A.M.? Can anyone corroborate that? Is there any particular reason you don't want to take a polygraph test?"

"I'll be there in five."

"'Kay. Thanks."

I hung up, wondering if I should run upstairs and tell Cookie, but her car hadn't been at our apartment building. I'd tell her later.

I walked the two blocks to Pari's shop and went in the back door. She'd prepared for my visit. Door to the public area closed. Shades on. Coffee brewed. Good girl.

The minute I stepped inside, however, I felt it. The tremble in her voice may have been slight over the phone, but the tremble in her emotions felt like the earth shaking under my feet. Alarm rushed up my esophagus and tightened around my throat, almost cutting off my air supply, which was a rather extreme reaction to Pari's emotional state.

Then I realized I was mimicking her physical response to whatever had her on edge. It had to be bad. Pari was as cool as a cucumber in the Arctic. Her vocabulary didn't include the word *panic*.

I feigned nonchalance and strolled into her office. She was sitting at her desk, pretending to work in a red, sleeveless halter that showcased her ink.

She looked up and acted surprised to see me so soon, but I felt relief flood every cell in her body.

"Oh, hey," she said, all sunshine and smiles.

She stood to hug me, then gestured toward a chair. I sat across from her and took the cup she offered. She made a killer cappuccino.

"How have you been?" I asked in lieu of moaning aloud after my first sip.

"Good," she lied. She sat back down, chewed at her lips for a few minutes, then stabbed me with the most serious expression I'd ever seen her wear. Not that I could see much of it from behind her dark glasses, but still.

"I may have inadvertently murdered someone."

I choked softly, then questioned her with raised brows.

"They found a body."

"I guess that's better than losing one."

"A guy's."

"Okay."

"The only thing he had on him was a card from my shop."

"Well, you do own a tattoo parlor. It's not odd that somebody would have your card, right?"

"Right." She twisted her hands together. "There's that, but I'd written my name and cell number on the back."

"So, you knew him?"

"I told the cops I didn't."

"You lied to them?"

"Yes."

"Care to explain why?"

"Because, like I said, I may have killed him. Well, Tre and I may have killed him. But we didn't mean to."

"Then I think technically that would be manslaughter. Not murder. I'm sure they'll understand," I said, tossing my own lie into the conversation.

"What? Oh, right. Manslaughter. Is it still manslaughter if it's self-defense?"

"Why don't you start at the beginning?"

She gathered her resolve in one shaky breath and plowed headlong into her story. "Well, as you know, Tre and I have been seeing each other off and on for a while now."

"How is Tre?" Tre was one of her artists. One of her tall, dark, delicious artists. "Still painfully gorgeous?"

"Oh, yes. Among other things."

"Okay, I'm with you so far. Off and on. Painfully gorgeous."

"So, it was during one of our off times that I met a man named Hector Felix. Tre had gone to California to visit family for a few days when Hector comes in with a couple of his friends wanting a tattoo. A Native American symbol for prosperity. Or maybe porn. I can't remember. Anyway, I gave him some ink that night, and he was just so charming."

"Aren't they all?"

"And thoughtful."

"Yep."

"And, well, loaded."

"Ah."

"He asked me out, and I just thought it would be nice to be taken somewhere special for once."

"Macho Taco not doing it for you anymore?"

"We went out, but it didn't take long for me to realize he was bat shit. In the most sincere sense of the term. Guy was crazy, Chuck. Certifiable. He was possessive and jealous from day one. Like he didn't even try to hide it. You know, most of the time, the really bad ones at least put on a show at first. Make you think they won't break into a jealous rage just for you thanking the waiter."

"When it's obvious like that, it's an entitlement thing."

"Makes sense. I'm not sure what came over me, why I did it, but I went out with him a second time."

"You didn't."

"I did."

"You shouldn't have."

"I shouldn't have. I should have broken it off immediately."

"Why didn't you?"

One dark strand fell loose from her hairband. She tucked it behind her ear. "You'll think I'm shallow."

"Pari, there's no shame in wanting something secure."

"Oh, no, that wasn't it. I just wanted to drive his Lamborghini."

I fought a grin. "Ladies and gentlemen, the Pari we all know and love. Speed freak."

"It was so stupid of me. I broke it off after the second date."

When she mentioned the date, I felt a ripple of repulsion shudder through her. "What happened?"

She shook her head. "It doesn't matter. Bottom line: nobody leaves Hector without Hector's permission."

"He actually said that?"

"Repeatedly. He harassed me for weeks, but he didn't do anything that the cops could trace back to him. Nothing I could call and report him for. Everything he did would have been his word against mine, and it started out small. The mirror on my car had been broken off. There were bullet holes in the plate glass windows up front. Then it all just escalated. My electricity got turned off. One of my regulars was assaulted when he left the shop. Then one day I came home to find all my clothes cut into pieces.

"When I confronted him, he said he tried to warn me. That I could never prove a thing. And that he had a lot of friends who could attest to his whereabouts."

"So, you did try to report him?" Normally, filing a police report would be the first thing I'd tell a client to do, but this situation had gone beyond that. I grew worried there *would* be a police report out there with both their names on it—a.k.a. evidence.

"No. I wasn't born yesterday, Charley. I know how these things work. He has money and connections and shady friends. Nothing I accused him of would've stuck."

"That might be a good thing since you told the detective you didn't know him."

"It was stupid, though. I should've told the truth. I just panicked."

"I'm so sorry about all this. I wish you would've told me."

"Seriously, Chuck? You had enough problems to deal with. How often does your pregnant best friend have to seek sacred ground just to stay alive?"

"Well, there was that."

"Also, by the time he started harassing me, you'd forgotten all about me."

"What?" I stabbed her with my best horrified expression before realizing she wasn't speaking metaphorically. I'd literally forgotten her. In my own defense, I'd forgotten everyone. "This happened during my stint in Amnesia-ville?"

"Yes."

"Gawd, I'm the worst sort of friend."

"True. You could try to think of others occasionally."

"But you know, you could've called Uncle Bob."

"I didn't want anyone else involved. By that point, I was embarrassed."

"You're too hard on yourself."

"No, I'm too smart for that shit. I mean, money? Seriously? The guy had the personality of bulldozer. But those wheels, Chuck." She clamped her hands at her heart. "Twenty-inch polished aluminum alloys with Brembo brakes."

"And some girls like diamonds."

She snorted. "Please. Give me a 6.5-liter V-12 with a seven-speed manual transmission over a rock any day."

"So, what happened?"

"A few nights ago, he came to the shop after I'd closed. Tre was back from California, but he'd already gone home for the night. Hector, as usual, was wasted. He attacked me. Said the only way a bitch left him was in a pine box."

"Dude had serious abandonment issues."

"Among others."

I gave her a minute to gather her emotions. It didn't take long.

"Bottom line, he flat-out tried to kill me."

I eased forward and took her hand. Tears slid from behind her dark glasses. She swiped at them angrily.

"He was . . . he was choking me."

I squeezed her hand to cover up the anger spiking inside me.

"He was so strong. I've taken self-defense and martial arts classes my entire life, and I still couldn't fight him off." She bit down and turned her face away. "I was on the verge of blacking out when Tre came back to the shop. He'd forgotten his wallet."

"Thank God," I said.

She nodded and swallowed hard before continuing. "He hit Hector with a baseball bat I keep for protection, but it barely fazed him. Whatever designer drug he'd taken was powerful. He went after Tre like a raging bull. We fought him for what seemed like hours before Tre finally got him in a headlock. He choked him out, and when Hector came to, he bolted."

"Wait, he ran out?" I asked, a little surprised.

"Yes. But by the time it was said and done, there was blood everywhere. All over my office. All over the floor. All over the walls. Hector stumbled out after being beaten bloody, and two days later they found his body in the desert."

"How long had he been dead?"

"According to preliminary reports, about two days."

"The detective told you that?"

"Not exactly."

Dread clenched my throat. "Pari, you didn't."

"I did."

"Okay, that's it. No more hacking government databases until all this blows over. They can trace that shit, you know."

"I panicked."

"I don't blame you. But, Pari, why didn't you call the police that night?"

"Tre convinced me not to. He knew him. Or, well, he knew his mother."

"And?"

"Her name is Edina Felix. She's a very powerful matriarch in El Paso."

"Matriarch?" An odd term.

"She runs a few legitimate businesses that Tre swears are a cover for a huge crime ring."

"Oh. That's . . . ambitious of her."

"Let's just say the mental illness was inherited, from what Tre told me."

"In what way?" I asked, growing even more concerned.

"They found the last girl who dumped one of her sons bleeding out in an alley with her face slashed."

I eased back into the chair.

"They never pinned it on Hector, of course, but that poor girl. . . ."

"You keep saying *girl*. How old was she?"

Pari pulled off the sunglasses and pinched the bridge of her nose. Waves of terror washed over her. I had never known Pari to be afraid of anything. Or anyone. She was tough, resilient, and irreverent to anyone who tried to control her. But Hector really scared her.

"Pari? How old?"

"Sixteen," she said at last. "The girl was sixteen."

A shock wave rocketed through me, causing me to flinch visibly. Sixteen? Who does something like that to a sixteen-year-old?

"It was a few months ago," Pari added.

"How old was Hector?"

"He was thirty-two.

"So, he was a child molester, too?"

"It would seem so."

"Did the girl die?"

"Tre didn't know. He didn't think so, but her family moved away."

"I need to talk to Tre."

"Good luck. He's gone."

"What do you mean?"

"He didn't stick around to be sliced up and left in an alley," she said in his defense. "He took off the day after Hector attacked me."

"He just left you here?"

"What? No. It wasn't like that. He begged me to go with him. It's a little different when you have a business. I can't just abandon my customers and leave town."

"You can, actually," I said, encouraging that very thing.

"Chuck, you know I can't." Her expression urged me to look for the deeper meaning, and it took me a moment to realize she was talking about the terms of her probation.

"Pari, even people in your situation can leave town with permission."

"Not me. My probation officer's a dick. I'm thinking about asking him out, though. He has an incredibly sexy sneer."

I laughed softly. "Do you have a number where I can reach him? I have some questions."

"For the love of God, Chuck, you're a married woman. Why do you need to talk to my probation officer?"

"Tre," I said, coughing on a half-sipped, half-inhaled sip of coffee. "I need to talk to Tre."

"Oh. Okay."

I handed her my phone, and she typed it in. "So, which detective came to see you?"

"Is *godlike* one or two words?" she asked, concentrating on my phone.

"Tre's that good in bed?"

"Yes. Yes, he is." She finished and handed it back. "Oh, and it was a Detective Joplin."

I groaned aloud. Could this day get any worse? "Joplin hates me."

"He didn't seem the most pleasant sort of guy. He seemed . . . dogged."

Pari was still terrified. It trembled just beneath her colorful yet steely surface. I could hardly blame her. Joplin terrified me, too. She needed answers. And closure. And I needed to pray that Hector's death was not the result of the fight. Knowing she'd killed someone, even in self-defense, would devastate her.

"Okay, if Joplin comes back, don't give him anything. He'll take the slightest crumb and run with it, so don't say a word. Lawyer up and call it a day."

"But won't that be admitting something happened?"

"If he comes back a second time, hon, he'll already know. But don't worry. I'll find out if Hector died as a result of the altercation. In the meantime"—I scanned the walls of her cluttered office—"how much do you like this building?"

7

I'll tell you what's wrong with society.
No one drinks from the skulls of their enemies anymore.

—T-SHIRT

Pari refused to let me burn down her place of business-slash-apartment to get rid of the evidence. Blood splatter was impossible to scrub away. So, instead of solving a crime, I was going to have to cover one up. But I had an inkling how to do exactly that. I just needed a little help from a friend.

Thus, I tried repeatedly to call said friend, a clairvoyant named Nicolette Lemay who could see people's deaths through their eyes via a series of hellacious dreams. Thank God for psychotherapy.

Since she didn't pick up, I could only assume she'd either blocked my number—understandable—or she was at work. Hoping for the latter, I hightailed it back to the office, hopped in Misery, then drove to Pres, where she worked in post-op.

Ten minutes later, I was standing in front of a nurses' station, waiting for her to pop out of a door. Any door would do. When she did, choosing to emerge from one appropriately marked Gastroenterology: Exit Only, she took one look at me, then slowed her step in surprise.

She only knew the bare minimum where I was concerned, but it was enough to set her on edge. She recovered after a moment and picked up her pace again, but it was a long hall.

A natural beauty, Nicolette had cinnamon-colored skin and hip-length black hair currently pulled back and stuffed under a cap. Her crowning achievement, however, were her eyes. Large. Dark. Seductive. The kind people paid a fortune for in liners and false lashes to try to duplicate.

"Charley," she said, stopping in front of me. "What are you doing here?"

This may have been a bad idea. She was nervous to see me. It radiated out of her rather like the perspiration covering her brow and upper lip.

"I just came by to say hi." This was going to be awkward to get out of.

"No, you didn't." Her lids narrowed. Then she leaned closer and whispered. "Did something happen?"

"Well, yes, but not in that way. Speaking of which, you seem really nervous. Is everything okay?"

"No, I just thought I might've been dreaming there for a minute."

"Hopefully not," I said, leaning in for a hug. "Every time you dream of someone, they die a few days later."

"Not always."

"Really?"

"Yeah, sometimes they die that very day."

I laughed softly at her teasing. "So, how's that going?"

"Okay," she said, lifting a slim shoulder. "No murders lately or I would've called. I've only had three incidents since we met, and they were all natural causes."

"Well, cool. Cool." I studied the wallpaper. A stapler on the desk. A basket of pens with a yellow ribbon around it.

Nicolette giggled. "Are you going to tell me why you're really here?"

I bit my bottom lip, realizing what I was about to ask might sound bad. But it was now or never.

"Can we go over here?" I motioned for her to follow me until we were a few feet from the nurses' station and hovering near the entrance of a waiting room with a nervous looking couple inside. "I have a favor to ask. A big one."

"I'm intrigued."

"I'm glad, because this might sound bad, so I want you to keep an open mind."

"Charley, I may not have known you for very long, but you did me a huge favor once. I figure the least I can do is repay the gesture."

"Nicolette, you don't owe me anything. You know that, right?"

"Of course. Still, good karma is good karma."

"True." Gosh, I liked her. "So, can you steal a few pints of blood for me?"

The surprise on her face glowed. Clearly, she hadn't expected me to ask her to commit a crime. Strange.

"Can I ask why you need them?"

"You probably don't want to know."

"Hmmm." She pursed her lips, pondering her answer, trying to decide how to word it, how to put it as delicately as possible. "No."

Oh, well, that was easy. " 'Kay. Thanks for your time."

She laughed softly and pulled me back when I tried to walk away. She leaned close and said, "It's not that I won't. It's that I can't. Every pouch of blood has to be signed for."

"Really? Do they get stolen often?"

Nicolette shrugged. "It is what it is. The only way to get blood without getting caught on Candid Camera would be to knock off a blood bank or a mobile collection van or something."

"That's it," I said, my mind racing.

"I was kidding. You know that, right?"

I started backing away. "No, yeah, totally." I had a heist to plan. "Thanks so much." I waved as I headed toward the door. "Oh, hey." I turned back. "Did your mother ever marry you off? Last time we spoke, she was going to take out an ad."

"Yeah, that didn't really go well. She's worried my eggs are going to dry up and I won't be able to give her grandchildren."

I snorted. "Aren't you a little young?"

"That's what I said. She told me we have a genetic disorder called early onset egg dysplasia."

That time I laughed out loud. Then I stopped abruptly. "Wait, is that a real thing?"

She folded her arms at her chest and grinned. "No, it is not."

"Well, good luck with that."

"Thank you."

I called Cook on my way back to the office. "Hey, Cook. I need you to see if there are going to be any mobile blood collection vans out tonight."

"You mean like a Red Cross kind of thing?"

"Exactly. I need to knock one over ay-sap."

"As in rob? You're going to rob a mobile blood collection unit?"

"Affirmative."

"May I ask why?"

"Because I figure robbing a mobile will be easier than robbing an established blood collection business. A building would have better security."

"I'm sure they have wonderful security. But I meant, what has possessed you to steal blood?"

"It's for a project."

"What kind of project?"

"A . . . bloody one."

"Charley."

"Look, just trust me. I need blood from lots of different people."

"Did you ever think that the blood you are planning on stealing was meant for a purpose? What if someone dies because the hospitals run out of their blood type?"

"You did not just put that on me."

"Damn sure did. Where are you?"

"In Misery, both literally and figuratively, behind Calamity's."

Cookie's head appeared at a window above me. "Why are you just sitting there?"

"Because I don't want to get out yet."

"Why don't you want to get out yet?"

"Because I'm waiting for the angry archangel looking in my driver's-side window to *go away*!" I yelled the last two words, hoping beyond hope Michael would get the message. He was a messenger, after all.

Alas, he did not. He stood his ground, towering over me like an ominous statue, the combination of dark hair, silvery eyes, and massive wings breathtaking.

"There's an angel standing beside your car?"

Another face shone in the window, a round one with a veil and a habit, in the nondrug sense.

"You have a visitor."

"I see that." I waved excitedly at my homegirl Sister Mary Elizabeth. She lived at a local convent. The same convent that took Quentin in when he had no one and nowhere to go. He was special, and the mother superior sensed that. I would be forever grateful to them. "I'll be up as soon as I ditch the cherub."

I hung up, then rolled down my window. "I gave at the office."

"Rey'azikeen has been awakened."

An electrical current rushed over my skin. No matter how many times I saw one, being so close to an angel, especially an archangel, was a surreal experience.

"Yeah. I know. I woke him. Accidentally. But I'm working on it. I have a plan. Will you go away now?"

"For the third time, a volatile god is loose on this plane."

"And that's my fault?"

I rolled up my window and opened the door, encouraging him to move aside. He stepped away so I could get out.

"Look, I get it," I said, slamming the door. "But this god just happens to be your Boss's little brother. Isn't there some kind of concession? Some kind of special dispensation for family members?"

"Yes. Three days."

"I can work with that. Three days. We can get the supplies we need, meet back at—"

"The three days that have already passed."

I blinked in surprise, then slowly glared up at him. "Are you messing with me?" I'd wondered that about this particular angel more than once. Did supreme beings have a sense of humor? I'd always doubted it, but who knows?

"I am not."

"You know what? You have your rules and your laws and your decrees, and I've been pretty good about following them."

"It."

"What?"

"You've been good about following it. We gave you only one rule—a life may be restored only if the soul has not already been freed. Only if it has not left the vessel and entered our Father's kingdom."

"Dude, I know the rule," I said, trying not to let the resentment I felt filter into my voice. I could've brought three people back the other day. Instead, I had to follow the rule. My rule. Created, I was certain, for me and me alone.

Two women came out of the restaurant and walked past us. Their expressions made me remember that the average joe couldn't see Michael unless he wanted them to.

"Come here," I said, leading him to an alcove that only I fit into. His wings were too tall, even folded as they were. "Okay, yes, you expressly gave me only one rule, but I assumed I had to follow the other ten as well. Amirite?"

He inclined his head, just barely, in acknowledgment.

"And I follow them without question." When he arched a skeptical brow, I added, "Most of the time. My point is that I've been a pretty good grim reaper. I've done my job without complaint and . . . wait." My brows inched together. "So the three days started the moment Rey'azikeen was awakened on this plane?"

Incline.

"In other words, they're coming to an end."

Incline.

"Okay, tall, dark, and silent, what exactly happens when the end comes? Will he be cast off this plane like I will if I break my one and only rule?"

He tilted his head to the side as though studying me. "No."

"Then what?" I did actually have a point with the line of questioning I'd chosen. I was gathering intel. What options, when it came to Reyes, were there? Would Michael trap him? If so, how? "What will you do when the countdown—thanks for the heads-up, by the way—comes to an end?"

He stood a moment, contemplating how much to tell me. At least that was the only reason I could think of for drawing out his answer. When he finally spoke, it was with a sadness I had yet to receive from him. But his words, as tenderly spoken as they were, siphoned the breath from my lungs.

"We will send an army. We will slay him if we can."

The world slowed around us, and I didn't know which one of us was doing it. Everything stilled. The cars driving on the side street slowed, then came to a complete stop. A couple of college kids out for a jog froze in midair. A bird coming in for a landing on a Dumpster hung suspended in flight, a beautiful testament to its ability. And sound ceased to exist.

"Michael," I began, but my voice failed me. I had to swallow and then try again. "Michael, there were two malevolent gods on this plane, and you did nothing about it. You never intervened. Why now? Why with Reyes?"

"They did not threaten the very existence of every sentient being on this planet."

"They were malevolent," I argued. "Of course they did."

"They were amateurs. Schoolchildren. Bullies playing pranks."

"They killed people," I said, astonished we were even having this conversation. "They killed people I loved. People Reyes loved."

"And you stopped them. Both. Which proves my point."

I scoffed breathily and turned my back to him, placing a hand on the cool brick wall to steady my shaking legs. "And Reyes? What is he? A malevolent god like the others?"

"Rey'azikeen is a general. Trained in combat. Able to kill both physically and mentally, he is a master soldier and manipulator. He has proven what he is capable of countless times. It must end, Elle-Ryn-Ahleethia."

An army. Of angels. Cutting into him. Stabbing him. Bringing my husband to his knees. Stealing his last breath.

"Is this your Boss talking?"

"It is my Father's will, yes."

I leaned my head against a brick. Either Reyes learned to behave and play nice with the other kids on the playground or his Brother would send an army to strike him down. And I thought *my* family was dysfunctional.

Remembering I was not above begging, I whirled around to face him. "Give me more time, Michael. I can . . . I can bring Reyes back."

"Rey'azikeen is feral."

"I can rein him in." I glared at the celestial being towering over me. "I can tame him." Surely, somewhere inside him, a part of Reyes was still . . . Reyes. Surely I could tame the beast. "Give me three more days."

He bowed his head and closed his eyes as though communicating with heaven directly, then he opened them just as quickly. "You have one."

And he was gone.

He vanished before my eyes. Traffic restarted. The joggers continued their journey. The bird landed with one elegant swoop. And sound rushed at me from all sides.

One day. I dug out my phone and checked the time. Twenty-four hours to trap my husband and knock some sense into him.

8

Why is it so hard to find an exercise bike with a nice little basket where I can put my vodka and nachos?

—MEME

I texted Garrett and informed him of our new deadline, then took the stairs two at a time.

Sister Mary Elizabeth stood in the middle of Cookie's office, hesitant to greet me.

I strode over and pulled her into a hug.

"Are you okay?" she asked, concern lining her pretty face.

"Yes. Michael is just a little prickly sometimes."

"Michael? *The* Michael?"

Sister Mary Elizabeth could hear the angels in the heavens. The news. The gossip. The turmoil. But she couldn't see them. I could understand her fascination. Their immense power almost bowled me over every time I met one.

"What's up, buttercup?" I asked, peeling off my jacket.

"It's the angels."

"It usually is." I offered her a cup, then poured one for myself.

"They're in an uproar."

"They usually are."

"What did Michael say?" Cookie asked.

"Pretty much that in a nutshell. They're upset another volatile—not malevolent, per se—god is loose on this plane, and they've given me a day to rein him in. Is that what you're hearing?" I asked the sister.

She nodded and sat in the chair across from Cookie. "I am a little surprised, however."

"By?"

"The fact that they gave you another day."

"Well, I did ask politely."

"But they never do that. They never waver."

"Gosh, I feel all special and gooey inside."

"Charley," Cookie said, sensing my agitation, "what happens if you can't get to him?"

I closed my lids to stop the wetness from forming behind them. They stung, but my chest stung more. Despite everything we'd done, to give us this kind of ultimatum seemed wholly unfair.

When I opened my eyes, Cookie's expression had shifted from worry to fear.

"They send an army," I said, my voice edged with resentment. "They cut him down."

A hand flew over her mouth, and Sister Mary Elizabeth hugged herself, worry lining her bright face.

"Sister, I'd be very open to some prayers if you and the other sisters would be willing."

"Absolutely. I know they will be. But I also have a message from the mother superior."

"Oh?" I took a long draft, daring the scalding coffee to burn my throat.

"She wanted you to know—on the down low, mind you—that, well, we suspect the Vatican has allowed Quentin to stay at the convent for ulterior motives."

"As motives so often are. What do you mean?"

"They're asking questions. About . . ." She cleared her throat and started again. "About your daughter."

And the hits just kept coming. I froze in place as a rancid kind of anger washed over me. It was one thing to go after me. It was another to go after mine.

"What do they know?"

"I have no idea. They're not very sharing. They've just been asking questions. The mother superior wanted me to tell you they're trying to be subtle about it, which has raised her suspicions even more."

"What does Quentin have to do with it?"

"We believe they're using him as an excuse to come into the complex and talk to the nuns. And they've questioned him, too. But I have to be honest. I think he knows what they're doing. His answers are always . . . vague."

That's my boy.

"Who are *they*, exactly?"

"A bishop from Santa Fe and another man. An investigator of some kind. And if I'm not mistaken, he comes straight from the Vatican."

I nodded. What the hell were they up to?

"I can let you know when they come back. If they come back. In the meantime, we'll pray for your success, Charley."

We stood, and she crushed me into a hug. She was strong for such a tiny thing.

"Thank you for bringing this to me, and thank the mother superior for me."

Sister Mary Elizabeth nodded, then hurried out the door.

"You've had quite the day," Cookie said.

"I can't help but wonder if everything we're working on is tied together somehow."

"I agree. Robert called. He said the first victim, Indigo Russell, had been in therapy for something that happened to her about a year ago. He's working on getting a court order to find out more."

"Good deal. I'm waiting on a call from Garrett. He's working a skip today. Something he couldn't get out of. A woman up on distribution charges decided she had better things to do than go to court. But he's promised to get back to me the minute he's tracked down the supplies we need. Any news on a mobile blood collection unit?"

"There's one operating at an event tonight, some kind of charity fair."

"Perfect."

"I thought we decided you were not going to steal blood."

"I'm not. I'm going to borrow some. Speaking of which, what are you doing tonight?"

"I'm not robbing a mobile blood collection van."

"Excellent. Neither am I."

"Then why—?"

"We aren't robbing the van. We're stealing it."

"Oh. In that case, I'm in."

I decided to hunt my old friend Rocket down. He could have some information on Reyes—namely, information concerning Reyes's human side. Is it still there? Is it something that can be saved? Or is he 100 percent deity? Is my husband truly gone?

Rocket, who died in the fifties, lived in an abandoned mental asylum. The same asylum in which he'd endured terrible things. The same asylum in which he'd died. I couldn't be entirely positive, but I suspected he'd had electroshock therapy. His mind, part of it at least, had been erased. He was a child trapped in a man's body.

But Rocket was a savant, especially when it came to the departed. He knew the name of every human in history who'd died. Would my husband be on that list?

I was so deep in thought, I didn't realize I'd turned down the wrong street. I pulled a U-turn and tried again, then realized I was on the right street. But it was different.

I pulled up to the locked security gate that led to the asylum. It was the right gate. I was at the right place, but the building, the asylum, had been destroyed.

Practically falling out of Misery, I stumbled to the entrance and scanned the area. Debris from the building lay in massive heaps. Thick slabs of crumbling concrete sat scarred with thin scorch marks. The entire property had been leveled.

Reyes. It had to be Reyes.

I pressed my hands over my mouth to keep from yelling Rocket's name. Had Reyes hurt him? Could he?

Without a clue as to how long I'd been standing there, I finally snapped to my senses and pressed shaking fingers to the keypad that opened the security gate. A couple of kids on bikes rode up. I listened as they spoke.

"I told you it was gone, *pendejo*. It was there yesterday, and today it's gone."

"Wow," the other one said.

"Right? My mom called the cops. She thought we were having an earthquake last night."

I whirled around. "Last night? This happened last night?"

The smallest one nodded. "My mom freaked. There was a loud crash. The building was there, then it wasn't."

"That creepy building has been there since I was a kid," said the ten-year-old. Eleven at the most.

"It was here for decades," I said, a pain throbbing in my heart. "I can't believe it's gone."

"Hey," the small one said, "you know the code? You know who owns this building?"

"Yes." I opened the gate and stepped inside the chain-link fence. Swallowing past the lump in my throat, I said, "I do."

"Oh, man. Do you know what happened?"

"I don't." I looked at the rubble that used to be Rocket's home. "But I'm going to find out."

I walked around the massive pile, careful where I stepped. Once the kids had pedaled out of sight, I started calling for Rocket.

"Rocket, are you here?" I tried to find a way into the middle. The walls where Rocket had written name after name in preparation for Beep's army were nothing more than debris, fragments of an incredible mind. "Rocket?"

I could've summoned him, but he had to be scared and disoriented as it was. Despite my best effort, tears slipped down my cheeks.

"Strawberry?"

Strawberry Shortcake, or Rebecca Taft, her real name, lived with Rocket and his little sister, Blue. I could only hope she hadn't been here when this happened. I couldn't believe Reyes would do something like this, but who else? He knew how to hurt me. He knew where to insert the knife to do the most damage, and he'd started with my beloved Rocket's home.

Then I heard him.

"Miss Charlotte?"

I spun around, trying to localize the sound.

"Miss Charlotte?" Rocket repeated. "I didn't say anything, Miss Charlotte."

I grew more frantic with each heartbeat. "Rocket, where are you?"

"Down here."

I stumbled up a mound of debris. A small opening between slabs of concrete showed a route to the basement, and the part I stood on looked like it could collapse at any second.

"Rocket? Are you down there?"

His face appeared in the opening at last, round and bright.

"Rocket." I put my hand through the opening.

He reached up and took hold of it. "I can't find Blue. I have to find her. She'll be so scared, Miss Charlotte. You have to come help me."

He tugged on my arm. Rocket, completely oblivious to his own strength, could pull it completely off if he were scared enough. Or suck me down into the debris.

"Rocket, I can't get down there."

"I'll help." He tugged again, and the debris shifted beneath my weight, lowering at least a couple of inches.

I had to wrench my hand from his grasp, peeling my fingers out of his meaty fist, or be pulled under.

"I can't go down there, Rocket. It's too dangerous."

"But I can't find her, Miss Charlotte."

I lay my forehead on a slab of concrete in frustration. I could summon the departed, but only if I had a name to summon. Everyone called his little sister Blue, but that wasn't her real name. I couldn't call her.

Or could I?

I may not have been able to summon the little doll, who'd died of dust pneumonia at the age of five, but I could certainly call her.

"I'll be right back, Rocket."

With each move carefully calculated, I eased off the pile of rubble, slipping once and almost falling to my death—or to the rest of my horribly maimed life. After regaining my footing, I noticed the kids were back, only they'd brought reinforcements. There was now a veritable hoard of bicycle-laden street urchins, watching my every move from beyond the chain link.

My next moves would probably seem a little silly, but that was my middle name.

"Blue!" I called out her name, which seemed a little old-school, but a girl's gotta do what a girl's gotta do. "Blue, sweetheart, where are you?"

Rocket appeared at my side. "Is she here, Miss Charlotte?"

I threw myself into his arms. "Rocket, honey, are you okay?"

Putting him at arm's length, I pressed my palms to his face to check him over.

"I'm okay, Miss Charlotte. I didn't say nothing. I promise."

"What?"

"I didn't tell him. Not nothing. He was so mad."

Gooseflesh erupted over every part of my body. "Who are you talking about, hon?"

"I didn't tell him, Miss Charlotte. I would never. That's breaking rules. No breaking rules. But now I can't find Blue."

"Rocket, sweetheart." I tried to bring him back to me. "Was it Reyes? Did Reyes do this?"

His impaired gaze landed on me in confusion. "No, ma'am. Not him."

Relief flooded every cell I possessed. But then who? "Do you know who did it?"

"It only looked like him. He was so mad, Miss Charlotte."

My lungs seized when I realized what he meant. It only looked like Reyes but wasn't him. This was not happening. "It looked like Reyes?"

"Reyes Alexander Farrow," he said with a nod. "Only not. Not anymore."

I sank onto a concrete slab, the edges jagged but also burned. Parts of the surface had been charred. Narrow black strips lined parts of the crumbled walls with tiny burst patterns. Almost as though the building had been struck by lightning over and over.

Reyes had been covered in live electrical currents when he came out of the god glass. Could he use it as a weapon? Is that what did this?

Rocket spun in circles, calling out his sister's name to no avail. I stopped him with my hands on his shoulders. "Rocket, I need to know, is Reyes in there anywhere? Is there still a part of him inside?"

Rocket's expression turned grave. "I didn't see him, but I wasn't looking neither. He's not dead. Reyes Alexander Farrow. He's not dead and gone. Not yet."

"Not yet?" I asked, elated. "Is . . . is his time coming?"

He bowed his head and went to work. When Rocket searched his data banks, he sometimes blinked in rapid succession. He was doing that now, and I realized I was holding my breath in anticipation.

"His time is moving. It won't stop."

Okay, no idea what that meant, but I was going to take it as a good sign.

"Blue!" he called out again.

I followed suit, calling out his sister's name. The kids looked on with both curiosity and apprehension, not sure what to think of my conversation with Rocket, an entity they could not see.

Most of them, anyway.

I noticed one of the bicyclists' coloring was a little off. He was one of the younger ones, his bike, a dark maroon, now only a faded version of that once vibrant color. The boy looked alarmingly similar to the smaller kid I'd spoken to earlier.

When my gaze landed on him, he raised an arm, extended an index finger, and pointed to a copse of trees on the north side of the property.

I turned and saw a slight discoloration behind a row of bushes.

"Blue?" I said, stepping closer.

Rocket followed, hope burning in his eyes.

"Blue?" I asked as I got closer.

Suddenly and without hesitation, the little girl whirled around and ran into my arms. *My* arms. I knelt down and caught her, wrapping said arms tight around her tiny body. She sobbed onto my shoulder as Rocket ran toward us.

"Blue?" He stumbled beside me and wrapped us both in his cool embrace.

In all the years I'd known Rocket, Blue had never let me get within ten feet of her. She either hid behind her brother or stayed away altogether. But now, today, she was letting me hug her. Letting me comfort her.

I stroked her hair, a short, dark bob, and rocked her while Rocket cried against us. And a vengeful kind of fury sparked inside me, kindled by my love for these two.

A few kids took out their cell phones and began filming. Kids these days. I could only imagine what this looked like. Sadly, I could not have cared less.

I glanced at the departed boy and silently thanked him. He didn't react, just watched. Even after the other kids left to show their friends the video of the crazy lady, the young entity stayed behind.

After Blue had spent all her tears, she leaned back, looked at her big brother, and patted his face a microsecond before jumping into his arms.

"I'm so sorry this happened, Blue."

She'd buried her face in Rocket's shirt, but she nodded, acknowledging my comment. Also a first.

"She didn't tell him neither, Miss Charlotte."

"What?" I asked, alarmed. "Rocket, tell me what happened."

"He came here. He was so mad. He wasn't him anymore, but he came here, anyway. That's breaking the rules, Miss Charlotte."

I patted his back and rubbed Blue's. "I know, hon. But what did he want? What didn't you tell him?"

"Where it was."

Confusion swept through me. "He was looking for something?"

He nodded. "We didn't tell him, though. Neither of us. We would never."

"Rocket, honey, what was he looking for?"

"The embers."

"The embers?"

"The ashes."

"Ashes from what? Rocket, what does that mean?"

"It means—"

Before he could get out another word, Blue slammed a hand over his mouth.

Disappointed, I started to protest, but she slammed a hand over mine as well, then she took it away and held an index finger over her mouth to shush us.

They straightened and glanced around as though searching for something. I joined them but saw nothing even though they must have. Their heads swiveled in the same direction, and a microsecond later, they vanished.

I turned so fast I almost fell, but I saw nothing out of the ordinary.

Just in case, I put my hand to the ground and lifted Artemis from the earth. She materialized beneath my palm and did a quick inspection of the area, sniffing and pawing at the debris. Finding nothing amiss, she gave up the search and assaulted me, knocking me to the ground and pinning me there while she licked my face.

I laughed and looked over at the boy, finally wresting a smile out of him.

9

I'm not saying I don't like you.
I'm just saying I'd unplug your life support to make a pot of coffee.
—MEME

The boy disappeared down the street before I could talk to him. He wasn't ready for the likes of me. I got that. Some days I felt the same way.

I called Cookie on the way back to the office.

She picked up, saying, "Davidson Investigations."

"Cook, I called your landline. The one to your apartment."

"Oops. Sorry, boss. How'd it go with Rocket?"

"Blue came to me."

She let out a soft gasp. "Blue? *The* Blue? The same sweet girl you've been trying to make contact with for . . ."

"Ten," I offered.

"For ten years?"

"The very same. Cookie, he destroyed the asylum."

"What? Reyes?"

"He leveled it."

"Oh, my God, Charley. I'm so sorry. I know what that place meant to you."

"And to Blue and Rocket. I don't like to be a negative Nancy, but this day has sucked."

"You need tacos." She knew me so well.

"I do. But that'll have to wait. We're doing this, Cook. We're going to try to trap him the moment the sun sets."

"Why when the sun sets? Are his powers diminished?"

"Sadly, no. I just figure fewer people will happen to spot us if we wait until dark."

"Oh, yeah, that's a good reason."

"I just wanted . . . you know . . . if anything should happen—"

"Don't you dare." She paused when her voice hitched. "Don't you even think about it. Besides, we're going to be there, Robert and I."

"Not this time, Cook."

"What? We agreed this morning. We're part of the plan."

"You were a part of it. I don't think Reyes is in there anymore. You should have seen Blue and Rocket. He left them terrified. I don't know what he's capable of now, and I just can't risk you and Uncle Bob. Not this time."

"Charlotte Jean Davidson," she said, slipping into her mommy voice.

"I love you so much."

"Charley, damn it."

"I keep telling people, *Damn It* is not my last name. It's not even my middle name."

"No, your middle name is Cookie Is Going to Kick My Ass Next Time She Sees Me."

"That's it, I'm legally changing my middle name."

Before she could make it even longer, because that one was going to be hard to explain at the registrar's office as it was, I hung up. No way was I risking my best friend's life. I'd already put her through so much, and she stuck with me, no questions asked. There was some cussing and name-calling and a little bit of hair-pulling, but no questions. And Cookie's hair grew back better than ever.

Rey'azikeen destroyed a precious memorial. The mere thought left me livid. It was time to hunt him down. To be done with this. To find out if Reyes was in there somewhere despite what Rocket said or not. Either way, I had to know.

I pulled into an empty parking lot on the outskirts of town. The land was part of the Sandia reservation, and the building used to be a casino, but the Sandia Pueblo built another one, bigger and brighter, a couple of years prior. So, lucky for us, this one lay abandoned.

Garrett was already there. I stepped out of Misery and started toward him just as Osh drove into the parking lot in a flat black Hellcat. My knees weakened at the sight of it.

Just as we did, Osh left his car lights on to illuminate the playing field. He grinned and stepped out wearing his usual attire minus the top hat.

"Do you think he'll come?" Garrett asked. He took the rifle off his open tailgate and loaded it.

I shrugged, my nerves making me seasick. "What do you think?" I asked Osh as he walked up.

He'd been busy checking out the horizon as the sun dipped past it. "I have a feeling he's already here. I think he follows you pretty much everywhere."

"I haven't felt him."

"I could be wrong. I just have a hunch, and if that hunch proves correct, he may know about our plans to trap him."

Garrett finished loading the rifle. He nodded. "Ready as I'll ever be."

After swallowing hard, I nodded back, and we took our positions.

We walked to the middle of the massive lot and stood in a triangle about twenty feet apart from each other.

Osh seemed to sense my distress. If he'd seen what had come out of that glass, he would've been more distressed himself. Then again, we were talking about Osh. Osh'ekiel the Daeva. The slave demon from hell, and apparently slaves weren't treated any better in hell than they had been on Earth.

"I can take him," he promised. "At least long enough for Swopes to get a shot." He looked at Garrett. "Just don't hit me."

"Hold him as still as you can."

When we'd settled into silence, I bowed my head and whispered my husband's name. Normally, I could summon a departed or Reyes or even an angel just by thinking a name, but Rey'azikeen was proving a little trickier in every sense of the word. I didn't know what to expect. I didn't know who to expect.

"Reyes," I said softly, reaching out with my mind.

Nothing. Naturally. Because it couldn't be that easy.

Then I remembered going through this exact same scenario three days ago when I attempted to pull Reyes out of the god glass. It didn't work then. No idea why I thought it would work now. Wishful thinking, I supposed.

I tried again. "Rey'azikeen." Nothing. Flashbacks of that night started playing in my head. "Rey'aziel," I said, the name he used in hell.

But still nothing.

"What can we do?" Garrett asked.

"I don't know. I'm trying my best."

"It's okay, love," Osh said. "If he doesn't want to be summoned, he won't be."

"I'll try again. I'll . . . I don't know . . . I'll force him."

With teeth locked, I concentrated on the beautiful man I'd married, the father of my child, the keeper of my heart, and said his name again. The name he was most likely going by now. "Rey'azikeen."

I felt a pulse in the core of my abdomen. My lids flew open. The wind had picked up and whipped my hair around my head.

Osh offered me an encouraging smile.

"Rey'azikeen," I said again, only louder this time, and I was rewarded with a warmth, a heat that washed in me and over me and through me as though I were nothing but air. He was close. We all knew it. But getting him to appear, to materialize, could be difficult.

And then I realized something. I looked at my two companions. "He's teasing us."

Osh agreed. "He's fucking with us."

Frustration cut into me. I looked toward the heavens and shouted, "This is the worst day ever!" Not that it would do any good, but for some reason I felt better.

"I was afraid this would happen," Osh said. Then he grinned, his white teeth flashing across his handsome face. He gestured at Garrett with a nod. "You're up."

Garrett slung the rifle over his shoulder and started toward me.

I took a step back in suspicion. "What? What did you two come up with?"

Garrett's gait was confident, purposeful. He didn't stop until we were barely inches apart, then he wrapped his arms around me, and said, "This," a microsecond before he planted his mouth on mine.

Shock immobilized me for what seemed like an hour. Garrett's mouth was hot against mine. Smooth. Tantalizing.

Understanding the point, I softened against him. Tilted my head for better access. Opened my mouth.

It surprised Garrett if the gentle intake of breath between our mouths was any indication, but he got over it quickly. He slid his tongue past my lips and explored to his heart's content, the kiss leisurely. Languid. Sensual.

Then again, for his plan to work, he had to make it good.

The wind whipped around us, pushing and straining to tear us apart. I wrapped one arm around his neck and kept one planted on his rib cage. Mostly in case this did actually work and he needed to get to his gun quickly.

"There!" Osh shouted above the roar of the now hurricane-strength wind.

What happened next seemed to play out in slow motion. Osh sprang forward, scrambling to attack Reyes, but his movements were slow as though swimming in molasses. The same with Garrett. He pushed me back before grabbing the gun and pulling the stock to his shoulder, but what would normally have been lightning-quick moves had decelerated to a dreamlike sequence of events.

I turned just in time to see Reyes, or Rey'azikeen as was most likely the case, appear in the distance. He walked toward me. The winds didn't affect the billowing darkness that surrounded him. Smoke cascaded off his shoulders and down his body to pool at his feet. It stirred with every step, thin bolts of electricity crackling and curling over him. And underneath it all, his fire. Always that fire. That reminder of his upbringing in hell.

I realized Reyes had slowed time. Osh could correct for that in a few moments, but Garrett, being human, could not.

Still, Reyes didn't stop it altogether. He could have, but he didn't.

I watched as he strode closer and closer. Osh dove toward him, and Garrett aimed the rifle at his midsection. He pulled the trigger, and Reyes easily sidestepped both Osh and the dart that was meant to tranquilize him.

He stopped short in front of me as the other two recovered and prepared for the next attack. Unconcerned, Reyes reached over, grabbed a handful of my hair, and pulled me roughly against him.

"You dare summon me?" he asked, anger sparking in his dark irises.

I lifted my chin, just as angry. "You destroyed Rocket's building."

I had to take advantage of his nearness, so I prepared for step two. Reyes hadn't been tranquilized, but that would have been a precautionary measure only. I'd needed him close. Physically close. This close.

I raised a hand to his chest and started to say the words that would bind him to this world, but before I got out a single consonant, he dematerialized.

I stumbled forward and then whirled around, searching for him. I could still feel his blistering heat on my skin, as though, like Icarus, I'd traveled too close to the sun. But I couldn't see him.

"Reyes!" I yelled as time bounced back, the wind even stronger.

Osh and Garrett regained their bearings and joined forces in front of me, expecting Reyes to come at us head-on again. But this being was not Reyes. This being was Rey'azikeen.

I felt the nuclear-like heat at my back a split second before an arm slid around my throat from behind. Another snaked across my midsection, and then his mouth was at my ear. His voice, smooth like butterscotch, caressed every part of me when he said, "Hold your breath."

I drew air into my lungs just as the world fell away.

10

God is love,
but Satan does that thing you like with his tongue.
—BUMPER STICKER

Reyes shifted onto the celestial plane and took me with him. The wind, like acid in this realm, stung my skin, but his arms wrapped around me were far more unsettling. Which version of the man I loved held me?

He tightened his hold, and even though I didn't think I needed air on this plane, needed to breathe in this realm, I squirmed against him as panic took root. "Let me go, Reyes."

His mouth at my ear again, he said, "This is what happens when you summon a god."

Despite the anger in his voice, despite the brutality I knew him capable of, part of me relished the embrace. I couldn't help it. I had loved this man for so very long, centuries if not eons. I leaned into him.

He pushed me off him but kept a firm grip on my left arm, presumably so I wouldn't dematerialize and escape. But I had no intention of leaving.

I did, however, try to jerk my arm free. His grip tightened in response. I refused to react. To give him the satisfaction.

Instead, I lifted my chin and dared him to do his worst.

The grin that slid across his painfully handsome face caused a pang of both sympathy and longing in my chest.

He practically scowled in response, clearly disgusted with me. "You're still in love with him," he said, his gaze boring into mine. "You believe that somewhere inside me is your Reyes. Your Rey'aziel." He pulled me closer. "But what you don't understand is that I was always lurking." He clamped his free hand around my other arm. "I am not Reyes." He pulled me close enough to see the sparkling flecks of green and gold in his coffee-colored eyes. "I am not Rey'aziel." He walked forward, pushing me until he'd backed me into a wall of some kind. A rock, its sharp edges cutting into my skin. "I am Rey'azikeen." He tightened the vise-like grip he had on my arms. "A god, even stronger now, thanks to you."

His dark gaze shimmered from underneath his lashes, cold and unforgiving. At least that's what he'd have me believe. But I felt a turbulence beneath his cool exterior.

"Why stronger?" I asked, my mind racing to find a way to get him back to the earthly plane. To bind him to it. To strip him of his powers until we could locate the human part of him.

"I learned from the best." His sensual mouth tipped up at one corner. A corner I'd tasted so many times. My mouth salivated to do it again. "Like you, I ate the flesh of my enemies. I devoured the criminal god Mae'eldeesahn and the demon assassin Kuur."

I stilled in surprise. That meant the killer, the being that had mutilated and murdered three people back on Earth, could be neither of them.

But it meant something more. It meant that he'd had to go to battle with a malevolent god. He'd had to not only survive a hell dimension but fight just to stay alive.

My throat constricted at the thought. I trained my expression to stay neutral. Empathy was not something Reyes appreciated. I imagined Rey'azikeen liked it even less.

"But you are still the best, are you not?" he asked.

"The best at what?"

"At devouring your enemies."

I had to keep him talking. Perhaps I could do the same thing to him he'd done to me. If I concentrated, could I shift and take him with me to the earthly plane? "Why did you level Rocket's building?"

He brushed a finger along my neckline. "Why do you care?"

"Because I love him."

He looked away, his sculpted jaw clamping down in frustration.

"I love him, and you scared him and left him homeless for no reason."

"I had a reason," he insisted, his heated gaze back on mine. "And you know it."

I was going about this all wrong. Honey attracted, not vinegar. "I know what?" I asked, softening my voice.

"I know you should never have sent me in there."

"I am well aware of that, too. But it was your idea."

He frowned. For a split second, he slipped and showed his hand. He didn't remember. He thought I sent him in there. I sent him to hell.

"I would never do that to you."

"You can't help it," he said as though finally understanding me. "You lie even when I know the truth. That was the second time you sent me into a hell dimension and the second time I escaped." He wrapped his hand around my throat and lifted my chin with his thumb. "Whatever will you do next?"

I'd forgotten. According to Garrett's research, I had indeed sent him to hell, but it was in lieu of the one his Brother had created for him. It was a hell from my home world. My home dimension. It was not as harsh as the one Jehovah had wanted to send him into. The one I'd eventually send him into.

"I didn't mean for you to have to escape. I tried to get you out."

He tightened his grip. "You failed."

The resentment he harbored stung. It was as though I was talking to a stranger. A powerful, unpredictable, volatile stranger, and yet one I knew so deeply. Loved so deeply.

"Is that why you're angry? You think I tricked you into going into the god glass? Is that why you're killing people?"

His brows slid together, completely taken off guard before he recovered again. "Yes," he said, lying through his perfect teeth.

His initial reaction spoke volumes. I'd blindsided him.

Elation soared out of me, a caged bird set free. Reyes didn't kill anyone. Neither did Mae'eldeesahn or Kuur. Then who? Two of the murders were in broad daylight, a place no demon could go. What else could do such a thing?

"Where is it?" Reyes asked, growing impatient.

I blinked back to him. "Where is what? What are you searching for?"

His gaze dropped to my mouth. Lingered there. "This does not have to go badly for you. Just tell me where it is."

"No," I said, frustrated.

His laugh held no humor whatsoever. "You can hide it, but know this: I'll find it eventually." He pressed into me. "And when I do, I'll not be kind."

"Then I won't be, either."

He lifted a brow. "What are you going to do? Are you going to devour me, god eater? Are you going to swallow me up as though I never existed?" He leaned closer and put his mouth at my ear again. "Perhaps I'll eat you first."

Every time he pressed into me, my body betrayed me, and a rush of heat flooded my abdomen. A Pavlovian response to his nearness. His scent. The fullness of his sculpted mouth. The width of his shoulders.

It was my turn to lean closer. To put my mouth at his ear. To flood him with warmth. I rose onto my toes and whispered, "You could eat me now."

Surprised, he jerked back, his gaze wary. Disbelieving. "You forget," he said, his deep voice softening, "I am not Rey'aziel. I am not Reyes."

Molding my body to his, I said simply, "Close enough."

Without warning, I crushed my mouth to his.

He stiffened for all of three seconds before surrendering. He kissed me back, long and hard and sensuously. Then he stopped. Just like that. And stepped back. He wrapped a hand around my throat again and pushed me against the boulder, pinning me to it.

Holding me perfectly still, he let his gaze travel the length of my body, pausing on Danger and Will Robinson, a.k.a. my breasts. With eyes glistening as though hypnotized, he flattened his hand to my stomach.

At first, I had no idea what he was doing. I only felt a tremendous heat in my abdomen. But his efforts were of the more visually motivated variety. I looked down to see him singe my clothes, set them on fire, and watch them burn.

Flames licked up my skin, caressing it. Ashes that were once my sweater floated away in the acrid environment, leaving only flesh in its wake. He knelt and explored every inch of my exposed stomach with his mouth, his tongue tracing exquisite lines. My skin was still so hot that the wetness from his mouth evaporated, causing trails of smoke to rise off me.

I dove my fingers into his hair and laid my head back, reveling in the feel of his ministrations. Scorching. Blistering. Decadent.

The flames continued upward, baring more and more flesh, and with each newly freed centimeter came a rush of pain, a slight sting when my skin met the abrasiveness of this plane. And then his mouth was there. Cooling. Soothing. Bathing me in desire.

Before I knew it, Danger and Will Robinson lay bare. He locked his mouth onto Will's nipple, his tongue feathering over her sensitive peak, as Danger spilled heavily into his palm.

His thumb brushed her nipple, and a jolt of arousal shot straight to my core, as though a string pulled taut connected the two. Its tug and release vibrated inside me every time he suckled the dark pink crest. Then he switched, his teeth grazing deliciously, hardening Danger's nipple to a small, tight peak.

He moved one hand to the front of my jeans and began burning them away as well. The heat scorched my abdomen, both inside and out, as molten lava pooled between my legs.

I parted them. Just a little. Just enough to give him access as my jeans were slowly incinerated. He slid his fingers between the cleft, fondling, massaging, caressing before sliding them inside, deep enough for the promise of orgasm that lurked on the horizon to rush forward, growing closer with every thrust.

I gasped, taking in tiny sips of air as the sensual pressure rose higher and higher.

He lifted one of my knees over his shoulder, urging my legs farther apart, and pressed his mouth to my center. He parted the folds with his tongue, sliding it between them and feathering it over my clit. My body jerked involuntarily, the titillation exquisite.

The air in my lungs thickened in anticipation. I curled my fingers tighter into his hair, and he growled, the sound spiking my pleasure even further.

Every cell in my body sizzled with the searing heat swallowing me whole. Every molecule of blood boiled, expanding inside me, swelling until my skin was too tight for my body.

His own clothes burned away, the ashes floating on the wind. He locked his arms under my knees and rose, his torso sliding up mine, his forearms parting my legs even farther as my feet left the ground. Anchored against the boulder, he held me suspended in midair, his muscles contracted to a marble-like hardness, his erection pressing into the crevice between my legs.

He nibbled my neck, trailing hot kisses to my ear, each one causing a quake of desire to lace down my spine.

Then he entered me, slowly, so slowly, his erection filling me to exquisite totality. He pulled out until only the very tip of his cock remained inside, then he eased back in, the pace agonizingly calculated. He repeated the process, ever so slowly, until the orgasm lying in wait shivered with impatience, begging to be released.

His mouth still at my ear, he spoke, his voice deep and smooth and intoxicating. "Who am I?"

I shook my head, unable to stop what was coming. Begging it to hurry.

He pushed into me harder. "Who am I?"

"Reyes," I said between gasps.

Bracing one of my knees with his hip, he grabbed a handful of hair in warning and said from between clenched teeth, "Who am I?"

I dug my nails into his steely buttocks, pleading with him to move faster. "Rey'aziel."

He jerked my head back but didn't increase his torturous speed. "Who am I?"

I grabbed handfuls of his hair as well. Squeezed tight. Jerked back. Then, refusing to give in, I said, "My husband."

That surprised him. He tensed as his climax grew closer. I felt his as easily as I felt mine. The blood rushing through his veins. The spasmodic tightening of his muscles. The sweet sting of orgasm just over the horizon.

I wrapped my arms around his shoulders and locked my legs around his waist, clinging to him, encouraging him to let go. He braced his hands on the barrier behind us and tried to steady his breathing as his lower body rocked into mine.

It was enough. The slow throb pulsing through my body rushed forward and exploded inside me. I cried out as hot waves of pleasure spilled out and flowed over every inch of my skin.

Reyes wrapped his arms around me and sped up at last, increasing the euphoria already pulsating through me. I dug my fingernails into his shoulders. He sucked in a sharp breath and lost the fragile hold he'd had on his control completely.

He slammed into me, his thrusts long and hard and deep, until his body went rigid. He shook violently as his muscles strained, absorbing the crush of orgasm, the exhilaration of desire rushing through him.

The growl that escaped him, so primal and animalistic, caused another wave of elation to wash over me, and I clung to him, reveling in his climax.

When it was over, he kept me close, panting into my hair, until something changed. He tensed. Lowered me to the ground. Stepped away from me. Even the hot, acrid winds of this plane couldn't prevent a chill from surging across my skin where his body had been.

I looked up at him in wonder. He seemed . . . surprised. Stunned. And a little angry.

Why? Because he'd actually enjoyed our union? That was something we'd always been good at.

He started to dematerialize, and before I could get the words *Reyes* and *wait* out, he was gone. Just like that.

I stood there swimming in confusion. At least Reyes had seemed as confused as I was. Was I just seduced by my husband or something else? Which part of Rey'azikeen craved me with such wild abandon? With such delicious debauchery? Or was that my husband making an appearance?

Then again, did it matter?

Slowly, reluctantly, I shifted back onto the cool earthly plane.

My two cohorts were leaning on Garrett's black truck. They straightened, their expressions a combination of concern and alarm as they stared at me a solid minute. Then, coming to their senses in unison, they sprinted toward me, not slowing until they skidded to a halt barely two feet away, ignoring the clearly marked boundaries of my space bubble.

When Osh tore off his duster and hefted it around my shoulders, I realized why. I glanced down to see nary a stitch in sight. My skin, covered in black soot and a fine sheen of sweat, was still smoking. Tiny ghostlike spirals wafted off me.

I could only imagine what my hair looked like.

I should've been mortified as Osh draped me in his duster, but my mind was elsewhere. Too stunned to worry about my public display of indecency.

"Charles?" Garrett said, bending down until our faces were level. "What happened? Did he hurt you?"

I shook my head. "He didn't do it. He didn't kill those people." I looked down. "Where are my boots?"

"Come on, sweetheart." Garrett scooped me up into his arms and carried me to his truck.

"Wait. Misery." I held out a hand to her, possibly exposing Will Robinson in the process. "Misery."

"Your state of existence?" Osh asked, a grin in his voice.

"We'll come back for her," Garrett said.

Osh ran around the truck to open the door. Garrett lifted me inside, but I threw my arms around him. My breath hitched, and I fought tears with everything in me. When Osh raised his brows—probably because the duster slipped off my shoulders—I grabbed his shirt and pulled him into the hug as well.

They let me hug them while I fought for control over my emotions.

Garrett wrapped an arm around my shoulders and Osh around my waist.

I didn't know how long that went on, but Osh finally pulled me out of my state of shock by asking, "So . . . threesome?"

I released them at last, pulled the duster around me the best that I could, then schooled my features to show a bravery I didn't possess.

"I don't know who he is," I said, lifting my chin. "I don't have a clue. But I do know that he's searching for something. Hunting."

Garrett's forehead wrinkled. "You don't know what?"

Shaking my head, I said, "No, but he destroyed Rocket's asylum because he wouldn't tell him where it was."

"Is it bigger than a bread box?" Osh asked.

"It could actually be a bread box for all I know. Rocket called it the embers and the ashes."

Garrett bowed his head in thought. I looked into the black distance, searching for other meanings. Embers and ashes. That certainly sounded like the god inhabiting my husband's body. Was it the ashes from something important?

"The god glass," I said, thinking aloud. "Maybe he wants the ashes from the pendant?"

"Glass doesn't turn to ash when it's burned," Garrett said.

"True. And why would he go to Rocket?"

Osh raised his head and stabbed me with a rare serious expression.

I perked up, hoping he'd thought of an answer. He tucked a lock of hair behind his ear, looked in the general vicinity of Danger and Will, then said, "Can I have my jacket back?"

11

Never ask a woman who's eating ice cream
straight from the carton how she's doing.
—BUMPER STICKER

There was nothing like a shower to give one perspective. I turned off the water just as a dark shadow slipped past my periphery. I whirled around but saw absolutely nothing.

Stepping out of George, I wrapped myself in a towel and walked to my bedroom.

"Reyes?" I asked aloud. Of course, I didn't get an answer. Even if he were there, he wouldn't have answered me.

The room seemed so big without him. Cavernous and empty. Not a place I wanted to stay much longer, so I dressed in a hurry and called Garrett.

"Hey, Charles. Everything okay?"

"Yeah. What are you doing?"

"Feeding my box turtle."

After a long pause, I asked, "Is that a metaphor for something?"

"Not especially. How are you?"

"Better. But I need you and Osh for another job."

"Does it involve hunting down a god who abducts you out from under our noses, takes you to another plane, and incinerates your clothes in a bizarre mating ritual that only another god must understand?"

"No. It involves flirting."

"We'll be right there."

I walked to Calamity's for a quick bite before the big night out.

The place was hopping. Not literally because it wasn't a dance club, but it was full and loud enough to drown out the noise in my head. Almost.

I'd ordered my favorite food of the week: green chile chicken enchiladas. Sustenance should help the gurgling sound my stomach insisted on making when I didn't eat for a few days. And maybe it would help me think better. I gave my brain a good racking, but still nothing. What could Rey'azikeen be searching for? What would he need on Earth and why? The questions wouldn't stop, and now we had a time limit.

Oddly enough, the dull roar of conversation soothed me into a more relaxed state. I watched a woman flirt with a guy at the bar who was more interested in the bartender than her. The male bartender.

I looked on as a table of men watched a server's ass so blatantly, all their heads tilted at the same time as she passed.

I caught a woman pour half her drink into her date's glass when he got up to go to the restroom. And I saw—

God. I straightened in my chair. I needed to talk to God. He was the one putting a time limit on everything. He was the only one threatening to cast His brother from the plane. I just needed a sit-down with the Big Guy. I could buy us more time. Me more time.

"I wouldn't recommend it," a male voice said from behind me. A male voice that I knew better than my own.

My pulse skyrocketed as Reyes stepped around the table. Even in a sand-colored T-shirt and simple blue jeans, he looked magnificent. Wide, powerful shoulders. Sinewy arms. Strong, almost elegant hands.

"You wouldn't recommend what?" I asked him.

"Talking to my Brother. He's . . . antisocial."

"Must run in the family." The molecules in my body began to vibrate with his nearness, desiring an encore of our earlier activity more than it desired air.

He reached down and caressed my face, his long fingers gentle.

I lifted my chin, refusing to be baited. If he wanted to talk, he'd sit down and we'd talk. I was finished chasing him.

A lopsided grin adorned his dark features. He bent until our mouths were almost touching, then asked, "Was it good for you?"

I jerked awake, blinking back to awareness, slowly realizing it was, once again, only a dream. I filled my lungs and slowly released the air. How the hell was he doing that?

"You weren't burned."

I turned to see Osh standing over me. Garrett walked in the door and headed toward us as Osh sank into the seat across the table.

"Your clothes were incinerated, every stitch of clothing gone, but you didn't have a mark on you."

"I can't explain it," I said.

"Can't explain what?" Garrett asked, sitting beside me.

"Why I wasn't burned."

"Um, you're a god?" He took a menu, pretending to peruse it, but I felt the uncertainty quaking beneath his steely exterior.

Osh was a little harder to read, but if I had to put a finger on his dominant emotion, I'd say it leaned toward a grim kind of acquiescence. If he had to take Rey'azikeen out, he would. He wouldn't like it, but he'd do the job that was set forth the moment I sent Reyes into the god glass.

We ordered and ate in relative silence. Both Osh and Garrett were flirted with mercilessly, which would be good practice for later. Glances from across the room. Subtle innuendoes hidden in a smile.

Another potential suitor even bought all three of us a drink. Very diplomatic of her considering the fact that she only had eyes for Osh, but even more so considering the fact that she was in her late sixties. If she were older, say a few hundred years older, she'd be perfect for the immortal slave demon.

"Watch that one," I told him, lifting my glass to her in salute.

She did the same as a wolfish grin widened Osh's mouth. "Why? More sex and less complications."

I slammed my eyes shut. There were just some things one did not need to know about one's future son-in-law.

"Thanks for getting Misery back to me."

They grunted as men are wont to do. But Garrett's emotions were all over the place.

"Are you okay?" I asked him.

He plastered a neutral expression on me that fooled no one. "Why wouldn't I be?"

"I'm okay. You know that, right?"

He nodded silently, then downed the rest of his beer.

"Okay, then." I put my hands on the table and rose. "Are we ready to do this?"

Garrett slammed his glass down and glared at me. "He took you."

Osh and I both went stock still as one might do when facing an angry predator.

After a moment, I replied to him. "Yes, he did. But I'm okay."

"Right out from under us. He took you, Charles."

I nodded. Nothing I could say at that point was going to help his acceptance. He felt helpless. Which was about the worst feeling in the world.

His hand gripped the glass tighter as a server eased up to us. "Would you like another one?" she asked him.

"We can't fight him," he said to me.

I thanked the server before addressing him. "I know."

"You're right," Osh said. "We can't." He turned a purposeful gaze on me. "But you can."

"No, I can't, Osh."

"Not with that attitude, you can't. You need to remember your place. You need to remember what you're capable of."

"I get it, Osh. I have a history. I used to apparently devour other gods."

"You ate them like cotton candy at a carnival."

I sat back and crossed my arms. "I can't do that to my husband."

"He's not your husband," he said softly.

I refused to listen. I knew Osh would take this course of action. He didn't have much of a choice, but that didn't stop me from resenting the implication.

"I'm not going there, Osh. Not yet."

"Just keep it in the back of your mind. The time may come when you'll need to cowboy up."

When I didn't respond, Osh sat back down, and both he and Garrett went back to nursing their drinks.

"Also," Osh said, unable to help himself, "I wanted to address the fact that you give new meaning to the term *smoking hot*."

Reluctantly, Garrett laughed, and the tension in the air evaporated. I was beginning to wonder if that wasn't Osh's superpower.

"Are we ready?" I asked them. We did have a job to do.

They both offered hesitant nods, before Garrett asked, his mouth half full of carne adovada, "What are we doing again?"

Osh took one last bite of his burrito and nodded his approval of Garrett's question.

"*We* aren't doing anything. *You two* are flirting."

"Sweet," Osh said.

It amazed me how he could look like a high school student one second and, well, an older high school student the next. Kid looked like a kid. I almost felt bad about pimping him out, but a girl's gotta do what a girl's gotta do.

I texted Cookie, and she met us in the parking lot, her all-black attire and black ski cap not at all suspicious considering she normally looked like a Jackson Pollock.

"Great choice," I said. All that was missing was black face paint.

"You think?" Her nervousness was charming. She gave Garrett and Osh a quick hug. "I've never pulled off a heist before. Oh, and I have black face paint if we need some."

Every ounce of strength. That's what it took not to giggle. "Well, it's not really a heist, and we haven't actually pulled anything off, yet."

"Right, right." She drew in a deep, calming breath.

We started toward Misery while Osh and Garrett climbed into Garrett's truck.

"And just so you know, I'll have your six through this whole thing."

"Good to know, Cook."

"Or, say, your seven thirty. Whatever you need."

Every ounce of strength. "So, what did you tell Uncle Bob?" I asked, unlocking Misery's secrets. And her doors.

"That we were going to a movie."

I bit my lip, then asked, "And he bought that?"

"Of course, only his exact words were, 'Tell that niece of mine if she gets you arrested, I'll make sure she never sees the light of day.' "

"So, he totally bought it. Awesome."

We hopped in Misery and headed to a little place I liked to call Pari's Plausible Deniability.

"Want to tell me what happened tonight?" she asked.

"Oh, right, well, I had green chile chicken enchiladas, and Garrett—"

"Okay, fine. You don't want to talk about it, you don't want to talk about it. But just so you know, when my best friend comes back from a mission to capture a god naked with her hair on fire—"

"My hair was on fire?"

"—I'm going to ask questions."

After a quick hair check, I took a left on San Mateo and headed north. "I'm sorry, Cook. I was going to tell you. It didn't go as planned."

"I assumed that. Did you learn anything, at least?"

"I learned that Rey'azikeen is just as good at coitus as his alter ego."

Cookie gasped, then her eyes glazed over and a tiny corner of her mouth twitched. I let her stew in her own thoughts.

About thirty seconds later, she leaned close and said, "Tell me everything."

I laughed and, well, told her everything, enjoying every sharp intake of breath, every sigh of pleasure, every "Oh, my God" and "Oh, no, he didn't." I knew I could count on *the Cook* to make me feel better.

Speaking of which, while Cookie was in the throes of amazement, I asked her if I could call her Walter. As in Walter White. As in the Cook.

She didn't answer. I took that as a yes.

As we got closer to our destination, Walter sat stewing again, only this time she stewed in a stock made of sautéed astonishment, pureed bewilderment, and raw, undiluted desire. After all we'd been through, I loved that I could still dazzle her. I was worried she'd grow tired of my tales and my life would become mundane in her eyes. But so far, so good.

"I know it's here somewhere," I said, trying to find the place.

Garrett was following me, and I couldn't help but find it reminiscent of the blind leading the sexy-but-also-blind. Which would explain the phone call I received from that very man.

"Do you know where you're going?"

"Duh."

"We've made three U-turns."

"I'm getting a lay of the land. You know, memorizing our escape route should we need to haul ass."

"Charles, where are we going?"

"I'm not 100 percent positive. Walter wrote down the address, but she's in a state of shock at the moment."

"He burned off your clothes?" Walter asked. At least she was talking again.

"I just remember the place seemed cocky."

If it were possible to actually ground out a sigh of annoyance, Garrett just did it. "How can a business be cocky? And who the fuck is Walter?"

"There it is!" I pointed with way more enthusiasm than I should have and pulled into the parking lot of a large, menacing-looking building with a smaller one in front. "Welcome to the law offices of Dick, Adcock, and Peterman. See? Cocky. They had to know what they were doing when they partnered up."

"What we need is in a law office?"

"No. What we need is in the huge building behind the law office."

We pulled around to the side of the law offices to make it look like we were visiting our lawyer—in the middle of the night—and not breaking into and entering the building behind it.

Nicolette Lemay, my nurse friend with the freakishly cool gift of clairvoyance, albeit selective, walked out of the shadows and toward us, scanning the area as she hurried across the lot. Which didn't look suspicious at all.

She met me as I slid out of Misery. "Are we really doing this?" she asked, her nerves supercharged. "I may be a nurse, but I panic easily."

I laughed. "No worries. I have a plan."

Walter gaped at me from the passenger's seat. "*You* have a plan? I thought this was Garrett's plan. Or Osh's plan. Or Pari's plan."

Speaking of whom, Pari pulled up in a little red Dodge Dart, got out, and walked up to my open window.

I greeted her with a nod, then looked back at Cookie. "What are you trying to say, Walter?"

"I'm trying to say that your plans never work."

"What? My plans always work most of the time, unless they're carried out on a Friday. My Friday plans never pan out."

Walter got out of the Jeep and walked around. I was pretty sure she checked out Misery's ass on the way.

"Hey, Pari," she said.

"Hey, Walter." Pari caught on fast. Faster than some people who shall not be named . . . Garrett.

We walked over to his truck. Garrett rolled down his window. "What are we doing?"

"Well, that depends. There are two night guards here, and I'm not sure which one is on duty. If it's the female, Garrett's on. If it's the male, this whole thing will rest in your hands, Osh."

"Ten-four, boss." A master flirt, he jumped out of Garrett's truck, a little too happy to oblige.

Garrett was a little more hesitant.

"If it helps," I added, knowing it would, "she won Miss New Mexico when she was twenty-two."

That brightened him right up. He climbed out of his monster truck—boys and their toys—and spoke softly to Osh a moment.

"I can't believe you let her plan this," Walter said to them, admonishing.

"Walter," I said, my tone more admonishing. "Ye of little faith. Maybe you need to stay in the car."

"No way. And why are you calling me Walter?"

"You said I could."

After making introductions in which Pari's heart went pitter-pat for Garrett and Nicolette's did the same for Osh, we headed to the front entrance of the building and peered through the plate glass.

"I don't remember agreeing to changing my name," Walter said.

"Probably all the meth. It's the female guard." I turned back to them. "Swopes, you're up."

Osh seemed disappointed.

I patted his shoulder. "It's okay. We still need you. I just had my nails done."

Garrett looked inside. "I thought you said she won Miss New Mexico."

"She did. I told you, when she was twenty-two."

He deadpanned me. Hard. "And when was that? The fifties?"

"Swopes, she's not *that* old. Now go do your thing."

He grinned. "Just kidding. She's cute. This'll be fun."

"You're such a slut."

He shrugged and nodded toward Osh. "Make it good."

Osh's grin turned downright evil.

"Not too good," Garrett clarified, but Osh had already fired.

He swung, so very much harder than anyone had expected, hitting Garrett's left eye and the bridge of his nose.

Garrett's head jerked back, and he stumbled a couple of steps. Then he pressed his hands to his face and doubled over, cursing like a drunken sailor on leave. But it worked. Blood slipped between Garrett's fingers.

He straightened and glared at Osh.

"What?" he asked, the picture of innocence.

Then Garrett glared at me. "This is the worst plan ever."

"See?" Walter nodded. "Told you. Nobody ever listens to me."

After offering Osh a bloody middle finger, he stumbled to the glass doors and knocked.

The rest of us hurried to the side of the building where we could watch to make sure Garrett got in.

When the guard opened the door, Garrett turned on the charm, spouting something about being mugged and his cell battery dying and could he borrow a phone and maybe use the restroom.

But I had to stop and think. "Do people get mugged in Albuquerque?" It didn't feel right. "Do we say mugged? And if not, what do we say?"

Everyone ignored me as the female guard opened the doors, and her heart, wide. She could not escort him into the building fast enough.

He gave us a furtive thumbs-up and slipped inside.

"That'll keep her busy," I said, rubbing my hands in anticipation. "Time to break and enter this puppy."

We walked around to the back entrance of the building, Walter getting more and more nervous. "I'm so bad at breaking and entering."

"Walter, no one is judging you. Not on this. However, you will be graded on your floor routine."

Nicolette was in heaven. I slowed to chat with her. "You seem to be having fun."

"Yeah, I don't get out much." She leaned close and gestured toward Osh. "And he's cute."

"Yes, he is."

Nicolette was amazing. Who was I to thwart true love? He might become my son-in-law if the events I'd seen in my one glimpse into the future panned out, but that was a long way off. He could do with a little grounding here on Earth. It would keep him honest.

"Just so you go into this with your eyes open," I said to her, "he's a former slave demon from hell and lives off human souls. Don't kiss him on the mouth. Like ever."

Her eyes rounded to saucers and her pulse sped up and she was so in. I could tell by her puppy dog expression. Also a tiny drop of drool dotted one corner of her lovely mouth.

Oh, yeah. She was a keeper.

"What about security?" Pari asked.

"I know a guy who knows a guy. It happens to be down at the moment. No cameras. No alarms. Nothing."

"Which is why they're paying full-time security guards," Walter said.

"Exactamundo. Pari? You're up."

Pari scrambled up the steps to a loading dock and, after much ado and a few curse words, picked the lock on the back door. I could've picked the lock myself, but Pari was faster. My lock picking skills were akin to an '86 Yugo in a race with a Bugatti Chiron.

We were like a special ops team. It gave me goose bumps.

We hurried inside, and then I laid out the plan.

"Okay, to save Pari's life and preserve her freedom—but mostly to save her life—Nicolette is going to draw blood from everyone for an art project. Not much. Maybe like a gallon or two each."

"A pint," Nicolette suggested. "Half if we don't want to risk anyone passing out when we make our daring getaway." She was really good at this stuff.

Angel had popped in and stood nonchalantly behind Nicolette, interest evident in his glistening eyes, but the minute I explained my plan, he started to back away.

"Hey Angel. You're just in time. We need a lookout."

He gestured with a nod, but continued backing away. "I just remembered, I have anywhere else to be."

"What's wrong?" I asked him as he paled before my eyes. It amazed me the departed could do that.

"I don't really like the sight of blood."

I blinked. "Says the departed gangbanger with the gaping chest wound."

He looked down. "That's different."

"Not really." Before I could say anything else, he was gone. Little shit. That got me nowhere fast. Who would be our lookout?

I turned to Osh, but Nicolette stood pinching the bridge of her nose. She glanced back at me.

I pointed to the space Angel just vacated. "Angel doesn't like the sight of blood."

"Let me get this straight," she said, suddenly annoyed.

I straightened in alarm. What'd I do now?

"We broke into a plasma center so I could draw blood from everyone for . . . an art project?"

"Yep."

Walter furrowed her brows. "I thought you said we were stealing a blood collection van."

"Nope. Too easy to track down."

"And this is going to save Pari's life?" Nicolette asked.

"And ignite her creativity. Two birds. One stone."

She planted both her palms on a desk as though for strength. "You do realize I could have stolen the supplies from the hospital and done this at, say, your office? For example?"

I gaped at her. "Seriously? We didn't need to risk felony charges and a life behind bars?"

She let a humorless smile thin her mouth and shook her head. Well, everyone in the room shook their heads, seeming a little frustrated with me. Everyone except Osh. He'd found a machine that made pretty sounds when he pushed the buttons on it.

"You said you couldn't steal blood from the hospital."

"I can't. That doesn't mean I can't take a few supplies. It's still illegal, but it can be done."

"You could've said something thirty minutes ago," I said under my breath.

"You didn't let me in on the plan until now."

"Told you," Walter said, gloating. She was so not getting invited to the office Christmas party.

"Well, crap." I glanced around. "Okay, so how about we just steal the supplies from here and go back to Pari's?"

"That works," Nicolette said, suddenly her perky self. She hurried to the supply room, which Pari also picked, and took everything she'd need to drain us all dry. If she were a serial killer, or a vampire, this would be a prime opportunity for her.

When we finished plundering the place, I dragged Osh out of a reclining chair in which he'd fallen asleep and we filed outside, no worse for the wear.

I sprinted to the front of the building and knocked on the glass doors. Both Garrett and the security guard looked up at me, Garrett confused and the security guard miffed.

They walked to the doors, and she unlocked them. Before she could say anything, I began the show.

"Garrett! Oh, my God!" I rushed forward and threw my arms around him. "What happened? Who did this?"

"I was mugged."

"Do we say *mugged* in Albuquerque?"

He glared at me.

"I'm so sorry. I'll take you to the hospital."

Disappointment lined the guard's face. But it quickly transformed into confusion. "Wait, I thought you said your name was Reyes. Reyes Farrow."

After I gaped at him for an eternity, an eternity in which he struggled to conceal mischievous grin, I turned back to her. "It is. It's Reyes Garrett Farrow. Not Reyes Alexander Farrow." I snorted and waved a dismissive hand. "That's another guy altogether."

She wrinkled her forehead in suspicion.

"Gotta go," I said, hurrying him along. "Have to get this man to a hospital for multiple stab wounds."

"He was stabbed?" she asked with a concerned gasp.

"Not yet, but the night is young."

Garrett wrapped an arm around me, and I helped him to his truck, where Osh was sitting. In the driver's seat. He started to order him out when I said, "We have to make this look good," and led him to the passenger's side.

"That was fast," he said. "Did you get what you needed?"

"We did. We just got the supplies, because apparently that was an option, and Nicolette is going to draw our blood at Pari's place."

"The mighty Charles Davidson stole?"

"Hey," I said, offended. "I've stolen before."

"Mm-hmm."

"Also, I left a hundred on the desk with an apology note, but don't worry, I disguised my handwriting."

He deadpanned me. "Did you disguise your fingerprints?"

Crap.

12

If I were a Jedi,
there's a 100% chance I'd use the Force inappropriately.

—TRUE FACT

"This is the weirdest idea you've ever had," Pari said when we got back to her apartment. "I love it."

I giggled. "I figured you would."

Nicolette took a little blood from all of us, and Pari mixed it, along with a dash of CAM phosphor, into a paint that matched her office walls. She then, with the help of a black light, created a beautiful mural right on top of the blood splatters that were already there, because no amount of cleaning ridded a scene of forensic evidence like that. Ever. Not without replacing the wall, anyway.

Pari applied a few more strokes, then did a test. She turned off the black light and turned on the regular lights. The new paint blended into the old, barely noticeable. One would have to be hard-pressed to figure out where the old paint ended and the new paint began.

But when the lights were out and the black light turned on, a gorgeous motif of bold strokes and sharp edges, punctuated by a skull here and there, shone through. It was an insanely cool effect.

"Camouflage," Walter said before washing down a bite of pizza with her beer. "Genius."

We all sat around Pari's office and the back room of her thriving tattoo business, watching her work. I sat on the floor and used Osh's leg as a headrest. He'd claimed the sofa in Pari's office, and Nicolette, having completed her mission and safely disposed of the hazardous materials, sat on the armrest on the opposite end. He'd moved his legs so she could sit down, but Nic was too shy for that.

Garrett had stolen Pari's office chair and was busy tearing into a slice of double pepperoni when Pari pinned him with her best inquiring stare.

"Well?" she asked him.

He nodded, then swallowed hard. "Incredible. You need to come to my house."

"Yes, you do," I said. "It's very brown."

"I like brown," he said, defending his domain.

"I like brown food," I offered. "Coffee. Chocolate. Caramel. How about you, Walter?"

"Tell you what," she said with a humorous smirk, "you stop calling me Walter, because if you don't, it will stick for years, and I'll let you name the girls."

I perked up. Literally. I pushed off Osh and sat up straight. "For reals?"

"Yes. Just leave me my dignity."

"What? Dignity's overrated."

"That's the deal."

Damn, she was a hard negotiator. "Oh, hell, yes." I jumped up and started pacing. "So many options." I stared at her girls, a.k.a. her breasts, a long moment, and brainstormed. "Thelma and Louise? Sonny and Cher? Laurel and Hardy? Oh, my God. My brain is going to explode."

One of Pari's artists was giving an older woman her first tattoo. The woman was not taking it well. Her screams of agony were mucking up my concentration.

"You know," Nicolette said, taking a sip of her own beer, "if any of us die under suspicious circumstances, Pari is screwed. She has our DNA all over her walls."

Pari stopped and turned toward me with a gasp. "She's right. What if you guys are murdered?"

I sat back down in front of Osh, leaning against the sofa, forcing him to scoot his legs to one side. "If something untoward does happen, we'll just have to make sure we're murdered far away from here. Right, guys?"

Everyone raised a beer in salute.

"No getting Pari convicted of our murders," Osh said.

Pari, pleased with our solemn-ish oath, went back to work. "You know, this could be my new gig."

"Painting blood on people's walls to cover up a crime scene?"

"While that does have a morbid sense of coolness to it, no. Creating paintings with CAM phosphor. To the casual observer, they could be everyday scenes. You know, boring crap. But once the black light comes on, they could be dark and broody and ominous. Only in neon."

"I would expect nothing less from you. Butch Cassidy and the Sundance Kid?" I looked back at Cook with hope in my eyes.

She thought a moment, then shook her head and took another bite.

Not giving up, I went back to work. "This could take a while."

"I know what you're doing," Garrett said. Only he was standing right over me.

I looked back at his former seat behind Pari's desk and then back at him, wondering if he'd gained some kind of supernatural ability of which I should be made aware.

He sank to the ground next to me just as Osh's legs wrapped around my torso, jump-starting my suspicions.

I put down my pizza and offered them my full attention. "I take it this is some kind of intervention."

"Something like that," Osh said.

Cookie sat on the sofa next to Osh. "We're worried about you, hon."

"*Et tu*, Walter?"

"Don't blame her," Garrett said.

I tried to stand, but Osh kept his legs locked in place.

"Charley, you know I have your six," Cookie said, before examining our positions in reference to one another. "Or, like, your 9:45. Either way, we're all here for you."

"So what's this about?" I asked my interrogator.

Garrett pressed his lips together in thought before answering. "We have less than a day to figure this out, to bring Reyes back, or have him either cast from this plane or cut down, and we're here doing art projects and eating pizza."

I cringed and lowered my head. "I know. I'm just . . . I'm fresh out of ideas. I have no clue what to do."

"Bet you a nickel you do," Osh said, offering me a reassuring squeeze.

I wrapped an arm around his leg. "You don't understand. I don't know who he is."

"He's Rey'azikeen," Osh said.

"Exactly. We tried the whole luring-him-into-a-trap thing. That didn't work."

"Or did it?" he asked. "What did we learn from that?"

"That I'm completely incapable of resisting that man in any form."

"No," Garrett countered. "We learned that he is completely incapable of resisting you."

I lifted a shoulder into a half-hearted shrug. How would that knowledge help us?

"And," Osh added, "we learned that you are unwilling to do what is necessary."

"What does that mean?"

"You're a god, Charles," Garrett said. He put a hand on my knee to calm me. "You're the First Star, like in the book."

I deadpanned him. "That's a children's book."

"And it's one I'm convinced is telling your story."

Osh leaned forward and wrapped his arms around my neck, offering me a reassuring hug. "I agree."

"What book?" Cookie asked.

"I'll show you later, but I don't get what any of this has to do with anything."

"You can defeat him," Osh said. "If you're willing to."

I broke free and stood. Nicolette's dark eyes had rounded, and Pari had put her masterpiece on hold to listen.

"I get it. I've eaten other gods. I've even done it in this form. On this plane. I devoured the god Eidolon, but he was evil. Reyes is not."

"We aren't talking about Reyes," Osh said. "We're talking about Rey'azikeen."

"Okay, fine, what do you know about him? I mean, surely you'd heard of him even in hell."

"Of course I had. We even knew that Lucifer's son, Rey'aziel, was created using the god Rey'azikeen's energy. I just didn't know that the godly part of him was still . . . in there."

"Then, okay, what do you know about him?"

He leaned back on the sofa and stared at me from underneath his dark lashes. After a long moment, he said, "I've only heard rumors. Slave, remember? I didn't exactly have access to classified information, even in hell."

"And? What did the rumors say?"

"There were rumors that he was the creator of what we called dark matter, not to be confused with the theoretical gravitational force that binds the universe together. This dark matter was, well, dark."

I pulled Pari's desk chair around and sat. "Explain."

He shook his head. "I just know the rumblings that permeated the underbelly of hell saying that he creates dark matter, and that dark matter is the darkness that swallows the light. It's the evil that swallows the benevolent. It's why he's so good at what he does."

"Why? What does he do?"

"You misunderstand. That's not the worst part."

I shifted in the chair and raised my chin, preparing for anything. "I'll bite. What's the worst part?"

"There were other rumors. Rumors that were spoken in hushed tones like some urban legend that kids are afraid to talk about."

"What did they say?"

"They said that Rey'azikeen didn't create the dark matter. They said that he *was* the dark matter. It was a part of him and that the dark matter came from his soul."

Was all this true? Was the god Rey'azikeen truly so dark, so scary, that even the demons in hell only dared to whisper about him? "Why would such a thing be so hushed in a place like hell?"

"Because he's the sibling of the God Elohim. It's like a television evangelist with a brother in prison. It's . . . dirty."

My hackles rose to razor-sharp spikes. "Reyes is not dirty."

"Hey," he said, raising his hands in surrender. "You wanted the rumors, you got the rumors. That's all I know."

I wasn't entirely certain I believed him, but I was worried Nicolette would never be the same after this, so I dropped it. For now.

I stood and started pacing again. "This is my fault. If he does something awful or gets kicked off this plane or killed or all of the above, it's my fault."

Osh stood and blocked my path to get my attention. He put his hands on my shoulders, and said, "No, sweetheart, it's not. You just need to make a decision. If he does stir up shit, are you willing to do what it takes to stop him?"

Cookie and I stayed with Pari after everyone left to make sure she was okay. An hour later, she kicked us out, saying even she needed sleep. She did look exhausted. Stress had a way of aging a person.

So, Cookie and I drove home and sat in my apartment, the cavernous room seeming to swallow us. Or maybe I just wanted it to.

Reyes was still there, inside Rey'azikeen. He had to be. Either that, or the god Rey'azikeen desired me just as much as my ethereal husband did.

But why would he? In his eyes, I was human. Nothing more and nothing less. Sure, a god lay underneath the flesh and blood of my human side, but it was apparently a god he had never liked. According to tidbits I'd heard here and there, in our previous existence, we had been enemies. So I was human. Strike one. And an enemy. Strike two.

Then why seduce me? Why bring me to my knees?

Perhaps that was the point. To bring me to my knees. To show me what he was capable of in any form. To show me what I was incapable of in any form—namely, resisting him.

I hadn't even considered going to bed when I got home. I knew what would happen the moment my mind drifted. He would invade. And, as bad as I hated to admit it, his invasions were like water on a parched desert. I craved them. Thirsted for them.

Bottom line, I missed my husband.

But he was toying with me. The god Rey'azikeen. Keeping me awake. To disorient me? To distract me? To impair my judgment or slow my reflexes?

It would help if I could figure out what he was searching for so blindly. It would give me the upper hand, especially if I knew where to find it. But I'd searched the apartment for signs of the god glass. It had shattered when he'd come back through it. I found nary a sliver of glass, much less its ashes.

Then the ashes of what? The embers of what?

My mind was too worn to think about it anymore.

Cookie had no inclinations toward sleep either once she found out there was a set of children's books that supposedly mapped out my entire history in a few thousand words. No way was she going to drop this. So, she raided her closet for soft clothes, as did I, except I couldn't wear her clothes, so she sent me home to raid my own closet, and we sat in my apartment, drinking the elixir of life out of coffee mugs that advised any passersby A FUN THING TO DO IN THE MORNING IS NOT TALK TO ME.

My soft clothes felt heavenly. Probably because the bottoms had little angels on them perched on clouds. An inside joke from Mr. Farrow himself. My T-shirt, which read MAJESTIC AS FUCK, wasn't quite so angelic.

"I can't believe you didn't tell me about these," Cookie said, reprimanding me.

"I only learned about them this morning."

"Which gave you an entire day."

She had me there. We both read in silence, Cookie on book one, *The First Star*, and me on book two, *The Dark Star.*

The book began with the First Star—me, if Garrett were to be believed—hunting and fighting malevolent gods that were tormenting kingdoms throughout the galaxies, both known and unknown to seers like the one who wrote the book I was holding.

In the seers' eyes, she was a hero, fighting injustices from one kingdom to another, using her wits to outsmart her enemies and her strength to battle them, for the more she fought, the greater their numbers. Fortunately, the more battles she won, the stronger she grew. With every victory, the star consumed her enemy. She gained its power until she became a star a hundredfold strong.

She became known throughout all dimensions as the Benevolent One, the Sentinel, the Star Eater.

But then came her downfall. She fell in love with one of her prey, the Dark Star, the most beautiful star in all the heavens. The most beautiful and the deadliest.

He'd been born with a very specific purpose: to use his darkness to create realms with no windows so that those cast inside could never again see the light the heavens had to offer. They would live in eternal darkness and damnation.

But over the millennia, he had grown too dark. His immeasurable power uncontrollable. He became a threat to those benevolent stars who would rule their kingdoms with kindness and tolerance.

And so, the Dark Star's Brother, Jehovahn, summoned the Star Eater.

The Dark Star, upon hearing this, grew enraged at the betrayal and ravaged Jehovahn's kingdom and its people.

Yet inside he grew anxious. Impatient, even. He'd heard stories for centuries about the First Star. He longed to meet her. Hungered to battle her. Despite his immense power, she was stronger. Her strength surpassed any star's from any kingdom in the known universe, and he wanted nothing more than to devour her whole.

But she made a show of truce. She met him among the rings of Saturn, stood before him in all her glory, so bright she nearly blinded him, and offered the Dark Star mercy if he surrendered to her demands.

He declined her offer with a shadowy grin, and what would later become known as the Battle of a Hundred Years began.

The harder he fought, the more ground he lost. She was his equal in every way.

With each new battle, with each new blow, she begged him to surrender. Promised him quarter. But he wouldn't hear of it.

When it became clear, however, that he could not beat her, a thought came to him. He could make use of the beauty he was famous for. He could make her fall in love with him.

And so, during the next days of battle, he purposely let her get closer than was comfortable, for she could easily devour him whenever she chose. But he worked to earn her affection. He touched her face. Pressed against her. Brushed his mouth across hers. With each lingering touch, he courted her. Enticed her. Invited her to love him. Not realizing he had unshielded his own heart in the process.

His efforts were for naught, however, for the First Star had loved him always. Had longed for him always. Which was why he was still alive.

"Are you sure these are children's books?" Cookie asked after a while.

"I was just wondering the same thing."

We eyed each other a moment, then went back to reading.

At night, the Dark Star worked hard to create a kingdom within a kingdom just for her. A lightless realm within another galaxy far, far away from her own. One where she would live out eternity alone and miserable. Slowly going insane.

"A lightless realm?" I said aloud. "A hell dimension? Did the author mean a hell dimension?"

"What?" Cookie asked, absorbed in her own book.

"In the book, the Dark Star creates a lightless realm to capture the First Star. Does he mean a hell dimension?"

Cookie thought a moment, then nodded. "Think about it. What is hell but a place of torment? And how tormenting would it be disconnected from all light? Men have created tortures with that very thing in mind."

"True."

We went back to reading again.

When the realm was finished, when the constructs were in place, he pretended to surrender. Pretended to be in love with her. Pretended to swear his fealty.

She dropped her guard for only a second, but it was long enough for the Dark Star to cast her inside, lock the gate, and destroy the key.

He had won. At last.

The victory that had been so far from his grasp was suddenly his. But for some reason, he didn't celebrate. He grew even more disenchanted with the world and even more tortured than he had been. Darker than he had been. For he realized too late that his love had not been a pretense.

And she was gone. The kingdom he'd created was impregnable. No way in and no way out. Thus, the Dark Star raged against all creation for centuries. Until he had another idea.

Beneath his Brother Jehovahn's kingdom lay a lightless realm with fire so hot, it would melt anything it touched. But the Dark Star knew all the secrets of the realm, for he had created it. He knew how to handle the fire. And, more importantly, he knew how to steal it.

So, in a moment of desperation, he stole into the lightless realm and took the fire it held so dear. Without thought, he used it to melt the gates of the kingdom he'd created and release the First Star.

But she had been imprisoned for so long, the First Star's mind had been compromised. She ran and hid among the other stars in the heavens, wondering if her mind was playing tricks.

Jehovahn had grown so angry at His little brother's actions, He came up with a ruse of His own. He commissioned the Dark Star to create his best lightless realm, one that was even more inescapable than his last.

The Dark Star wanted to go after the First to explain, but Jehovahn told him He needed the realm immediately for a malevolent ruler that, because of the Dark Star's imprisonment of the Star Eater, the only sentinel in the heavens, had become too callous. Too brutal.

So, the Dark Star created a lightless realm even worse than the last and encased it in Star Glass. He gave it to his Brother, explained how to open and close the gate, then went in search of the Star Eater. Went in search of his true love.

The First Star, having regained her senses and realizing what the Dark Star's Brother was up to, begged Him to let her cast the Dark Star into the lightless realm of her own kingdom, for it was not as severe. Not as cruel. In fact, it was a virtual paradise compared to the one the Dark Star had unwittingly created.

If Jehovahn would allow this, she would do the Brother a favor in return. Anything he asked of her.

"Even though My little brother sent you to a lightless realm of his own making, trapped you in there for centuries, you would forgive him?"

"I would and I have," she said, for she loved him, and love is forever.

Jehovahn allowed her to cast the one she had grown to love into the lightless realm of her kingdom, but the Dark Star, betrayed yet again, vowed revenge.

He easily escaped the First Star's realm, only to be followed out by two other stars, malevolent ones, who used the lightless realm he'd created for Jehovahn, the Star Glass, to capture him and take him to the ruler of the realm beneath, the realm made of fire.

For stealing his fire, the goblin ruler used the Dark Star's immense power, his infinite energy, to create a son. A son with a map through the void of the oblivion that lay between realms. A map that had been branded on his flesh. He would use the son to help him escape his lightless realm and battle for the heavens in which the Dark Star's Brother shone. The heavens he would one day rule.

The son, now having no memory of his former life as a star, was tested at every turn. If he failed, he was beaten. If he succeeded, he was beaten harder. On and on, over and over, until he fought back. Until he learned to kill. Until the darkness swallowed him whole.

His goblin father, pleased with his dark son's progress, watched him rise through the ranks of his army to become a general.

The father's dream was getting closer and closer to becoming a reality, but the son could not completely forget the brilliant star he'd once seen. Glimpses of her flashed in his mind's eye, and he longed to see her once again.

So, the dark son used the map to navigate the oblivion between the realm beneath and a kingdom he did not recognize.

Then he saw her, shining brilliant in the distance, brightest even among a billion other stars. She spoke to another Star, a familiar Star, and he realized she was going to be sent to that Star's kingdom as one of its own. To advocate. To lead the lost.

Just before she was sent to the kingdom to become a guide there, she turned and saw him. And she smiled. She smiled a microsecond before she disappeared into the ethereal winds that would sail her to her new life.

Being closer to the kingdom, the son decided to join her. He gave up everything, even his memory, to be born into the kingdom as one of their own.

But his goblin father, upon learning of his son's deceit, sent emissaries to the kingdom to foil his son's plans. And so the dark son, born to good parents, would soon see how cruel his goblin father could be. For when the First Star was born into the kingdom, her departed mother's soul shining around her, she saw him. She saw his darkness as he waited. She saw his ruination. And she was afraid.

For her sake, the dark son retreated to his life of misery, the life his goblin father had arranged for him. He would emerge only when the First Star needed him. Only when she was in distress. He would help her, but her fear kept him at arm's length. Never to touch her. Never to know her.

But he watched over her as she grew up and fulfilled her duty to the kingdom's Star. The Star known as Jehovahn.

"Are you finished?" Cookie asked, tapping me on a leg with her book. Having read the first one, she sat waiting impatiently for the next.

But I sat completely stunned. "I just don't see how this can be a children's book," I said, repeating our earlier sentiments. "Much less an internationally bestselling one."

"Is it . . . accurate?" she asked.

"I don't know. It certainly seems so."

I'd had every intention of reading the third book, but I needed time to absorb what I'd just read. While Cookie read, sucking in a soft breath here and there, I made more coffee, because one needed copious amounts of coffee when one couldn't sleep, then I announced my need for fresh air. Cookie barely took note. I threw on some shoes and a jacket and went for a walk.

The crisp night air felt good. I walked to the UNM campus and strolled the beautiful grounds.

The book, for all intents and purposes, was spot-on. At least from what I'd been told. I still didn't remember much of my godly past, and it had been suggested that the God Jehovah had taken some of my memories. But why would He?

The only fallacy I'd found was in the telling of who created the hell dimension within the god glass. From everything I'd been told, Reyes didn't build that hell dimension. God had built it for His little brother. But with the author so right on everything else, why would he get that wrong?

"Given up on me yet?"

I turned to see Reyes following me, strolling aimlessly just as I was. Or pretending to. His walk was that of an animal, full of power and grace, stalking its prey.

I continued my walk and let him follow, not knowing if we were in a dream or reality. Maybe it was both.

"Never," I said, dipping my fingertips in a fountain as I walked. "They're coming for you. The angels."

"Aren't they always."

"They're sending an army."

"To do what? Glare at me harshly? They cannot take me down, and they know it." He stepped closer. "But you can. Shall we meet on the battleground and finish what we started?"

His suggestion startled me. The battleground? I could no more imagine myself doing battle with a god than I could imagine myself hula dancing. "Is that what you want?"

"I want the embers." His voice, deep and bourbon-smooth, trickled over my skin.

"I want world peace," I said, tired of fighting. Of battles. Of conflict.

Then he was at my back, wrapping his arms around me from behind, one at my waist, one at my neck. He buried his face in my hair and growled.

I'd craved him so badly, I sank against him, fitting my body into his as though we were puzzle pieces. As though we were lock and key.

"I didn't betray you," I said, remembering the book and how the Dark Star had believed the First had betrayed him.

His mouth found my ear, his breath hot against my cheek, when he said, "Of course you did."

And just like every other time Reyes had entered my mind, I jerked to awareness. I whirled around, seeing only the deserted campus.

Did he truly believe I'd betrayed him? If anything, it was the opposite. He'd betrayed me, or the First Star, whatever the case may be.

I needed answers, and this was getting me nowhere. It was time for a sit-down. I hurried home and found Cookie reading the third book.

"I'm going for a drive."

"Okay," she said, waving one hand absently, completely absorbed in the book.

"I'm going to have a little talk with Reyes's big Brother."

"Good for you, hon."

After grabbing my bag and keys, I left her to her own devices, but just as I closed the front door, I heard her belated, "Wait, what?"

13

Apparently, "Just fuck me up" is not
an appropriate coffee order at Starbucks.

—MEME

I drove out to our old stomping grounds, a gorgeous abandoned convent that Reyes bought when I was pregnant with Beep. It sat nestled in the Jemez Mountains, about an hour northwest of Albuquerque.

I maneuvered Misery around trees and through a dry riverbed until the convent came into view. We'd lived there for eight months, and seeing the structure again caused a gentle ache in my heart. It seemed like years since I'd seen it. In reality, it had only been a few months. Wait, no, two. Only two months? It boggled my mind.

I searched for the hidden key and found it in a fake turtle beside the door. Better than a real turtle, I supposed. I opened the door and toured the place, using the flashlight on my phone. Stepping out the back door, I could see the clearing where Cookie and Uncle Bob married, the copse of trees where a group of hellhounds snarled and snapped at me, the well I'd fallen into and had a child. Not a typical birthing story, but definitely one for the record books.

I sat on a bench surrounded by mesquite and summoned Michael. We were on holy ground, after all. He should feel right at home.

It took only a thought to pull him from his dimension into mine, but it would take a lot of talking to calm him down. Apparently, angels didn't like to be summoned. I could hardly blame them. I didn't even like to be texted most of the time.

He appeared before me, his massive wings slightly open as though readying for flight. Or a fight. Either way. His silvery eyes bored into mine, his hand resting on the sword at his side as he took a step closer.

"You should take care, Elle-Ryn-Ahleethia."

"Thank you," I said. "I'll do that. But first, I want a word with your Boss."

His head tilted to the side as though curious about me. "Good luck with that."

"Now, please."

The look on his normally stoic face was one of incredulity. "Have you ever heard the phrase *be careful what you wish for*?"

I bowed my head and stared at him from underneath my lashes, concentrating as hard as I could. Not on Michael, but on his Father. On Reyes's Brother. I didn't know His real name. I only knew the names we humans had given Him. Then again, maybe I didn't need it.

With deliberate intention, I focused all my energy and whispered one word. "Now."

Michael transformed into a sea of smoke and vanished, and for a moment I thought I'd lost the game.

Then I felt it. A power like nothing I'd ever experienced. Like nothing I'd ever dreamed possible. It flowed through me as though I were a veil of silk filtering its essence.

I whirled around to find . . . Him.

The power emanating out of Him was impossible to mistake as anything other than Jehovah. I stood motionless as I took in the form He'd chosen: a young boy of Indonesian descent. Interesting, since the books I was reading were written by an Indonesian boy.

"You rang?" He said, His voice like an ocean drowning me in its warmth. He sat cross-legged on a boulder a few feet away.

"I read the second book."

"And?" He asked the question as though He already knew I'd read it. Then I realized He did. I had once dissipated and joined all living things around me, and I knew everything about each and every person for a thousand miles.

"Is it true?"

"Which part?"

"I'd always thought You created the god glass for Reyes. You'd built a hell dimension just for him."

"Did I?"

"That's what I'm asking."

"Hell dimensions aren't really My thing."

My thing? His colloquialism surprised me.

"Then it's true? You tricked him into creating it all the while knowing You'd lock him inside?"

"You forget the most important part." He lifted a knee and planted an arm on top. "He created a hell dimension solely for you as well."

"But he released me."

"Ah, yes, when he realized he loved you. Is that how the story went?"

I knew I didn't have a lot of time. God had to be a busy Guy. I wanted to ask my most important question, but I also longed to understand their relationship. The dynamics of it. The form. "If the story is true and Reyes creates hell dimensions, why do You have him do all Your dirty work?"

He didn't take offense. He leaned back in mild interest. "We are gods, are We not? We create. We shape. We mold. Rey'azikeen is no different. He just thinks a little darker than most. He *is* a little darker than most. That darkness he embodies comes in handy."

"Are You saying the darkness Reyes creates is truly from him? A part of his essence?"

"We all have Our strengths."

Talking to God was as bad as talking to Michael. I sighed and said almost hesitantly, "I'm told we were once friends."

"We were."

"I wouldn't know. I don't remember. Did You steal my memories?"

"That was part of the agreement. It's all in the contract."

My lids widened. "There's an actual contract?"

He laughed softly. "No. And if there had been, you would've been in breach, wouldn't you say?"

"Why?"

"Your job was to either tame My brother or devour him. It would seem you did neither."

"Is that why You would send an army after Your own brother?"

"He must be stopped. You had your chance, so . . ."

"What did he do that was so bad?"

He lowered His head as though overtaken by sadness. "That is between Us."

"I need more time."

"I gave you a day. You've squandered it."

"No. I just . . . I don't know what to do. How to reach him."

"It won't matter either way."

"You don't know that." I stood and started toward him. Michael appeared instantly, blocking my path with a steely arm.

"I'm not giving up on him. I'll fight alongside him if You send Your army."

His gaze traveled the length of me. Assessing. Analyzing. "You win. I'll give you eternity."

I narrowed my lashes. "There's a catch."

"Isn't there always?"

"What is it?" I asked through clenched teeth.

"You won't need an eternity. He'll find what he's looking for, and you'll have a decision to make."

"Okay, when will he find what he's looking for?"

"Within hours. Unless you find him first."

Before I could ask anything else—for example, what Reyes was looking for—He and Michael both disappeared.

I sank onto the bench again. I'd at least gained more time. Or had I?

Even driving back to Albuquerque as dawn broke over the horizon, the colors splashing across the sky like watercolors dropped from heaven, could not bring me out of my agitated state. I couldn't decide if I should be depressed or in a full-blown state of panic.

Artemis, sensing my mental issues, sat across the console, her ass in the backseat, her head in my lap. She'd popped in to comfort me. The fact that her giant head made driving a little trickier than usual meant nothing in the grand scheme of things. She was a keeper. And thankfully, while my arms had to rest on said giant head, the steering wheel was not an obstacle. For her.

I scratched her ears. "We have to come up with a solution, girl. If you were an angry god, what would you be searching for?"

I had only hours before Reyes would find whatever that may be. I needed to know now. His finding it would force me to make a decision. Unless it was a nuclear warhead, I couldn't see why I would have to make a decision. I was so bad at decisions. And decision fatigue was a real thing. I'd read about it.

"What would a god need? More power? We have a lot as it is."

Artemis had deigned to clean my entire arm, licking me from wrist to shoulder. Because my clothes were no barrier against her tongue, a tongue that went on for days, she could lick me from head to toe unhindered.

When she went for the armpit, however, I had to put a stop to her ministrations. I had just put on deodorant. And I was ticklish.

"Maybe he's searching for something we could never have access to. Like"—I grabbed my hair with one hand and pulled—"like what? What would a god need?"

The only thing I could come up with was the god glass, but it had been destroyed. He was searching for embers and ashes. Okay, so like the remains of a volcano? A nuclear explosion? A campfire?

I ground my teeth as Artemis, reacting to my frustration, hopped up and dove for my face. Thank Reyes's Brother I wasn't wearing any makeup.

Wait. I perked up. Well, first I fended off the ninety-pound Rottweiler, eased off the gas, and swerved back into my own lane. Then I perked up. Maybe I could trick Reyes into telling me. If I summoned him, I could offer to help. I could assist him in his search.

"I wouldn't suggest it."

His voice, like warm honey, washed inside me, weakening my already strained muscles.

I glanced to my right. He sat in the passenger's seat, his shoulders wide, his knees spread, his body almost too big for the small space.

Artemis jumped, then eyed him, unsure if he were friend or foe. Slowly, she crawled into my lap, all ninety pounds of her, and looked back at him with a whimper. I was right there with her.

He'd turned to where his right shoulder leaned against Misery's door so he could face me. His dark eyes shimmered in the dawning light, absorbing the colors, reflecting them back at me. His straight nose and full mouth sat at such perfect angles, they screamed sensuality without the slightest effort. Like a supermodel or a cover boy.

I tore my gaze off him and concentrated on estimating the distance between cars since I had to look around Artemis to see the highway and anything on it. Rush-hour traffic had already begun. Commuters from Bernalillo and Santa Fe peppered the road into Albuquerque, making my job that much harder.

"You wouldn't suggest what?" I asked him, taking comfort in the fact that Artemis stood as a barrier between us. I'd wrapped one arm around her to keep her calm.

"You tricked me once."

"And you tricked me."

He sat silent for a long moment, then said, "You remember."

"Not really. I just read an unauthorized biography of us. It was very . . . enlightening."

His brows slid together as though trying to understand my meaning.

"Reyes, what are you looking for?"

"So you can help?" he asked with a scoff.

"So I can stop you. Apparently, I'm going to have to either way." When he didn't comment, I continued. "What are you looking for?"

He pressed his lips together and turned to stare out the window. "I don't know. He won't tell me." He turned back to me, his gaze so stunningly beautiful, it pained me to look at. "He won't tell me, but he'll tell you."

A horn sounded beside me, and I jerked the wheel to the right, snapping out of the dreamlike state Reyes had held me in. Dreaming again. Damn it. I pulled over to the side of the road. To calm my nerves. To catch my breath. Then something hit me. Artemis really was in my lap. She'd seen him. I hadn't been dreaming.

Losing the feeling in my legs, I started to scoot her off my lap when Angel popped in, sitting right where Reyes had been.

"Did you see him?" I asked.

Angel frowned at me, then laughed when Artemis jumped into his lap. "Who?" he asked between chuckles.

"Reyes. He was just here."

"No, *loca*, he wasn't."

"It *was* a dream?"

He shrugged. "I have no idea. Either way, Reyes wasn't here. Rey'azikeen may have been, but not Reyes."

"Ah, right. You guys love pointing that out."

Spotting a lull in the traffic, I pulled back onto the interstate just as my phone rang.

I answered it. Or I tried to.

"Where are you?" Cookie asked before I even got a *Charley's House of Butterfly Genitalia* out. "Are you okay? Why did you leave?" Cookie bombarded me with questions, not actually giving me time to answer any of them. "Have you read the third book yet? I've been calling for hours. Where did you go?"

I finally had to interrupt her. "I'm fine, Cook. I'm on my way back."

"Did you get any sleep at all?"

"Not this week, but as soon as I wrangle me an ornery husband, I'm hibernating. For, like, a year. Maybe two."

She began to calm. "Are you okay, hon?"

"I should be asking you that. Did you get any sleep?"

"No. Well, I dozed a little. In your apartment. Robert woke up, found me gone, and put out an APB, but he called it off when I went home. That's not why I'm calling. You really need to read this book. The last one? It's about the two stars, you know, you and Reyes. But why does the author call you stars? Why not just come right out with it and call you gods? Does he know what you are? And how did he see all of this?"

As Cookie prattled on, clearly having had one too many last night—coffees that is—I let a loud yawn overtake me.

She stopped. "I'm sorry, hon."

"It's okay. I'm listening. Keep going. How did he see all of that. Got it."

"Charley, you're pulled in so many different directions, I don't know how you do it."

"Right? I put in my bid for the Elastigirl serum, so the minute the scientific community gets its act together and creates something more useful than Viagra, I'm set."

"Then sign me up, too."

"Wait," I said as the perfect solution hit me like a hurricane. "I've got it. Ari and Lola! Get it? For the girls?"

"No. Okay, that's funny, but no."

"Ah, man."

"I like it," Angel said, contemplating my choices.

"Thank you. Also, I talked to God."

A long silence ensued in which I debated a mocha latte with whipped cream or a mocha latte without, before Cookie asked, "God? As in *the* God?"

"The One and Only. He's very cryptic."

"Aren't they all?" she asked.

She had a point. Gods tended to be a secretive and mysterious lot. Except for me. I was an open book. Literally now that there was an unauthorized biography floating around.

"You're still alive, so the meet and greet must've gone well."

"Super. I'm no closer to solving our fugitive-husband dilemma, but I now have an eternity to do it. Or a few hours. It's a toss-up."

"Well, okay, then."

After assuring Cookie everything was copacetic and I was on my way back safe and sound, we hung up and I gave my full attention to the bloody departed teenager with a Rottweiler in his lap. "What's up, *mijo*?"

"Hector's gone," he said, grunting under Artemis's weight while fending off a thorough face-washing.

"Oh, I'm sorry. Who's Hector?"

"Hector Felix? The dead dude you wanted me to investigate?"

"Oh, right."

"Also, I need a raise."

"Okay, but only because you asked nicely. Hector's gone?"

"Yeah, you know, not on this plane, and I don't think he went to a good place."

"Yeah, I didn't figure he would. Did you find out anything that will help Pari?"

"I like her. Does that count?"

"No, but I like her, too."

"So, I think these football players may have killed Hector, but I don't know for sure."

"Really?" I asked, surprised. I took the Central exit and narrowly missed a woman in a yellow Audi who couldn't decide which lane she wanted to be in. "Oh, my God. Just pick one."

"After Hector left Pari's place, he went to a bar and started shit with these Lobo football players. I don't think he was the smartest guy."

"No, he was not."

"All I got from Domino—"

"Domino?" I asked.

"Yeah, you know? Domino? The dude who's always at that bar on San Mateo."

"Oh, that one," I said, infusing my voice with my second favorite -asm: sarc.

"You met him once. He hit on you, almost blew your cover."

"If I had a nickel for every time a departed—"

"He was a PI, remember? He wears that Hawaiian shirt?"

"Oh!" I said, pulling into a Java Juice drive-through. "Magnum."

"No, Domino."

"No. Yes. I mean, he was going through a Magnum PI stage when he passed. I didn't know he'd been a real PI."

"Okay, whatever, he was there that night. Said your guy Hector came in drunk off his ass. The barkeep asked him to leave. He got rowdy. Threatened to kill him and his whole family. So these football players step in, right?"

"Mm-hmm," I said, half listening. It was go time. I had to make a decision. I was so bad at decisions.

"They tell the guy to go home and sleep it off, so he pulls a gun."

"Got it. A gun." My turn was coming fast. It was now or never. I pulled up to the speaker and said with all the confidence I could muster, "Yes, I'd like a mocha grande with . . . no, *without* whipped cream. No, with. No. Yes. With. Definitely with."

The clerk laughed softly, her voice sweet for so early in the freaking morning. "Can I get you any breakfast?"

She did not just ask me that. "No. Yes, okay, I'll take one of those . . . no, how about a . . . no, not that, either. Never mind, that's okay. Wait, yes. Yes, I would like one of those English muffin things with egg and ham and cheese? Or a chocolate croissant. Whichever is easiest for you."

She laughed again. "How about both? Then you can decide later."

Oh, she was good. "Sold."

I pulled around to the window before she could ask me anything else as Angel gaped at me. "What the fuck, Chuck?"

"What? I'm having a difficult time making decisions lately. It's called decision fatigue."

He continued to gape.

"It's a real thing."

"You need medication."

"I read it on the Internet."

"My mom has anxiety. You need to talk to her."

I paid the clerk, then turned to him. "Your mom has anxiety?" I asked, suddenly worried. "Why? What's going on?"

He shrugged. "I don't know. Just life. That's why I need a raise."

I made a mental note to check up on her. I paid Angel by putting money in his mother's bank account. It used to be anonymous, but she found me out a few months back and refused to take my money. Sadly, cash deposits made at night are almost impossible to trace. Especially when the depositor wears a ski mask and rockin' pair of thigh-highs.

"Here's your change," the clerk said, completely unmoved by the chat I was having with my passenger's seat.

"Thanks, hon."

We pulled out and drove toward my humble abode-ment just as I got a text from Amber. Her message sent a shiver of worry down my spine. It read, *What does it mean when someone you're investigating threatens to kick you in the face and sell your teeth on eBay?*

I texted her back, using Siri so I could text and drive without killing someone. *I'd say it means you may have found your man. "May" being the salient word. Now just figure out his motivation.*

Hers, she texted back. *She's an assistant volleyball coach.*

"What?" I shouted into Siri. I gave up and called the little stinker.

"Hey, Aunt Charley," she said, cheery as ever.

"What the hell? Why is an assistant coach threatening you?"

"Not me. Petaluma."

"Who's Petaluma?"

"She's our special investigator in charge of acquisitions."

I blinked in surprise, then asked, "Expanding already?"

"We have three cases now. How do you keep up?"

"Sweet pea, do you even know what acquisitions means?"

"No, but we heard it on a TV show last night. It sounds cool, right?"

"Totally. I want you to tell your mother everything you just told me. Maybe not the acquisitions part. And tell her to figure out who this assistant coach is."

"Oh, I know who she is."

"No, tell your mom you want dirt. Greasy, sticky dirt."

"Um, dirt. Okay. Is that a technical term I should be aware of?"

"Most definitely. Ask your mother."

We hung up, and I refocused on Angel. "What happened next?"

"Where were we?"

"Hector. The bar. The football players. The gun."

"Oh, yeah, so Hector pulls a gun, and one of the guys knocks it out of his hands all stealthy like. Then there is this huge fight, and they knock him out. They freak. The owner of the bar tells them to go home. He'll take care of it. They are all buddies, I guess. He doesn't want them to lose their careers over some piece of shit like Hector Felix."

That guy was seriously disliked.

"They leave, and the barkeep calls this other guy. Some friend of his, but before he even shows up, Hector wakes up. He tells the barkeep he's coming back to kill him and that he wants the names of the guys so he can kill them, too."

"Dude's got issues."

"But Hector leaves all beat up and covered in blood and shit. Then he ends up dead a few hours later. Interesting, don't you think?"

"Very," I said. "Which bar was that?"

"They aren't open. It's too early."

"But they serve food. They'll have deliveries."

"Suit yourself," he said with a shrug. "Trickster's on San Mateo."

I made a U-turn first chance I got and headed to Trickster's.

14

Some days I amaze myself. Other days I put my keys in the fridge.

—MEME

"Where are you?" Cookie asked when she picked up. I was sitting outside the bar, waiting for a delivery truck to show up.

"I'm at Trickster's. I need to talk to the owner. Can you get me a number?"

"Sure. Amber told me what's going on. What the hell?"

"Right? Some people, people I like to affectionately refer to as idiots, think they can talk to Deaf kids any way they want without consequences. I don't know what this chick's problem is, but I need dirt, Cook. Something with grease that will stick hard enough to get her ass fired."

"On it. Now, why are you at a bar at seven in the morning?"

I explained about the football players and had her scour the Internet for something, anything, that may have mentioned the fight that night. She promised to get back to me if she got a hit.

In the meantime, Angel left to check on his mother, and Artemis tore out of the car to chase some strange noise she heard in the distance, so it was just me and Misery. Left to our own devices. Would people never learn?

I grabbed my phone, checked messages, then bought a digital copy of the third book, *Stardust*, since I'd left the paperback copy at the apartment. I'd barely opened the app to read it when a delivery truck pulled up.

If Angel had been there, I could've asked him if the guy taking the delivery was the bar owner. Perhaps the departed man in the Hawaiian shirt waving at me from on top of the delivery truck would know.

I motioned him down with a wave of my own, at which point he took Angel's place in the passenger's seat.

He really did look like Magnum PI, if Tom Selleck had been a chubby, balding man in his early sixties. Otherwise, he'd nailed the look. The mustache helped.

"Charley Davidson, I presume." He held out a hand.

I took it. "Domino, I presume back?"

"That I am, ma'am. That I am. So, you're really bright. I remember you."

"Yeah, Angel told me you hit on me once."

"Only once? Must be losing my touch." He gave me a flirtatious wink and chuckled.

I laughed with him. It felt good. Not as good as the sip of mocha latte I took, but good nonetheless. "Is that the bar owner from the other night with Hector?"

"Sure is. Why are you so bright again?"

Taken aback, I stared at him until he became uncomfortable.

"So, yeah," he said, changing the subject, "that's your guy."

"Wait, you really don't know who I am?"

"Not a clue, sweet cakes, but we can change that real quick like." He wriggled his brows, and I laughed softly, trying not to encourage him.

"Well, that's refreshing. As far as you know, Hector Felix walked out of the bar alive and well."

"*Well* is a subjective term, but alive."

"And the guy the barkeep called? I'm presuming he was called in to clean up a sticky situation."

"That was the gist I got, but I had to leave right after Hector did. Had a date." He blew on his nails and polished them on his bright red tropical shirt.

"Okay. The barkeep, what's his name?"

"Parish. He's a pretty stand-up guy. Takes good care of the boys, if you know what I mean."

"I'm sure he does." If he was that involved with the football players, he could be providing something more than just pizza and beer.

I stepped out of Misery and walked up to Parish just as the deliveryman was finishing up.

"Mr. Parish?" I asked.

"Just Parish." He eyed me suspiciously. "Parish McCoy."

I held out my hand. He took it after a bit of hesitation.

"I'm Charley Davidson. I'm a private investigator looking into the homicide of Hector Felix."

The man paled several shades, but his emotions didn't scream guilt. They screamed, *That man was crazy and threatened to kill me and my family!* I could understand his misgivings.

"I'm not looking into the incident here. Not closely, anyway. I know you're friends with the football players. Do you believe any of them would have cause to come back and kill Mr. Felix?"

"Besides the fact that he threatened their families? Their careers? No. Not at all."

"I'll take that as a yes, but I'm more interested in the man you called after."

The stunned expression on his face told me he could not imagine where I was getting my information from.

"Someone else was there that night, Mr. McCoy. Someone you didn't see."

He ran a hand down his face in frustration and stepped back to sit on a cinder block ledge that lined the bottom of his establishment.

"I have no intention of telling the police what happened if the events of that night didn't play into Mr. Felix's death, but I need to know for certain. Do you still have the recording?"

"No." He coughed into a hand, and I could see his whole life flashing before his eyes. Not literally. He just had that kind of stress humming underneath his surface. "No, I erased it."

Now he was lying. Finally, a bargaining chip. "I'll tell you what, Mr. McCoy. You let me see the recording, and I won't involve the police even though my uncle is a detective for APD."

He paled even further. With shoulders slumping and hands sweating, he led me into his bar, a clean if not outdated watering hole. Then again, maybe disco was coming back.

"Dude, you have to ditch the mirrored jukebox from the '70s. Otherwise, nice place."

"Thanks." He didn't mean it. I could tell.

We walked to a back room, where he showed me the footage

from seven nights ago. Sure enough, Hector Felix was making a grand nuisance of himself. At one point, he got in the barkeep's face, waving a broken bottle at him, threatening to cut a bitch. Either that or he was telling the barkeep he had a cup itch. Since he didn't look like he wore athletic gear, ever, I leaned toward the former.

My lipreading kind of rocked.

Then came the gun and the football players, and, sure enough, one of them disarmed Hector with a move that one learned in the military.

"That guy," I said, pointing at the tall African American with the most incredible biceps I'd ever seen. "What's his story?"

He shrugged. "Military brat. His father taught him that move, if you're wondering. He ended up with a full ride because he's a badass tight end."

"No shit." Man, he had an ass. "You sure seem to know a lot about these guys."

"I don't have a family. They're all I got. I treat 'em well. If that's a crime—"

"Not at all, Mr. McCoy."

He wasn't lying, and he truly didn't believe any of *his boys* would have gone after Hector after the fight.

"I'll need their names and any contact information you have on them, just in case. And I'll need a copy of this recording." Before he could argue, I brought up another touchy subject. "What about the guy you called to take care of the situation?"

He bit down, not wanting to drag him into it.

"Mr. McCoy, I will keep you out of this if I can, but I do need the whole story."

"He's a friend. By the time he got here, I'd closed up shop. I didn't even tell him why I'd called. I didn't want him involved if he didn't have to be."

"He had no idea who Hector was?"

"No clue. And he couldn't have killed him, anyway."

"Why?"

"The man is seventy-eight."

My mouth fell open, but I quickly closed it. Gaping mouth wasn't a good look on anyone. "How was he going to help you clean up the mess?"

That time his mouth fell open. He couldn't fathom where I was getting my intel. It took him a moment to answer. Finally, he said, "He wasn't going to help me get rid of the body, if that's what you mean. He was going to help me"—he lowered his head, embarrassed—"help me call the police and turn myself in."

A tingling sensation ran up my spine. He was going to take the blame for the death, to sacrifice himself, for the players.

"It wasn't what you think. He was an ass. I'd planned to tell them that he attacked me. I had no choice but to fight back."

"But he was beaten up rather severely."

He reached over and pulled a baseball bat from underneath his desk.

"Pretty. What's her name?"

He grinned. "Betty."

I liked her. "Look, Mr. McCoy, I don't know how he died yet, but if he did die from the injuries sustained here—"

He held up a hand to stop me. "I understand." He pushed a button and gave me the DVD from the recording. "This is the only copy. If he did die from those injuries, I go with plan A. I'm good with that. I have a feeling a jury will sympathize."

"I agree. But just in case—"

"I know, I know." He wrote down the names of all the players that were there that night as well as his lawyer friend.

"No one will see this, Mr. McCoy, unless absolutely necessary."

"You gonna tell me who your informant is?"

I looked over at Domino. He sat at the bar, a mischievous grin on his face. "Tell him his brother told you."

Realizing that I was probably walking into a trap, I said, "Your brother?"

Mr. McCoy nodded. "Yep. That would be just like him to come back from the grave to haunt me. And get me convicted of manslaughter in the first."

I laughed softly. "If it helps, he still has a great sense of style."

That time, Mr. McCoy barked a boisterous laugh.

I walked out with Domino asking, "Why is he laughing? What's wrong with my sense of style?"

I would only go talk to the football players as a last resort. The odds of any of them hunting Hector down and finishing him off were slim at best. Why would they? They had their careers to worry about. Hector did threaten them, but without knowing their names, he would've been hard-pressed to find any of them.

On the way out, Cook texted me a picture of a woman, square-jawed with short brown hair and splotchy skin. I called my B.F.F.

"How'd it go?" she asked.

"Unless the injuries sustained in the fight had something to do with Hector's death, I don't want to bring this to the table. I do, however, want you to check arrest records just in case there's something we should know. I'll give you the names when I get back."

"You got it, boss."

"How's Amber's case coming? I take it this is the assistant coach?"

"It is. I don't have anything on her yet, but the coach has a serious social media addiction. I'll get something on her eventually."

"I just need enough to intimidate her. To scare the bejesus out of her. We can threaten a lawsuit and all kinds of other fun stuff. Is she Deaf?"

"Nope. She's hearing. A CODA. Her mother was Deaf."

A child of a Deaf adult. Oftentimes, CODAs were some of the strongest advocates in the Deaf community. But there were those rare cases where CODAs resented their Deaf and hard-of-hearing parents. They were cynical and apathetic to the extreme. I'd met a couple of them in the past. They had learned to manipulate adults at an early age. That tainted a person's soul.

"Okay, have we heard anything about Hector's cause of death?"

"Not yet. They're keeping it under wraps in the hopes of preventing violence between criminal factions."

"Damn. I need that info."

"We could always ask Robert."

"I hate to get him involved. The lead detective, Joplin, dislikes Uncle Bob almost as much as he dislikes me. And that's saying a lot."

"Well, I am Robert's wife. Surely he could share a little info. It's called pillow talk."

"You guys talk about dead people amid coitus as well?"

She laughed and hung up. In my face. That happened to me so often.

I hopped in Misery and settled onto Idris's lap—such a lovely place to be—but I'd barely turned the key before getting another call.

I picked up with my best professional greeting. "Davidson Investigations. We don't sleep so you can."

Oh, I liked that. I searched for a pen and paper to jot that down when a woman's voice came on the line. "Charley Davidson, please."

"This is Charley," I said. Giving up on the jotting things, I craned my neck to make sure I missed the Porsche behind me as I backed out. 'Cause that would be expensive.

"Hello, my name is Kathryn, and I'm a volunteer at Presbyterian Hospital. I'm calling to let you know that your friend was admitted a couple of hours ago."

I slammed on the brakes. "What? Who? Which friend?" Was she assuming I had only one?

"She wrote your name and number on a piece of paper. I don't usually do this, but she was insistent."

"Who?" I asked, dread seizing my lungs. "Who's there?"

"Oh, of course." I heard the shuffling of paper. "Okay, according to her license, her name is Nicolette Lemay."

I gasped. A horn honked behind me, as I'd only pulled out of my parking spot halfway, but I couldn't move. I could barely breathe. "I don't understand. I just saw her a few hours ago." Could something we did be the cause of her hospitalization? Did she get into an accident on her way home?

"I'm sorry. That's all I know. She's in intensive care, but I believe she can receive visitors."

"Wait, was it . . . did she get into a car accident?"

"I'm sorry—"

"Kathryn," I said, pleading.

After a hesitant sigh, she said, "From what I heard, no. I believe she was attacked. The police are here."

I couldn't tear out of that parking lot fast enough. I called Cookie on the way and told her what I knew. Then I hung up amid her protests, just barely catching her insistence upon meeting me there before the call disconnected

I slammed on the brakes under the Emergency Entrance Only sign and shoved Misery into park before bolting out the door and into the emergency room. After a series of unhelpful encounters, I made my way to the intensive care unit. Two patrolmen stood outside one of the glass rooms with a detective—it was Uncle Bob—talking to a doctor inside.

I sprinted to the room, but the patrolmen blocked my entrance.

"Uncle Bob!" I shouted, despite the glares I knew I'd receive.

He turned and came out to me. "Pumpkin, how did you get here so fast?"

"A volunteer called me. What happened? Is she okay?"

"Do you know her?" he asked, incredulous.

"Yes. That's why I'm here. Wait, why are you here?"

He cursed under his breath, then led me to the side to talk in private. "Sweetheart, she was attacked like the others. She barely survived."

"The others?" I stood there stunned, the truth staring me in the face yet my mind unable to grasp it. To get a firm hold. I swallowed hard, then asked, "The others? Like the one at the gas station yesterday?"

He nodded, and my hands flew to my mouth.

"Did she . . . will she . . . ?"

"They think she'll be fine, but her wounds are extensive. We can only wait."

I swallowed again and drew in a deep breath. "Uncle Bob, was she burned like the others?"

"Charley," he began, but I held up a hand.

"I need to know."

"Yes, pumpkin. She was. Her wounds are identical to the ones on all three bodies. The scratches. The bruises. The strange burn marks."

My knees weakened, and Uncle Bob helped me to a chair. He grabbed a cup of water just as Cookie ran up to us, panting and half-hysterical.

"How is she?"

"Do you know her, too, hon?" Uncle Bob asked.

She nodded, and he pulled her into his arms.

"I'm sorry, sweetheart. I didn't know."

"Is she . . . ?"

"They're hopeful. They said all we can do is wait."

"I need to talk to her, Uncle Bob."

"Pumpkin, she's unconscious."

"Uncle Bob," I said, injecting meaning into my tone. "I need to try."

He nodded and walked me into the room. I almost passed out when I saw her, and he had to guide me to a chair once again.

It was at that moment I realized Reyes was in the room. Why? Did my distress summon him as it had in the past? But that had been Reyes. Why would Rey'azikeen care if I were distressed?

I stood again, refusing to let him see me so, well, distressed.

Nicolette's dark hair had been partially shaved where a long gash on her scalp had to be stitched up. Her face was swollen, completely unrecognizable, and covered in scratches. But just like Uncle Bob had said, she had burn marks on her arms and feet.

My breath hitched in my chest as I walked up to her. Put a hand over hers. Closed my eyes.

"It's okay," she said from behind me.

I whirled around to see her standing in a corner, and panic set in. "No way." I walked over to her. "You get back in there. I can save you if you're still inside your body."

"Charley, it's okay. It's—" She stopped and gave me a once-over. "My God, you're beautiful."

"Nicolette," I began, but an alarm on her monitor blared, and a team of medical staff rushed inside.

After being ushered out, I searched the area for Nicolette and found her looking in from the outside of her room.

I hurried over to her. "Nicolette Lemay, get back in your body this instant."

"Okay," she said with a grin, "but you need to know."

"Right." I nodded. "Who did this, hon? What happened?"

"It's not what you think. It's . . . he . . ." She looked down as though confused. As though she was searching her memory. Just as she looked up, just as she opened her mouth to explain, she vanished.

She'd been thrust back into her body when they resuscitated her. Her heartbeat stabilized, but we weren't allowed to go back in.

"Uncle Bob, I need to get in there," I said through gritted teeth as a very nice security guard showed us to the door.

He. She'd said *he*. So, it was a person? But who could do such a thing?

"Okay, I'm going to have to do this old-school."

Cookie nodded in understanding, but Uncle Bob frowned, uncertain.

"Cover for me." Before he could ask, I shifted onto the celestial plane and sought out my friend. A friend I'd come to adore.

I found her lying down, but in this state, on this plane, she lay on a bed of yellow grass and small white flowers. She was lovely.

I touched her shoulder and healed her most life-threatening wounds. The swelling in her brain would diminish, and any internal bleeding would stop. I didn't want to heal her completely, not just yet, but this, I could do.

However, she remained unconscious. I let her sleep. She clearly needed it.

I materialized inside the women's bathroom and headed out to meet Uncle Bob and Cook. After a quick nod of reassurance, I glanced at the security guard.

"Where did you go?" he asked.

"To the little señoritas' room. Is that a problem?"

He scowled, annoyed, then led us the rest of the way out.

She was on the celestial plane. At least a part of her was. Her essence, perhaps? But humans weren't on that plane. Not entirely. Not until they passed, anyway. Maybe she'd shown up because she had been so close to death.

Or maybe there was more to it than that.

Either way, I needed to take a closer look at this case. It wasn't Rey'azikeen. I knew that beyond a shadow of a doubt. But the deaths did coincide with the shattering of the god glass. With the opening of the gates.

When Reyes had broken out of the hell dimension, when he'd shattered the god glass to free himself, he'd also freed everything inside.

The poor souls that had been trapped by the sinister priest darted straight through me, but I'd never felt or seen the priest, the evil man who'd put them all there in the first place.

A suspicion that had been simmering in the back of my mind reappeared. Being in a hell dimension for over six hundred years had to wreak havoc on one's mental state, and his hadn't been exactly stable to begin with. But if my suspicions were right, he hadn't gone to hell, the hell of this dimension, as I'd suspected.

If my suspicions were right, he was still on this plane.

But his presence on this plane didn't explain why those people had died in such a horrible way or why Nicolette was so savagely attacked.

I hurried back to the office to pore over the files for the hundredth time. I was missing something. I had to be. The connection. There had to be a connection, and I was missing it.

I grabbed the files off Cookie's desk, put on a pot of the good stuff, double the good stuff, then sat at my own desk to study. To dissect. To search for any commonalities between the victims. I combed through their files, but all I got was the usual, so I hit their social media sites.

Out of the three deaths, one man and two women, including the woman found yesterday morning in the convenience store restroom, only one had her social profiles set to private. Cookie had a way of bypassing those kinds of nuisances. I did not.

The other two victims, a woman named Indigo Russell, who was found in her home three days ago, and a man named Don Koske, who was found in his car the day after, seemed the polar opposites of each other. Taking into account the latest victims, Patricia Yeager and Nicolette, made the differences even more glaring.

An accountant, a recording artist, a court clerk, and a nurse.

Hopefully, a search of their social media accounts would give me a broader picture of their lives and habits. Something had to connect them. But three and two-thirds cups later, I'd found nothing.

"Think about it," Cookie said. She'd joined in the search. I now officially had a search party. She couldn't look at the pictures of the victims' bodies, but she was fantastic at poring over pictures on social media outlets.

"I'm thinking," I assured her. "It's all I've been doing for hours."

"Nicolette is a very unusual girl. She has a gift. A supernatural gift. Maybe she somehow lured the entity to her. Like, maybe—"

She stopped talking when I jolted upright and gawked at her, lids wide, mouth slightly open.

"You had an epiphany," she said, letting a grin cut across her pretty face.

"No, Cook. You did."

I grabbed my mouse and went back to Indigo Russell's Tumblr account. Something had caught my eye, but I couldn't put my finger on why.

"Look," I said, pointing.

Indigo had posted a picture about a year earlier. The image depicted a dark, leafless forest, stark and eerie, and hiding behind a tree lurked a demon with bright red eyes and sharp claws.

"It's not just the picture," I said, pointing to the description. "It's what she says about it."

"Every night," Cookie read aloud. "This is what waits for me every night since the incident." She looked back at me, empathy evident in the lines on her face. "Wait, what incident?"

I had gone back to staring at a picture of Indigo taken by a friend of hers on a camping trip. Ensconced in a sleeping bag, Indigo was barely awake when the culprit stole into her tent and snapped the shot. Her hair had been a mess, her face soft with the lingering remnants of sleep.

"Cookie, I've seen her. Look at the date of that picture." I sat back in thought. "Remember when we first met Quentin?"

"Of course, poor baby. He'd been possessed by a demon because he could see into the supernatural realm. Several demons had possessed people sensitive to their world. Because only those people could see you, and they were after you. They wanted to kill you."

"Yes," I said, pointing to Indigo. "Cook, she was one of them. I remember her that night."

"You mean during the fight in front of our apartment building?"

"The demons were using humans as both bloodhounds and shields so they could try to kill me. To kill Beep. My light wouldn't hurt them as long as they were inside a human. We had to literally pull them out before we could kill them."

I stopped and studied Indigo's features, her large eyes and long, dark hair, and I remembered her from that night. Sitting off to the side during the battle. Rocking back and forth, trying so desperately to shake off the demon inside her.

"She was one of them, Cook. She fought the demon with everything she had, but it still managed to control her to some degree. After the fight, after we killed all the demons, she ran off. I never found out her name or where she was from. Nothing. And she was right here in Albuquerque the entire time."

"And now she's gone," Cookie added. "Despite surviving that nightmarish ordeal, she's gone."

"Exactly. What if you're right? What if it works the other way? What if the same people who can see into the supernatural realm can be seen *by* the supernatural realm? What if they are targets because of it?"

"It would explain why both Indigo and Nicolette were attacked by a supernatural entity."

"And it could explain the others. We have no way of knowing. Unless . . ."

I thought back to the case of Joyce Blomme and the haunted house. I had been curious as to why Joyce, the departed grandmother and great-grandmother of the current occupants, could only see two of the three people in the house that night.

"I need to run an errand. To interview a potential witness." I could have called Chanel Newell, but I wanted to interview her face-to-face. To gauge her reaction to my questions, because most people who are sensitive to the otherworld had a difficult time admitting it, even to someone like me.

"Again?" Cookie asked. "You get to have all the fun."

"It's the woman from the other night whose grandmother was haunting her house but the grandmother thought that the granddaughter was haunting *her* house and I had to tell the grandmother that she had died thirty-eight years ago and that she was, in fact, the haunter, not the hauntee."

"Oh," Cookie said, standing to walk back to her desk. "Okay, then. I'm good here."

"Thought so," I said, unable to suppress a slight giggle.

I headed that way. Or tried to. The door opened before I could get to it, and one Detective Forrest Joplin stepped into the humble offices of Davidson Investigations.

I tensed. Mostly because he hated me with a fiery passion. He didn't understand how I solved cases. Thought Uncle Bob indulged me too much. Thought I used nefarious means.

He was right. I used any means necessary, but that was no reason to hate my innards. My innards had nothing to do with my cases.

"Detective," I said, sweet as could be. My world may have been coming to an end, my friends may have been attacked and suspected of foul play, my husband may have been turned into a volatile god, and I may not have slept in several days, but no way was I letting Detective Joplin know any of that. I beamed at him. "Fancy meeting you here."

Agitated, probably by my mere presence, he glanced at Cookie, then back at me. "Can we talk in your office?"

My smile widened. "Of course. As long as Cookie can be in there as well. I may need a witness."

"A witness?"

"You seem miffed. If I get another heated scolding because I solved one of your cases behind your back, I need a witness. You know, for when I file a complaint."

He raked a hand through his military buzz. "I'm not here to scold you, Davidson. I'm here to warn you."

I clapped in excitement. "Even better. Can we record it?"

He stepped closer to me. "Your uncle is snooping around my case, and if he's snooping, odds are you put him up to it."

I looked over at Cookie. Her face turned an odd shade of purple.

"Cook, you talked to Uncle Bob already? I thought that was going to be, you know, pillow talk."

"It was. That was the plan, but then—"

"Cookie," I said with a gasp, beaming at her with pride. "You got a quickie?"

"Charley, I hardly think this is the time."

I propped a hip on her desk. "Oh, it's the perfect time."

"I just asked him if he could check into that thing we were talking about when we were talking about, you know, that thing." God, she was good at collusion.

After another moment of awkwardness in an already awkward stalemate, my quota for the day had been filled, and I let her off the hook.

I turned to the surly detective. "Yes, I was just wondering if you had a COD on one of your victims. A man named Hector Felix."

"Why?"

"Right? It's such an odd name. It's like two first names put together. But I have no idea why anyone would name him that."

He bit down, his jaw working. "Why do you want to know?"

I had a feeling he was making nice in front of Cookie. That woman was invaluable in ways she couldn't even imagine. "I'm asking for a friend."

"That friend wouldn't happen to be a local tattoo artist?"

Cookie gasped. Loudly.

I slammed my eyes shut, then said, "No."

But he was already wearing a smirk when I opened my eyes again. "Well, they did date." He picked up Cookie's stapler. "He did blow her off." He set it down, feigning complete intrigue in mundane office supplies. "And poisoning is the number-one MO when females kill."

"Poison?" I asked, astonished. It took everything in me not to turn to Cookie for a high five. Pari was so off the hook, as were the Lobo football players.

"Yes," he said, missing my skyrocketing euphoria. "Less violent."

I almost giggled. "Clearly, you don't know Pari."

"Clearly, you do." He pinned me with a victorious smirk, which was so much more annoying than his smug one.

Oops. "Yes, but I also know she had nothing to do with his death."

"He'd also been beaten recently. Any thoughts on that?"

"Not that I can share."

"So, I can add obstruction to my list of grievances against you."

"You have a list of grievances against me?"

"Several pages' worth."

Dude did not like me.

"Either way," he added, "count your friend lucky. This was the last girl who tried to break up with Hector Felix."

I'd noticed the manila envelope in his hands but hadn't paid it much mind until he brought out an eight-by-ten glossy of a girl whose face had been slashed to ribbons.

My hands flew to my mouth as did Cookie's. She sank into her chair and stared in shock.

"Straight razor," he said.

The poor girl, a blonde in a light blue hospital gown, had about a thousand stitches closing the numerous slashes along her cheeks, forehead, nose, and chin. Each more gruesome than the last. She also had a swollen shiner and the whites of that eye were blood red, so she was probably beaten as well.

"Who would do this?" I asked, my chest constricting the flow and ebb of air to my bloodstream.

He took the picture out of my hands, stuffed it back into the envelope, then handed it back to me, as though to make a point. "Something to think about."

"Detective—"

"Mrs. Davidson," he said, then turned and strode out.

"Oh, Charley," Cookie said from behind her clasped hands.

I took the photo out. The woman's name, Judianna Ayers, was on the bottom.

"Okay," I said to the door Joplin had just walked out of. "I'll bite." I handed the photo, as badly as I hated to do it, to Cookie. "Get me everything on this woman. I have an errand to run. Be back in an hour."

"What did you mean, you'll bite?"

"He gave this to us for a reason, Cook. Asshole wants me to look into it? I'll look into it."

"You think he wants you to solve this woman's attack?"

"Maybe he can't pin it on Hector." I grabbed my bag and stalked toward the door. "But I damned sure can."

15

That which doesn't kill me,
makes me weirder and harder to relate to.
—T-SHIRT

I drove to Chanel Newell's house. I'd remembered her saying she had a few days off and she wanted to get a jump start on spring cleaning, so I hoped to find her home.

A white Encore sat in the driveway of the house I'd staked out only a couple of nights earlier. I walked to the door and knocked. Blue Öyster Cult filtered through the wooden door.

A girl after my own heart.

The door opened. "Mrs. Davidson," she said, surprised.

"Hey, Mrs. Newell."

"Chanel, please. Come in." She opened the screen door and ushered me inside. "The kids are at my sister's house. She's helping me out so I can get some cleaning done." She yanked off a pair of yellow rubber gloves and led me to the kitchen so she could turn down the music.

"And call me Charley. Please."

"Sure. Would you like some tea?"

"I don't want to keep you. I just had a couple of questions."

"Oh, okay."

She moved some magazines and papers off the kitchen table, embarrassed, and offered me a seat.

"Chanel, I am going to ask you an odd question, and I just want you to know that I am completely open to any answer you give me."

A nervous laugh bubbled out of her. "This sounds ominous."

"You let me into your home the other day, having no idea who I was when I told you I believed your house was haunted."

"Yes." She nodded evasively. "I did."

"Why?"

"Oh, I don't know. You had a card. You seemed legit."

I couldn't help but grin. "I think it was because you knew before I even said anything that the house was haunted."

"What?" She scoffed lightly. "No. Why—? How would I know such a thing?"

"I believe you're sensitive to the supernatural realm. And if I'm right, the supernatural realm is just as sensitive to you."

She tensed, and a line formed between her brows. "What does that mean?"

"Is your son also sensitive?"

After chewing on her lip a moment, she caved. "Yes. More than I am."

"But not your daughter?"

"No. It tends to run in my family. My daughter was my husband's. He passed away a couple of years ago."

"I'm so sorry, Chanel."

"We're doing okay, though. Better."

"I'm glad."

"What did you mean, the supernatural realm is just as sensitive to me?"

The last thing I wanted to do was frighten her, but she deserved to know. "I'm going to be honest, Chanel. I investigate, well, all kinds of anomalies. Even those with a supernatural spin."

"Okay," she said, growing leery.

"There have been three murders and an attack, and they look, as crazy as this will sound, to have a supernatural element to them. I could be wrong, of course," I added when she started to ease away from me.

Even the sensitive had a difficult time with my level of supernatural phenomena.

"But, sadly, I don't think so. I don't know if proximity has anything to do with what's going on or if there have been victims with the same type of wounds in other cities, but I need you to leave for a few days. Get out of town with your children. Especially Charlie."

Alarm stopped her in her tracks. "What are you saying? We're in danger?"

"I don't know. This is an educated guess at best."

"So, if we can see them, they can see us?"

I nodded, then turned to the other woman sitting at the table, the one I had yet to acknowledge, Mrs. Blomme. "What do you think, hon?"

She frowned. She'd been excited to see me when I first came in, but my message worried her.

"Can you see your great-granddaughter?"

She shook her head. "Not a bit. I've tried, too. I can see Chanel talk to her, but she just isn't there."

"I was worried about that. And that puts paid to it," I said, quoting Jane Austen. I turned back to Chanel. "Do you have anywhere you can go?"

Chanel, lost in my conversation with her grandmother, snapped back to me. "What? Well, yes, I suppose. I have a brother in south Texas. Will that be far enough?"

"I hope so. It's certainly worth the effort. I'll let you know the minute I get this straightened out."

"I'll keep an eye on them," Mrs. Blomme said.

"Chanel, I know you can see your grandmother, or see her essence. But can you communicate with her?"

Chanel shook her head. "I can't, but I think Charlie can."

"That little darling and his gravy boat," Mrs. Blomme said, slapping her knee in delight. "He's such a doll. I have a beautiful family, Mrs. Davidson."

"Yes, you do. Can you keep an eye on them for me? Come and get me the minute something seems amiss?"

She straightened and saluted. "Absolutely."

"You know how to find me?"

She cackled. "You're a little hard to miss."

"Thank you."

I left the Blomme-slash-Newell family to see what Cookie had discovered about our girl, Judianna Ayers, the woman Hector Felix took a straight razor to. But first, once inside Misery, I summoned Angel.

"*Hola, chica,*" he said, gesturing with a nod from my passenger's seat.

I shifted toward him, planting my knee on the console. "Hey, sweet pea."

He cringed at my term of endearment.

I ignored him. "I have a question for you."

He let out a long sigh and raked a hand down his face. "Yes, you can see me naked, but this is the last time."

"Angel."

"I mean it. There's only so much a man can take."

I coughed to cover my soft burst of laughter. He hated the fact that I didn't think of him as a man. Just because he was technically older than I was didn't mean I thought of him that way. He'd died at thirteen and still looked thirteen.

"Are you going to insist on making out again?" he continued.

I reached over and ran my fingers over the peach fuzz on his chin. "In your dreams, sweetness."

He caught my hand and raised it to his cool lips. If we hadn't been hit with a heat wave by the name of Rey'azikeen the Erratic, he would have held it longer. Instead, he lowered it and asked, "What's up?"

"Are there some departed who can't see humans? I mean, you can see anyone. And I remember the case with the three lawyers, Sussman, Ellery and Barber. They could see humans, too. But—"

"They'd just died," he said, interrupting.

"What?"

"The lawyers. They'd just died."

I shook my head, trying to understand, to think back to my cases and all the departed I'd worked with over the years. I'd started working with my dad, helping him solve crimes, when I was five years old, and in all that time, I'd never noticed the fact that some could see into the Earthly plane and some could not.

Despite the heat of the volatile deity lingering nearby, Angel had kept hold of my hand in his lap. He was getting braver by the moment, but I wasn't sure what Rey'azikeen could do to him. If anything. Although I had seen him choke Angel out once. Clearly, the teenager could be hurt.

"The fresher the death," Angel explained, "the more we can see."

I slumped against my seat, dumbfounded. "This is the first I'm hearing about this. How could I not know?"

He shrugged. "It's never been an issue before."

He was right. It had never been an issue, but it damned sure was now.

Then another thought hit me. Mrs. Blomme had been gone for thirty-eight years and could only see those humans sensitive to the supernatural realm. Angel had been gone for over twenty years. I took his hand into both of mine, and asked, "Angel, are you . . . losing the ability to see humans?"

He squeezed my hands. "Not yet. I don't know if it happens to all of us, but I guess it might someday."

"Why does it happen? What does time have to do with it?" It made sense. The priest had been dead for over six hundred years. It would definitely explain a few things.

"Think about it," he said, keeping his gaze averted. "Would you want to see people, dozens of people every day, if they couldn't see you back? It gets . . . lonely."

"Angel." I leaned forward again and placed my hand on his cheek. "You know, just in case, you might want to let me see you naked now before I lose the ability."

"Good try, gorgeous."

"Something to think about," he said a microsecond before he vanished.

Now in a state of melancholy, I called Cookie.

"From what I can tell," she said, knowing exactly why I'd called, "she's in protective custody."

"Really?" I said, impressed. "How'd you deduce that?"

"I have a vast underground network of spies, so I could tell you, but then I'd have to kill you."

"I see. How'd you really figure it out?"

"You don't believe me?" she asked, appalled.

"Not even a little."

"Robert told me," she said, giving in. "It's why Joplin's so frustrated. Well, one reason, anyway. I'm pretty sure he's sexually frustrated as well, but that's a story for another time. He'd been trying to pin something on Hector Felix for a couple of years to no avail. And then Hector ups and dies on him."

"The nerve of him," I said, my voice dripping with sarcasm. "Uncle Bob didn't happen to say where she was staying while in protective custody?"

"It's super hush-hush. Not even the captain knows. Robert didn't really say it in so many words, but I think it's an FBI thing."

"That's so weird. I just happen to know an FBI agent. A couple of them, in fact."

"Charley, you know they can't tell you."

"True. But that doesn't mean I can't accidently stumble upon information regarding the whereabouts of a certain traumatized young lady."

"And how do you plan on doing that?"

"It starts with an *A* and ends with an *ngel*."

"I already know where she is, boss," Angel said from the passenger's seat.

I jumped, nigh lodging my heart in my throat, then leveled a glare on him before hanging up with Cook.

He sat laughing, his shoulders, so close to being the wide-set chick magnets they'd promised to be, shaking. "You kill me," he said between chuckles.

"Oh, yeah, well, you . . . you laugh like a girl."

He laughed harder. "That's all you got? You need to get some sleep. You're losing your touch."

He was so very, very adorable. I loved every inch of his charming, inquisitive self. So, I knew what I was about to do was going to hurt me more than it hurt him.

I hauled off and punched him on the arm. Sadly, my attempt at payback only served to fuel his mirth.

I needed new friends.

"Whatever. I need you to go on a stakeout."

"I'm always on a stakeout."

"Because you're so good at it."

"True," he said, sobering. "Please tell me she's pretty."

"As a matter of fact, she is."

I filled him in on my plan, which involved us tricking one Special Agent Kit Carson of the F, B, and I.

"She's cool," he said when I was finished. "But this won't work."

"Why not?" I asked, offended.

"Just because you call her asking about this Judianna Ayers doesn't mean she's going to jump in her car and drive to where they're keeping her."

"True, but maybe she'll bring something up or make a call I can trace. Just take note of any addresses or phone numbers after we hang up."

"Will do."

He vanished just as my phone rang. Cookie was calling back, hopefully with the location of our girl and I could pull the plug on the sting.

"Charley's House of Snake Venom."

"I had a thought."

"Just one?"

"You said that this priest—"

"If it is the priest."

"Right, if it is this priest and he's attacking people who can see into the supernatural realm—"

"Exactly, but why? Why would he attack people at all?"

"More importantly, what's to keep him from attacking Quentin? I mean, Quentin doesn't just see into the supernatural realm. He can communicate with them."

"Oh, Cook," I said, my pulse suddenly rushing in my ears. "I didn't even think. Can you call Amber and have her get him a message?"

"Of course. But, not to shine a glaring light on the obvious, what's to keep the priest from attacking you?"

"I can handle him. Don't you dare worry about me. But Quentin . . ."

"I'll take care of it. Maybe we need to send him away for a while, too."

I bit my bottom lip in thought. "I wonder if he would be safer at the convent. You know, that whole sacred ground thing?"

"It's worth a shot."

"Okay, have Amber tell him to get his butt home pronto. Oh, and Pari," I added. "Can you call her? I'm about to sting Kit."

"Sounds . . . painful. I can definitely call her. Should I tell her to leave town?"

"Yes. She won't, but tell her to. In fact, send Garrett to watch her if he's finished with his skip."

"You got it. Any excuse to talk to that man."

"Right? Have you seen his abs lately?" A heat washed over me with the statement and it wasn't coming from inside me. I ignored it. Jealously was so unbecoming.

We hung up, and I set up the sting, otherwise known as Operation Spy on Kit and Get Her to Reveal the Whereabouts of a Certain Witness to a Crime Perpetrated by the Newly Departed Hector Felix. I was so bad at naming operations.

I dialed Kit's number and waited. She didn't pick up the first time, so I tried again. She was an FBI agent. She had important shit to do. Important shit I had no problem interrupting, so I tried again.

After the fifth call, she finally picked up. "Davidson," she said, her voice a little edgy. A little sharp. A little irked.

"Carson," I said back. "'Sup?"

"Okay, I'll be right there," she said to someone other than me. I hoped. "I'm headed into a meeting, Davidson. Is this business or pleasure?"

"It's always pleasure when you're involved, Kit."

"So, business. What do you need?"

"Oh, nothing too urgent. It's just, this woman came in with fresh cuts all over her face. It was awful, Kit. She wants to hire me, but I told her to go to the police. She said she'd already been talking to the FBI, but she was afraid for her life. She wants me to find her attacker."

"What?" Kit said, taken aback. "We already know who attacked her. Damn it. I'll call you right back."

She hung up before I could say, "Okeydokey." Thirty seconds later, Angel was back with a stunned expression on his face.

"I can't believe that worked."

"Told you. I should've gone to Hollywood. I could've been a contender."

"She just dialed the number to one of the agents watching your witness."

"In her defense, not many of their enemies can send in a departed teenager to spy on them and intercept the numbers of their outgoing calls."

"True." He repeated the number Kit had dialed to check on Judianna Ayers.

I called Cookie, relayed the message, then told her to work her magic. Five minutes later, as horrible as the truth of what we'd done felt, we had a location.

"No way could it have been that easy," I said, growing worried.

"I know, right? But this is the address that came up. That number is sitting pretty right there."

"But it's a witness protection gig. It can't have been that easy to get this information."

"I don't know what to tell you."

"You know what? I'm punching a hole in their security measures. Teaching them where they went wrong. Where they need to tighten up."

"Better you than a real enemy. Be careful, hon."

"Okay. I'll check it out. Thanks, Cook."

I headed to the address Cookie gave me in the South Valley off Fourth Street. Not the best part of town. Not the worst, either. There were some really cool historic houses in the district. It gave the area a certain charm not afforded the worse parts of Albuquerque. The war zones.

Knowing I'd never get through security to see Judianna and could be arrested just for trying, I did the next best thing. I bypassed security. I shifted onto the celestial plane, straddling the two realms, and walked through an exterior wall of the residence and into the bathroom, hoping beyond hope we had the right address.

I cracked open the door and listened. A TV blared from the living room, and two agents sat at a table nearby. Relief washed over me. We definitely had the right address. Now to find Judianna.

I started to sneak down the hall when I heard a soft voice behind me.

"I'll scream," it said.

I froze, then slowly turned to see the once-beautiful Judianna Ayers standing behind me with a toothbrush in her hand.

"I will stab you in the face."

She held it like a weapon, her toothbrush, all piss and vinegar.

She was scared. Anyone would be. But she had not done as I'd feared. She had not withdrawn inside herself and given up. She was a fighter. And she was threatening to stab my face with her toothbrush.

I liked her.

I glanced around, wondering where she'd been thirty seconds ago. So I asked. "Where were you thirty seconds ago?"

"In the shower."

Noting her fully clothed state, I looked her up and down, suspicion kneading my brows.

"The water in the sink doesn't work," she explained. "I have to brush my teeth in the bathtub."

"So, you climbed in?"

"Okay, fine, I was reading. Do you know how loud that stupid TV is? I have to come in here to read, and, well, throw in a couple of pillows and the bathtub is pretty comfortable." She turned on me as though snapping to attention. "But how did you get in here, and what do you want?"

Her stitches had been removed some time back. God only knew how long she'd been holed up in this tiny house with FBI agents dogging her every move.

"I was going to ask you if you killed Hector, but I can see that's fairly doubtful considering the bodyguards."

"Killed Hector?" she asked. She straightened her shoulders. After a moment of thought, she sank down onto the side of the tub. "Hector's dead?"

That was a definite no to the kill theory. "Yes, hon. I'm sorry."

"Oh, no, it's fine. He was an ass. It's just . . . shocking."

"I'm sure." I sat next to her and checked out the book she'd been reading: *Harry Potter and the Prisoner of Azkaban*. I knew I liked her.

"Wait, you thought I killed him?" Her skin stretched when she spoke, and some words were harder for her to pronounce, but she was healing remarkably well.

"Not anymore. And, no, not really. I just needed to make certain. But can you tell me about Hector?"

She lifted a shoulder. "He was violent, unpredictable, sociopathic."

"Besides that? He was apparently poisoned, and if you'd keep that to yourself for a bit, I'd appreciate it. I'm not sure I'm supposed to be repeating that. Did anything unusual happen while you were together? Besides the obvious."

"He'd been acting strange for about a month before I tried to break it off with him. Secret phone calls and meetings."

"Another woman?"

"Oh, no." She waved a dismissive hand. "That was a given with Hector. He never kept his liaisons a secret. No, this was different. He was . . . stressed. Worried. And believe you me, Hector didn't worry about anything."

"And you have no idea what was going on?"

"Not a clue. He never talked business in front of me."

I was having a hard time picturing this levelheaded girl, so smart and courageous, ending up with someone like Hector Felix. "How did you meet him?"

She laughed, but it was a hollow sound, full of resentment. "I was a model. He came to a show, flirted a little, and the next day I had a dozen roses show up on my doorstep along with a note saying that I was his."

"Ah. A traditional guy."

"It was so strange. At first it made me feel, I don't know, wanted. Safe, even."

"I understand that. But once you found out what he was like, why did you put up with it? With him?"

"Hector didn't give me much of a choice. I would still be with him if he hadn't tried to kill me one night. I decided nothing could be worse than living in fear. Not even death. So, I left him."

"He didn't take it well?"

"No. He did not. But I still had my career." She lowered her head as tears formed between her lashes. "I was a model."

I closed my eyes. "I'm so sorry, Judianna. I'm sorry Hector did this to you."

She glanced back at me in surprise. "Hector didn't do this to me."

"What?"

"Oh, no. This was a message from his mother."

I sat there speechless for a full minute until a knock sounded at the door.

One of the agents shouted through the door. "Judianna? Is everything okay?"

Hector's mother. I had to meet this woman.

"Everything is fine. I'm just talking to—" She looked at me. "What's your name?"

"Let me guess," a startlingly familiar female voice said. "Charley Davidson?"

Judianna lifted her brows in question. I could hardly shift now. I had no choice but to face the bleak, dead-of-winter music.

I nodded and stood to open the door.

"Carson!" I said a microsecond before a male agent slammed my face into the floor and cuffed me. That was so going to hurt in the morning.

16

It just occurred to me that you could substitute
Miranda rights for wedding vows. Verbatim.
—TRUE FACT

Thirty minutes later, I sat in the back of Kit's SUV with a bag of ice on my face. Not that I needed it. I'd heal almost instantly, but it looked good.

Kit climbed in the backseat with me while her partner in crime . . . solving, Special Agent Nguyen, sat in front.

"Charley Davidson," she said, opening a file she held, "as I live and breathe. You tricked me."

"*Tricked* is a strong word."

"What are you doing here?"

"Visiting an old friend."

"An old friend who just happens to be in protective custody?"

"Weird, right?"

"I would ask how you found her, but I'm not sure I want to know."

"You probably don't."

"What about how you got inside the house? A house, mind you, that has been completely compromised."

"I wouldn't go there, either."

"Okay, how about why are you here? Only the truth this time, yeah?"

"I'm trying to solve Hector Felix's death. A friend of mine, a friend other than this one, is a person of interest in it, and I want to make sure her name is cleared."

She nodded and opened the file.

"Do you have any clues into his death?" I asked, hopeful.

"Don't know. Don't care."

"Really? Why? Isn't that, like, your job?"

"We're after bigger fish, Davidson."

"The matriarch." It hit me why they had Judianna in protective custody. Hector's mother had ordered the attack.

Kit closed the file. "You are about thirty seconds away from fucking up my case."

"Come on, Carson. You know my record. We can work together on this."

"You're good, Charley, but not this time."

"What? Why?"

"We have someone on the inside. Someone with family connections. For the first time in a decade of investigations, we've managed to infiltrate their family. I can't risk his life, Davidson, no matter how much I'd like you on the case."

I fought the disappointment bubbling inside my chest and nodded.

"And I'm not going to arrest you even though I should. I don't want to bring any more attention to Judianna or this case than is absolutely necessary."

A get-out-of-jail-free card. I'd take it.

"But if I see you butting your nose into this case, Davidson."

"Kit, I'm only after Hector's killer."

"That's butting."

"Not this time. My case has nothing to do with Judianna, who's totally great, by the way."

"I mean it, Davidson. I don't want to see you anywhere near this family."

I let out a long sigh of surrender. "Fine. No going near the family."

"Swear to me," she said, like she didn't trust me.

I held up my pinkie. She glared, then kicked me out of her SUV. Two minutes later, she absconded with Judianna, heading north with a full security detail following.

Judianna must have had something good on Edina Felix, Hector's mother. Something solid. I couldn't mess that up if I just went to Hector's funeral, could I? I hadn't actually sworn. We never shook pinkies. And I really, really, really wanted to meet the woman Hector Felix called Mommy.

It seemed that shifting in and out of the celestial realm stirred up my anarchistic husband, or the anarchistic entity residing in my husband's body, even more. I'd felt him close all day, but when I shifted to sneak into the safe house, I'd felt a stronger version of his presence. His warmth. His energy. His anger. He obviously hadn't found what he was looking for.

I hadn't found what I was looking for, either, so we were even.

I walked back to Misery, climbed inside, and picked up my phone just as it rang.

"Hey, Cook," I said, turning the engine over and heading back to the office.

"Are you wearing a little black dress?"

"Not this month."

"How are your clothes as far as attending a funeral? Will you blend?"

"I won't stick out, but I'd rather change. I take it the funeral is soon?"

"Hon, the funeral is at two."

I held my phone out to check the time. "Oh, I have just under three hours."

"In El Paso."

"Texas?" I asked, appalled. "Why El Paso? I thought the Felix family was from Albuquerque."

"They have a few holdings here, but they're based out of El Paso."

"Wonderful. Okay, I can do this. I'll run home, grab some clothes, and change on the road."

"While you're driving?" she asked, equally as appalled.

"It's that or miss the whole thing. El Paso is three hours away. I can make it in a little over two without killing anyone. Yeah," I said, thinking out loud. "I can do this."

"Why don't you just do that teleportation thing?"

My shoulders sagged. "I'm just not that good. I could end up in Scotland again. Or Siberia. Or Mars."

"I'll get some clothes together and meet you out front."

"Thanks, Cook. I owe you."

"You already owed me. How'd it go with Judianna?"

"Kid's a survivor, through and through. And I didn't get arrested. So, you know, that's a plus."

"Good for you."

Ten minutes later, I sped into the parking lot of our apartment building, grabbed the bag out of Cookie's outstretched hands like a drive-through, slowed down and backed up to grab the coffee cup she held out, then peeled out of the lot and headed back to I-25.

The reality of what I'd done sank in about three miles later. I'd just allowed a woman with the worst fashion sense I'd ever seen pick out clothes for me. Clothes in which I'd have to appear in public. Not the best scenario, but I'd faced worse.

I figured I could wait and change as I got a little closer, so I turned to the heat emanating from the backseat. Seeing nothing, I decided to watch the road again. Going ninety-five in a seventy-five in Albuquerque traffic took concentration. And guts. Mostly guts.

"Are you going to talk to me?" I asked, speaking to the emptiness around me.

Nothing.

Either Rey'azikeen was sulking or he was figuring out how to kill me and drag me to hell. I could've summoned him, forced him to shift onto this plane, but I didn't want to do something so drastic in a traveling coffin. Bad enough that I was speeding.

"You know, you could do me a favor and keep a lookout for cops."

Nothing times two.

My record was clearly not improving when it came to tall, dark, and sulky. Maybe I would summon him just to piss him off. Maybe—

I stilled as a realization dawned. If the priest were on this plane, if he was attacking people, killing them, all I had to do to bring him forth was to summon him. But I'd need his name to do that.

Unfortunately, I didn't know his name. And I had no idea how to get it. He'd lived in the 1400s and had been locked in the hell dimension ever since.

I racked my brain trying to come up with a way to learn the priest's name. Researching something like that would take years, and there was no way to know if any of the records from his parish survived. But someone knew. Michael? Would he have that kind of information? And if so, would he share?

Rocket. Rocket would know. But his telling me would be breaking the rules. His own set of moral rights and wrongs that made sense to Rocket and to Rocket alone. Would he break the rules if it were super-duper important?

He would just have to. I would give him no choice. People were dying at someone's hands, and my best and only guess was the priest, unless Rey'azikeen had lied. Unless he hadn't taken out the two supernatural entities trapped inside the god glass with him, the demon assassin Kuur and the malevolent god Mae'eldeesahn.

"Why would I lie about something so trivial?"

I flinched and looked in my rearview. Reyes, or Rey'azikeen as the case would be, sat in the backseat, lounging like a delinquent schoolboy in the back of a classroom. Knees spread. Hands resting on his thighs. Expression dark as he locked his gaze onto mine in the rearview. His irises fairly sparked with energy.

It took everything in me to tear my gaze from his and focus on the road.

"You know the name," I said, almost accusingly. "The name of the priest."

"Yes," he replied as though teasing me. Tempting me.

It worked. I practically salivated for it. "May I have it?"

"Tell me where it is and you may."

"Reyes, look, I don't know what you're talking about. I need more information. I'll help you find it, I swear."

He turned away from me, frustrated. "I don't have more information."

"Okay." I frowned in confusion. "What do you have?"

"It is ashes. It is embers. That's all I know."

"The god glass? The pendant I sent you through?"

"Why would I need that?"

"If you don't know what you are looking for, why are you looking for it?"

"I do know. I just don't . . . have access." He rubbed the back of his neck in frustration.

"What does that mean?"

"It means that Rey'aziel is keeping it from me. He won't give me access to the information I need."

How could Reyes essentially keep something from himself? It made no sense.

Then again, if Reyes was keeping information from Rey'azikeen, it meant that he was in there. Somewhere. Somehow. Holding the information close. Denying Rey'azikeen access to that part of himself.

My heart left my chest and soared. Metaphorically. He didn't know what he was even looking for. He didn't know because Reyes was still in there.

"That's interesting," I said, trying to keep him talking, trying to think of a way to bring Reyes out, if that were even possible. "Do you know what it looks like?"

He scrubbed a hand over his face. "It's important that I find it."

"Okay. I can help."

The expression he rested on me next would suggest he didn't trust me in the least. "And then what, god eater? Will you sup on my soul?" His voice mesmerized. Flooded my body with warmth. Filled my cells with joy. Tugged at something deep inside me. "Will you swallow my heart and claim it as yours?"

I wanted to say, "Why not? Fair's fair. Mine belongs to you." But I didn't.

Apparently, I didn't need to. His face darkened, but not in anger. "Crawl back here with me," he said, his words so soft and deep I had to strain to hear them.

I fought the urge to let go of the steering wheel and do exactly that. "I can't," I said, shaking my head. "I have a funeral to go to. And you said it yourself. You're not my husband." I'd said it as a challenge, daring my husband to fight.

Rey'azikeen's next line of attack was his fire. He sent it out to caress my skin. I felt flames lick along the most fragile parts of me. The most delicate and sensitive and tender.

"Rey'aziel doesn't have to know."

I resisted the gravity of his presence and bit the inside of my cheek to clear my head. "Aren't you afraid I'll sup on your soul?"

He locked his gaze again, and moments passed until I blinked and broke the spell.

"I am," he said. "Afraid. I have been for hundreds of thousands of years."

"And yet there you sit. I must not be that scary."

"You're a fool."

I ignored the rankle his statement caused. "Why is that?"

He turned to stare out the window. "You should have devoured me eons ago when you had the chance."

I glanced over my shoulder. "If I had, I wouldn't have you now. I wouldn't have Reyes."

"You have neither of us. All you have is doubt and suspicion and animosity."

"You're wrong."

"You're naïve." When I failed to rise to the occasion and hurl insults back, he lowered his voice again. "Crawl back here with me."

"Give me the name of the priest."

"I don't know it."

I gasped. "You lied?" Disappointment swallowed me.

"Malevolent god," he said by way of explanation.

"No," I said, almost yelling. I finally pulled over, threw Misery into park, and faced him. "No. Not malevolent. Unruly, perhaps. Rebellious. But not malevolent."

Surprise registered on his perfect face, but he recovered quickly. And he grinned, as though the heavens had opened up and shone just for him. "Is that what you told my Brother when you begged Him not to send me into the god glass? The hell dimension He tricked me into making?"

"I don't know. I don't remember."

"I'm so close," he said. He leaned forward, took my hand, and laid it over his heart. "You could take me now. You'd be wise to do so. To devour me before I find the object of embers and ashes."

"When you find it, what will you do with it?" I asked, trying to eke out information, anything to clue me in to what he was searching for.

He shook his head. "That is not your concern. Your concern is only now. Only this." He leaned back and dropped his hands to his sides, laying himself completely open, daring me to devour him. Or fuck him. It was hard to say.

And, God help me, I wanted to do both.

"Time's up," he said. Then he was gone. I'd only blinked, and from one microsecond to the next, he disappeared.

I shuddered, his powerful allure so enticing, I could hardly form a coherent thought. But the tiny voice coming from my passenger's seat took care of all the yearnings, all the pangs of desire, in two seconds flat.

"Who was that?" Strawberry asked.

I gaped at her, absorbing her presence before throwing my arms around her.

Strawberry Shortcake, so named because of her pajamas, was a nine-going-on-thirty-year-old departed girl, half-sweetheart, half-demon child, who'd lived with Rocket at the asylum before Rey'azikeen tore it down.

She let me hug her for, like, an hour before getting enough and pushing me away.

"Where have you been, sweet pea? Were you there when the asylum was destroyed?" Maybe she knew something more about what Reyes was searching for.

"No. I was looking for my brother. I still can't find him. You promised you'd find him for me."

Her brother, Officer David Taft, had gone on sabbatical from the police force and hadn't been seen since. Uncle Bob didn't seem particularity worried when I questioned him about it. No one had reported him missing, but his only family was sitting in my passenger's seat, and she couldn't exactly call the cops. Still, he had friends. Or I'd assumed he'd had friends. None of them had reported him missing.

I'd planned on looking into his whereabouts when all hell broke loose. Literally.

"I'm sorry, sweetheart. I'll find him. Promise. But have you seen Rocket? Is he okay?"

"You'll find David? Pinkie swear?"

I held up my pinkie, wrapped it around hers, and swore on its life, apparently. I never quite got the pinkie-swearing tradition.

"Okay, where's Rocket, love?"

"He's playing."

"At the asylum?"

"No. With the other kids."

"The other kids?"

"The ones at Chuck E. Cheese."

I blinked, trying to picture Rocket playing with a roomful of children anywhere, much less Chuck E. Cheese.

"His favorite game is Whac-A-Mole. He thinks it's funny."

"Well, he's right."

"I guess. I have to get back. I've looked and looked for David. Your turn."

Before I could question her further, she was gone. And I was wasting time on the side of the interstate when I had a funeral to crash.

17

Apparently "spite" is not an appropriate answer to,
"What motivates you?"
—MEME

On the way to El Paso, I could think of only two words, two things that best described the place: *great* and *tacos*.

Okay, El Paso had a lot more to offer than great tacos. Like great enchiladas. Great tamales. Great gorditas. It took me a while, but I finally realized I was famished. And almost out of gas.

As the city came into view, I tried to change while driving, crossed the white line a few times, almost died twice, then finally pulled over before I killed someone. I slipped my clothes off to the glee of many a trucker and slid into the little black dress Cookie had found. The one I hadn't worn in fifty years. I could only describe the fit as tourniquet-like and thank the gods I hadn't eaten after all.

Unfortunately, Cookie forgot one little-black-dress fashion essential. Shoes. So, my ankle-high boots would just have to do.

I'd missed the church service for Hector but, thanks to the wonders of GPS, found the graveside service no probs. I threw a casual jacket over my shoulders and made my way to the throng of funeralgoers.

Most were dressed in black. The Catholic priest's robes waved in the wind as he gave his final soliloquy, praising Hector and his family for being such pillars of the community.

With the service already under way, I walked around the crowd until I could get a good look at Hector's family. Fortunately, no one stopped me. Bodyguards, as plentiful as they were, had the manners to keep a low profile. They didn't pat me down when I walked up. They did, however, keep a weather eye.

The priest ordered everyone to bow their heads in prayer, and they did. All but one. A woman in her fifties sitting in the front row kept her gaze locked on the coffin. She wore a black hat with a net pulled down over her face. Despite clear signs of distress—swollen eyes, red nose—she remained a statue, head high, jaw set, mouth firm. Hector's mother, no doubt.

I scanned not only the faces in the crowd but the emotions rippling through it. Amazingly, considering we were at a funeral, there wasn't a ton of grief. I'd felt more grief while having lunch at the Frontier when a news program announced that *Lost* was ending. The guy wasn't the most beloved sort.

Only one woman, the one I'd assumed was Hector's mother, Edina, had any real emotion churning inside her. She kept a firm hold on it, but mixed with the devastation was a seething, explosive kind of anger. The kind of anger that screamed vengeance. Whoever did kill Hector would someday face that woman's wrath.

I'd seen evidence of her wrath in the form of permanent scars on Judianna's face. Because she'd tried to leave her son. I did not envy the person guilty of killing him. What kind of atrocities would she think up for such a crime?

Another interesting character, a younger woman sitting right next to Edina, also wore all black with a net over her face. Hector had a sister named Elena. Perhaps that was Elena. I'd only seen one picture of her taken from a distance, so I couldn't be sure. But she was striking with charcoal hair and flawless skin the color of caramel.

What was even more striking was not her lack of emotion but the stable of emotions she did possess. Anger and something akin to hatred emanated out of her in hot, hostile waves. An interesting juxtaposition considering her brother had recently died.

But no one at the funeral took me by surprise save one. Aunts and uncles stood around, trying to cry for Edina's benefit. Nieces, nephews, cousins, and friends gave their respects as the funeral came to a close. Stoic bodyguards patrolled the area and kept an eye on their charges. But one person, one of the bodyguards, the one standing directly behind Elena, surprised me to such a strong degree, I almost gasped when I realized who it was.

He was barely recognizable. He'd gained mass since I'd last seen him in his patrol uniform, along with a sharp suit, even sharper haircut, and dark, perfectly trimmed stubble. Like most of the guards, he wore sunglasses, but I recognized him nonetheless. Officer David Taft. Strawberry's brother. The brother neither she nor Uncle Bob had seen in months.

No wonder Strawberry couldn't find him. He was a different animal. Almost unrecognizable. A chameleon, able to blend in with this lot. He'd have to be to survive, but the difference in his manner and appearance stunned me.

Ubie had told me Officer Taft could have taken another position, something undercover, which would explain why his new assignment didn't appear on his record, but I didn't believe it. How would APD not know if one of their officers joined another organization?

And now I knew what had happened to him. He'd joined the FBI. Kit told me they finally had someone on the inside, someone with connections to the family. I never dreamed it would be Taft.

Although he wore sunglasses, I knew the moment he spotted me. Anxiety spiked within him. And adrenaline. And annoyance. Jerk. He hardly owned the world. If I wanted to attend a funeral, I'd attend a funeral. And yet he didn't flinch. His stonelike expression remained completely intact.

I could practically feel him shooting daggers at me. With as much stealth as I could muster, I dropped my gaze and shook my head, hoping to get my point across. I had no intention or desire to blow his cover. Those things took years to build. The fact that he had gained access to such a close-knit family was both impressive and befuddling.

I couldn't help but wonder about his connection to the family. Was he from this area? Was he related?

After the funeral came to a close, a line formed for the condolences. I lined up, ignoring the fact that I could barely breathe in my little black dress, and passing out was a serious concern. I waited my turn regardless. I would get an even better sense of everyone up close and personal, as they say.

When I reached the grieving mother, I took her hand and offered my sincerest apologies. And I meant it. I could not imagine losing a child.

Mrs. Felix thanked me softly. Her fragile hold slipping, she sniffed into a handkerchief before regaining her composure and offering her hand to the next in line.

When I shifted my attention to Hector's sister, I didn't dare risk a glance at Taft. Even the smallest infraction could cost him his life. Or me mine. Neither was ideal.

I took her hand in mine and knew, beyond a shadow of a doubt, she'd done it. A ripple lay just beneath the righteous indignation. A ripple of guilt. She tried not to feel guilty. She truly believed her actions justified. I just couldn't quite suss out why. What motivated her to take her brother's life.

Still, the act alone was enough to startle me. To murder her own brother. Her own flesh and blood. I stood taken aback for a split second before recovering and offering her my sympathies.

But another emotion leeched out of her. Certainty. All-consuming, absolute certainty. She knew she would get away with it. She harbored zero doubt. Zero apprehension.

At this point, I could do one of two things. I could walk away and report my findings to an angry but ultimately grateful—one can dream—Detective Joplin, because no way was I telling my FBI buddy I'd disobeyed a direct order and come to the funeral. Or I could bait the guilty party and hope to shake something loose.

I realized something about myself in that moment. I loved to bait. And I really loved shaking shit loose. Loose was so much better than tight, thought the girl in the body cast. This dress was so going to Goodwill.

I leaned in to Elena as though to kiss her cheek and whispered, "What would your mother think?"

Elena yanked her hand back and stared up at me. I winked and went on to the next bereaved family member. When I'd finished offering my sympathies, I took out my phone, pressed the button to call Cook, and started toward Misery.

An arm linked with one of my own. I glanced to my side at Elena Felix as she matched my stride step for step.

She offered me a calculated smile. "Walk with me," she said, leading me toward a sleek black limousine.

"Of course." Not that I had any choice. I glanced over my shoulder and noticed two men following us, Taft and another bodyguard who resembled a well-dressed vault door.

"After you," she said, gesturing me inside.

No way was it going to be this easy. Still, I'd ruffled her. I felt tremors of trepidation in her the moment she walked up to me. Guilt did that to a person. I could have been talking about her use of cocaine when I asked what her mother would have thought. Or the fact that the sun rises and falls on a daily basis. But a guilty person will always, *always* apply what is said to what that guilty person did.

Elena ducked in after me, and Taft after her. The other man took the passenger's seat up front with the driver. After she got settled, Elena held out her hand for my phone.

I passed it to her, but she didn't bother checking it. I'd already dialed Cookie. The screen was black but if there was a God, and by that point in my life I was fairly certain there was, she'd picked up.

Elena handed it to Taft, a man I barely got along with and who had about as much use for me as a light bulb had a koozie. But he cleaned up well. I couldn't wait to tell Strawberry what her brother had been up to. If I lived that long. Then again, I was a god.

He put the phone in the front pocket of his jacket, mic side out.

Hopefully Cookie would be able to hear and ascertain what was going on. Or she'd think I'd butt dialed her again and hang up. I was so bad about that.

I decided to fill Elena in so she'd know what she was getting herself into should she start shit. She sat across from me with Taft by her side. Close by her side.

"I'm a god," I said matter-of-factly.

"Are you?"

"That's how I know."

She pulled the net up over her face and removed her hat as the driver started the limo. "And what do you know, Mrs. Davidson?"

She used my name. Admittedly, that threw me. "You're very well informed."

"I pay to be."

The driver drove us out of the cemetery and headed north in the opposite direction of the city.

Elena smoothed her hair and took out a compact. Checking her lipstick, she continued. "I also know that you're a private investigator who sometimes consults with the Albuquerque Police Department. Mostly with your uncle, an APD detective."

For a split second, I wondered if Taft had told her. But he couldn't have. Not without blowing his cover.

"Yes, he told me," she said when she noticed my sideways glance toward him. "And, yes, before you ask, I know he used to be a cop."

I schooled my features to stay neutral, but I'd rarely paid attention in school, so I had no idea if I was doing it right.

She put her compact away. "We dated in high school. When I saw him at a club a few months ago, I realized how much I'd missed him."

Was that what Kit meant when she said she had someone on the inside with a connection?

"Only he told me he was a security guard at New Mexico State. He lied." She gave him an admonishing scowl chased quickly with a flirtatious grin. "So, I had my men take him to an abandoned warehouse to . . . question him. Just a little. Nothing too dramatic."

Had she done the same to her brother? Questioned him?

"They were to kill him afterwards. Davey knows I don't like being lied to."

I glanced at him, but he sat completely stone-faced, giving nothing away.

I didn't have to see evidence of his emotional state on his face, however, to know what he was feeling. Underneath the calm, almost robotic exterior beat the heart of a man who was going to kill me if he ever got his hands on me. Anxiety churned inside him. Somehow his cover hadn't been blown. Somehow it all played into his new role in life. Even so, the situation was sticky. One wrong word could get us both killed.

"As you might imagine," she continued, "I wanted to know if he'd been sent. You know, in an official capacity. But before my men could finish the job, he took them out. All three of them. Singlehandedly."

Her pulse sped up at the thought of her boyfriend taking out three violence-prone men. Probably three of her best.

"An hour later, he showed up on my doorstep, after disabling two of my personal guards, mind you, and asked me why I sent my men after him when he only wanted to date me." She giggled and curled an arm into his.

"How . . . romantic," I said.

"My thoughts exactly."

She picked up a glass of champagne that had been ready and waiting for her and took a sip before continuing, and I couldn't help but wonder if she could be any more of a cliché.

"Once I showed him how impressed I was with his . . . abilities, he explained. He told me he hated being a cop. Hated the grayness of it all. He had a unique philosophy, you see. A person is either good or bad, but many cops are a lot of both. He didn't like the ambiguity of it all, so he'd been looking for a career change, one in private security. He wanted to land a good job before he told me the truth."

"A man after my own heart," I said, not sure if I was supposed to know him at this point or not.

"When I told him who my family was, what we did for a living, he shrugged and said, 'I was a cop, not a saint.'" She turned to him and ran a finger under his jaw as though he were her favorite pet. "That's when I knew I had a keeper."

"I'd say. And he told you all about me in the two minutes it took me to make it through the line? I'm impressed," I said through gritted teeth.

He didn't flinch.

"No," she said, "his exact words were, 'That's the woman I told you about. Be careful.'"

He ratted me out? Wait, he'd already told her about me? I sat appalled.

"It seems you're something of an urban legend."

Resisting the urge to blow on my nails and polish them on my shirt, I shrugged.

"He said you help your uncle with his cases and that his arrest record is impeccable because of it."

"I do what I can."

She lowered her head to apprise me with more purpose. "He said you're dangerous."

"You know it's funny. In all the time I've known him, he's never mentioned you."

She let a slow smile spread across her face to let me know just how unimpressed she was.

The neighborhoods ended, and we drove farther and farther into the country. This was not going to end well.

"I'm surprised your mother lets you keep him on," I said, "considering his job history."

"Please, some of our best assets are cops. Or ex-cops. Cops are people, too," she said with a wry laugh.

"I suppose they are."

"So, my question to you is, what did you mean?"

"Exactly that. I'm a god. It's hard to believe, but there you have it. Just wanted you to know."

"At the grave. What did you mean when you asked, what would my mother think?"

"Oh, right. I just wonder what she'll think when she finds out you killed your brother—a.k.a., her son? You know, just one of those random thoughts I have. Why is the sky blue? Why is a green chile green? What will Elena Felix's mother think when she finds out her daughter killed her son?"

The more I talked, the tenser Elena grew. A turbulent rage sparked inside her and then a vulnerability. She cast a sideways glance at Taft, who remained impassive, but I felt the jolt of shock rush through him. He didn't know. She hadn't used him to get her brother's body to the country for disposal. Interesting.

"I just can't figure out why," I said, trying to keep her talking. After all, the more she talked, the more Cookie could record. If she hadn't hung up on me.

Elena taking my phone worked out perfectly. I could hardly have stuck it down the front of my dress. A dress that fit like a condom. The outline would've shown clearly.

Of course, I had no idea if Cookie had actually picked up. Or if she'd turned on the recorder as was standard protocol anytime I seemingly butt-dialed her. We'd used the technique once before to catch a husband in the process of trying to hire a hit man to kill his wife.

But our approach was far from perfect. I seemed to possess some kind of disability when it came to butt-dialing people. Like the one time I butt-dialed Cookie, and she recorded an entire afternoon of me trying to learn to Jazzercise. Needless to say, she was not happy. She kept trying to figure out if I was really being attacked or if I was grunting and groaning from exertion.

"So, how about it? Why did you kill your brother?"

She scoffed, then raised her chin, annoyed. "Check her."

Taft did as ordered. He leaned forward and frisked me, running his hands up my hips and along my waist before reaching between my breasts to check for a wire there. He ran his fingers along the edges of my dress, brushing his fingers along the tops of Danger and Will, who were quite scandalized.

With his face hidden from Elena, he let a half-second grin slip, letting me know he was having fun. Since Elena could still see my face, I couldn't glare at him too blatantly, but I did stab him with my best scowl of annoyance.

Satisfied, he leaned back and nodded.

"As I was saying," she continued, "I . . . I didn't have a choice." She looked at Taft as though she weren't explaining to me but to him. "He'd been arrested. He'd made a deal. He was going to give the feds everything."

Ah. Of course. The secret meetings Judianna had told me about. The ones he'd partaken in right before she'd tried to leave him.

"I had no choice," she said, practically pleading with Taft.

He finally broke the stoicism and looked at her. Took hold of her chin and tilted her face up to his. "I would have done it for you, bunny. You should have come to me. But your mother can't know."

She nodded and snuggled against him. Her hero. He was better than I ever gave him credit for. Brad Pitt had nothing on this guy. Besides the fact that he was Brad Pitt.

"So, you poisoned him?"

She didn't answer, but how did she know Hector had made a deal?

I began to worry there was a mole at the FBI. A mole who had tipped her off. "How do you know all of this?"

"Hector told me."

Unexpected, but it made sense. If there'd been a mole, she would've known about Taft.

"He came to me, crying, saying Mom would never speak to him again. Please. She would never speak to him again?" She scoffed, embittered. "He was her baby boy." Her pretty face twisted into a sneer at the thought of him. "Her favorite from the day he was born."

"I take it you were older?"

"No matter." She looked up into the face of her one true undercover love. Poor thing. "I'm taking over soon, anyway."

"The family business? Mazel tov. Does your mother know?"

Taft smiled down at her, so good he almost convinced me. If I couldn't feel every emotion pouring out of him, I would've bought it, too. "She won't know what hit her."

Elena's smile turned to one of almost worship. I was certain she reserved that particular smile for when they were alone. Any woman that hungry for power would never flaunt her weaknesses so openly.

She reached over and knocked on her window.

The driver obeyed instantly. He pulled to the side and rolled to stop. "This is where you get out."

The driver had taken a side road with little to no traffic. There wasn't another car in sight. Or house. Or animal, for that matter. The Franklin Mountains rose to the north, and the Rio Grande sat to the west.

"Can you call me a cab?" I asked.

That calculated smile spread again. "You won't be needing one."

Uh-oh. Now it was my turn. For Taft's sake, I had to make it good.

I pretended to just now catch on, as though reality were finally sinking in. I straightened and looked around, fear rounding my lids.

"You don't have to do this," I said. "They'll know. Plenty of people saw me at the funeral. They saw me get in with you."

"What people? You mean my family and friends?"

Pretty much. I began to pant, my gaze darting around, looking for an escape. "My car. My car is at the cemetery. They'll find it."

"Your car is being taken care of as we speak."

No. Not Misery. She was innocent! "Taft, tell her. Tell her I can keep a secret."

She raised her brows at him in question.

He scowled at me. "She'll burn you the first chance she gets."

Her grin turned triumphant. "Would you mind taking care of this, sweetheart?"

Relief flooded every cell in his body. He may have been worried she'd have the vault door up front do me. "Not at all." He took hold of my arm and started to drag me out the door.

I put up as much of a fight as I could without actually damaging him. I did manage a punch to the side of Elena's face. She totally deserved it.

Taft took a handful of my hair and slammed my head into the doorjamb, somehow managing to hit only his hand but making a loud enough thud to convince our audience that he'd knocked me out.

I collapsed, growing listless as he continued to drag me out of the car and into the desert surrounding us. I came to just enough to help him half walk, half drag me toward an incline of rocks where no one passing by would see my body.

"No one's going to see me out here," I said, pretending to plead with him.

"That's kind of the point."

"They'll never find my body. I'll decompose and be all icky. And my ass. What'll happen to my ass? I mean, have you seen it?"

He almost grinned, jerking me along with him as I slipped and stumbled. "It's hard to miss in that dress."

"Right? Cookie chose it. I can barely move."

"I'm surprised you can breathe."

I stumbled again, wrenched my arm free and tried to run. He easily caught me and steered me closer to the rock barrier.

"Cactus!" I yelled.

He swerved.

"Hey, did you really take out all of her men when they abducted you?"

"Yes." He glared at me as though I were judging him. "I didn't have a choice, Davidson. They lived. You know, in case you're wondering if I've gone totally dark."

"They may have lived, but will they ever walk again?"

"Two will," he said with a shrug. "Eventually."

"Who knew *Davey* Taft was such a badass?"

He flinched and shoved me forward. I pretended to fall, which was hard unless I actually fell. So I fell, then turned and pleaded with him. He grabbed my arm and manhandled me to my feet quite impressively.

"Your sister is looking for you," I said, as we got closer and closer. "She can't find you."

"What? Why?"

"My guess? She doesn't recognize you anymore."

"What's that supposed to mean?"

"It means you are either very good at your job or you've really gone bad."

"Good. She doesn't need to see me like this."

I nodded in understanding. "You know, I can tell her it's all a show. She'll understand."

He shook his head, ashamed. But why? He was doing a bang-up job. I would totally have bought it.

Maybe that was the problem. Maybe he enjoyed the role too much.

"I'll tell her you're fine. That you'll be back soon."

"That'll work."

"If all went as planned, Cookie recorded that whole thing. I'll make sure Agent Carson gets a copy."

"Okay, but first, run."

I took off again, and a gunshot pierced the air with startling clarity. I fell forward as he stalked toward me.

"I shot you in the calf."

"Oh, I'm not dead yet?" I asked, surprised.

He leaned closer to grab my arm again and took the opportunity to stuff my phone down the front of my dress. Then he recited a number, and said, "Send it there, too."

I fought him as he hauled me to my feet. "Whose number is it?"

"Elena's mother."

I limped along as he steered me behind the barrier of rocks so no passersby would happen to see me from a vehicle, but not so far that Elena wouldn't see the job finished. That way, she wouldn't have anyone check later.

"Okay," I said when we came to a stop. I fell to my knees in front of him and begged, getting the bizarre impression he was enjoying it. "I just need to know. Are you shooting me in my head? Because I'm not having the best hair day as it is."

He slid a nine millimeter out of a shoulder holster inside his jacket. "This is going to have to be close, hon."

I couldn't believe it. He felt bad for what he was about to do. Fake kill me to save my life and probably his, too.

Then again, maybe he wasn't faking.

I narrowed my eyes in suspicion.

He grinned, aimed the gun, and said, "Say hello to my sister."

When he pulled the trigger, I realized he could have meant that in a couple of ways.

The loud crack thundered against the rock wall. I jerked my head back and collapsed onto the uneven ground. My hair would never be the same.

He fired two more times into the dirt beside my head to make sure he'd finished the job. That time I concentrated on *not* reacting.

As he turned and walked off, I said softly, "Be careful, Taft."

He holstered his gun and kept walking.

18

They say it's what's inside that counts.
I agree, but I'm keeping my hair appointment just in case.
—T-SHIRT

I waited a good ten minutes after they drove off just to make certain I wasn't still being watched. It was a tough ten minutes. Half my face was in the dirt, being poked by all kinds of native plants. My hair covered the other half. And trying to breathe without looking like you were breathing was harder than I'd imagined. Playing dead sucked. Especially when things started crawling on me.

All that was bad enough, but when Artemis appeared, excited I was on the ground ready to play, the whole plan turned south. Thankfully she only attempted CPR once by taking a diving leap onto my sprawled body. I grunted and finally gave up the game. Mostly because a coyote had come sniffing, trying to decide if he could dig in or if he needed to wait a while longer.

I sat up, startling the ragged animal, and attempted to brush some of the dry desert dirt off. I scowled playfully at the gorgeous creature. "Not today, buddy."

He ran off a short distance, then turned back to watch me. To calculate when his next meal would keel over for good.

After making it to a shaded boulder, I dug the phone out of my cleavage.

I put it to my ear and asked, "Did you get all that?"

"Charley, damn it."

I got that so often.

"What the hell?" she asked, clearly relieved I was still alive. "I didn't know what to do. It's been an hour since the gun went off."

"Ten minutes."

"Close enough!"

"Sorry, hon. But it was Taft. You knew I'd be okay, right?"

"No. How could I know you'd be okay? He fired a gun. Four times."

"Yeah, I think he was enjoying that. Did you get the conversation?"

She let out a long sigh, then confirmed target was acquired. God, I loved technical speak.

"Every word. What do I do with it?"

I looked around, ignoring the sullen god lounging on top of the rocky protrusion I'd almost died behind, and tried to figure out how I was going to get a ride back to Albuquerque.

"At first, I was thinking Joplin, but I can't risk all of that getting into the wrong hands. Send the whole thing to Kit with my apologies."

"Your apologies? What did you do now?"

"Disobeyed a direct order."

"Will she arrest you?"

"There is a strong likelihood, yes. Let her know I need Joplin to get the part about Elena killing her brother. The rest she can keep under wraps. Oh, and don't be surprised if she raids the place and confiscates the recording."

"I never am."

"How much do you think a cab back to Albuquerque would cost?"

"It would be cheaper just to buy a new car. Something cool. Like a Porsche."

Now, there was an idea.

An hour later, thanks to LoJack, Cookie found Misery. In Mexico. Most likely with the keys in the ignition, inviting grand theft auto.

I Ubered it to Juarez, which is apparently much easier than Ubering it *out* of Juarez. It took me a while to explain to the driver, who'd picked me up in the middle of nowhere wearing a little black dress, ankle-high boots, and a lot of dirt why I needed to hide in his trunk, but my passport and other paraphernalia were in my purse in the very Jeep I was headed toward.

At least it was if they didn't take it, but since the whole point was to prove I'd gone to Mexico and gotten myself dragged off and killed, never to be seen again, it would've been stupid for them not to leave it.

I promised him a huge tip, as in four figures, if he'd let me rest in his trunk. He was worried we'd get caught, but I assured him we wouldn't. If they did happen to open the trunk, which was unlikely, I'd just shift onto the celestial plane. I'd vanish.

He totally didn't believe me, though. Not the part where it was unlikely they would open the trunk but the part where I could shift onto the celestial plane and become Invisigirl. Strange how nobody believed that shit.

My other choice was, of course, to shift and go across incorporeally, but I still didn't trust the whole teleportation thing. I once had a nightmare where I'd shifted and tried to go on vacation in Ireland, only to materialize in the center of the sun. Probably because I had a nuclear-powered furnace asleep beside me.

On the plus side, I'd get a great tan.

We found Misery sitting alone on a dusty street with more than one hungry pair of eyes watching her. Just in case someone on Elena's payroll was still there, I paid a ten-year-old girl to steal it for me.

She picked me up a few blocks away, and I paid her and the driver, then headed back across the border, thankful I kept a hidden stash underneath Idris, my driver's seat. A hidden stash that contained my passport, five thousand in cash, and a travel-sized box of Cheez-Its.

Once I crossed the border, I called Cookie.

"So?" she asked.

"I got her back. It was a teary reunion. I told her never to do that to me again. Then I did that thing where I slapped her, then pulled her into my arms and cried. I think the Uber driver is scared of me."

"Charley, you are going to be the death of me."

"Sadly, you could be right. How are things on the home front? Any more attacks?"

"Not that we know of. Robert is going to call if he hears anything. Garrett's at Pari's, and Osh is at the hospital watching over Nicolette."

"Perfect. Oh," I said, remembering my mission. "Are you ready?"

"As I'll ever be." She had no idea what I meant, but she soon would.

"Wait for it . . ."

"I'm breathless with anticipation."

"Pico and De Gallo."

I waited, so proud of my creative mind, it was unreal.

"Okay, I like it, but which is which?"

"Cook," I said, disappointed, "do you even know your breasts?"

" 'Parently not as well as you do."

"Pico is your left and De Gallo is your right. Wait, hold on." I lowered my phone and tested the names out on Danger and Will. "Yes, that's it. Left and right."

She thought about it another moment, then said, "Okay, we have an accord."

"Yes!" Victory was mine at last. I did a fist pump, then choked on the dust I'd stirred up.

The trip back to Albuquerque was a quiet one, save the ninety-pound Rottweiler panting in my ear. She pawed at something crawling in my hair. It took every ounce of strength I had not to freak.

"It's a ladybug," Reyes said from the backseat, his eyes boring into mine via the rearview.

"Is that your new game? Show up uninvited just to fuck with me?"

"I'm trying to determine what Rey'aziel found so fascinating."

"Ah. Well, good luck with that. I've often wondered the same thing."

"There," he said, his brows furrowing. "That."

"That?"

"You're . . . humble."

I scoffed. "Hardly. Have you seen my ass?" I did have a nice ass, so the question bore repeating.

"Then, what is it?"

"Uh, reality? So, that's what's fascinating about me? My attitude? My humility? I knew the shock therapy I underwent in college would pay off."

"Pull over."

"Nope. Got a psychotic priest to find since you spent time with him in the god glass but never bothered to learn his name, so I can't summon him." I hadn't taken the time to change out of the dress yet. I tugged at the straps, vowing to pay Cookie back.

"Would you like me to rid you of it?"

"The priest?"

"The dress."

Damn him. "Damn you."

He laughed softly, his dark eyes glistening, his sensual mouth tilting slightly. It was Reyes. He was Reyes. If he were an angry god, why would he be there, dare I say *flirting* with me?

"Let me know when we get there."

"What?" I looked in the rearview, and he'd eased down in the seat, laid his head back, and closed his eyes.

He was snoozing?

I shook my head, unable to figure out what he was doing there. What his end game was.

"To find it," he said, his voice silky smooth and oceans deep. "Will you trust me when I do?"

I stared out the windshield at the long highway ahead of me. "As much as you trust me, I guess."

Rey'azikeen slept. He actually slept. I hadn't slept in four days, but he sat in my backseat and slept the entire way home. So beautiful it hurt to look at him.

But he was a god. Why was he sleepy?

As bad as I hated to do it, I stopped by the apartment for a shower and a change of clothes. I left Reyes in the backseat, hurried up to my apartment, tore through my closet, and hopped in a still-cold shower.

I needed to get to Rocket before any more time passed. I needed that name so I could summon the priest before he attacked anyone else.

Ignoring the dark whooshes I saw once again in my apartment—I could deal with them later—I threw on a clean a pair of jeans, sweatshirt, and boots. It had been dark for about an hour, but it was still early enough to head to Chuck E. Cheese.

I was just about to check in with Cookie across the hall when I heard her voice. Her loud voice. And she wasn't normally that loud. When I stepped into our living room, I realized she was in my apartment.

"Why, no, Agent Carson, Charley isn't here right now." She stood at my door and waved a hand at her back, signaling for me to get back.

"Her Jeep is outside."

"Right, it's not running right now."

"It's hot."

"It gets that way. Something about a thermometer malfunction?"

Kit sighed. "Fine. I'll go away, but if you would tell her I need to see her sooner rather than later, I'd appreciate it."

"Will do. Good to see you again. Hope the recording was all you hoped it would be."

"Oh, it was. And then some."

"Wonderful. Bye now." Cookie closed the door and sank against it.

I hurried to the door for a look through the peephole. They'd gone.

I sank against the door with her. "Thanks for that, hon. I can't be arrested right now. I found Rocket. I think."

She straightened. "Where is he? Is he okay? What about that sweet baby girl?"

"From what Strawberry said, they're all having a ball at Chuck E. Cheese."

"You're kidding, right? Which one?"

I blinked at her. "What do you mean, which one? There's more than one?"

"There are two on either side of the city."

"Damn it. She didn't say. Which one should I try?"

Cookie thought a moment. "Okay, the one on Wyoming is a lot closer. Try that one first."

"Gotcha. Do you think they're gone yet?"

"I have a feeling someone is going to be sticking around to see if you go back to Misery."

I deflated.

"You could stay here for a while. Get some rest. You were shot at today. I think you deserve a good night's sleep."

The word *sleep* gave me a deep longing in the pit of my stomach. And Rey'azikeen had been playing a bit nicer, just showing up and not digging into my brain. I wondered . . .

"No. No, I have to do this before anyone else gets hurt, Cook. There'll be plenty of time for sleep after."

"Well, I tried."

"Yes, you did."

"They may be watching Misery. Take mine." She ran across the hall and got her keys.

"Where's Amber?" I called out to her.

"Working on a school project before winter break. She should be back soon." She handed me her keys and a bottle of water before running to my living room and bringing back the third book, *Stardust*. "You know, in case you have to go on a stakeout or get stuck in traffic. You need to read this book."

"Okay. Hopefully I'll be back soon, hydrated, well read, and with good news."

"Don't get shot at again."

"'Kay."

I threw a scarf over my head and took the back exit. After narrowly missing a light post, I stole around the building to Cookie's aging Taurus, wondering if Reyes was still sleeping in Misery. His behavior made no sense, but I didn't have time to worry about it. As soon as I found the priest, there'd be plenty of time to capture Rey'azikeen and try to beat some sense into him.

I started to turn the key when I noticed two men in an unmarked government car at the exit to the parking lot. I ducked down, then craned my neck to check out the second exit and my only escape. Another unmarked car with two men drinking coffee. Four G-men on little ol' me. What the bloody hell? Kit must've been more than a little peeved I'd disobeyed her direct order. She was so touchy about those things.

I sank into the seat, frustrated. I could go in the opposite direction and slink down the alley, but I'd need a distraction. And I didn't dare pull Osh off Nicolette duty or Garrett off Pari. They needed to be there in case the priest showed up.

Cookie was my only hope.

In her defense, she could be quite the distraction when she put her mind to it. I turned the brightness on my phone down so as not to draw attention to the fact that someone was hiding in Cook's car, then I dialed her number.

"Did you get busted already?" she asked.

"Ye of little faith. I'm incognito in your car. They have both exits staked out, but if I had a distraction, I could sneak down the alley and avoid them altogether. At least, that's the plan."

"You're so bad at plans."

"Cook."

"Okay, okay, give me twenty minutes."

"Twenty minutes? What are you going to do?"

"Just leave it up to me."

Dread crept up my spine as she hung up. Oh, well. If I got nothing else out of it but sheer entertainment, it would be worth it.

Since I had twenty minutes to spare, give or take, I turned up the light on my phone and brought out the third book written by the prodigy from Jakarta, Pandu Yoso. The book titled *Stardust* that was supposedly about Beep.

It picked up where the second book left off, with the dark son, a.k.a., the Dark Star, a.k.a., Reyes, watching over the First Star while she fulfilled her duties in Jehovahn's kingdom. She had given up her kingdom to watch over His, all so Jehovahn would spare the Dark Star the torment of the lightless realm Jehovahn had tricked him into creating. The one encased in Star Glass.

The book basically described parts of her life, calling her the First Star and recounting events in her life as a physical being that had shaped her, including an indifferent stepmother, a betrayal by her best friend, and an uncle who loved her unconditionally.

It went through her first meetings with Dark Star, when she was still afraid of him to when she found his true self at last. His physical manifestation, dark and beautiful and untamed. They fell in love and collided, creating Stardust. Creating Beep.

And when she was born, the galaxies glistened in her eyes, for she was the daughter of the two most powerful stars in all the kingdoms in all the world, and she was destined to do great things. She was destined to save Jehovahn's kingdom.

I had to admit, the kid nailed it. According to other prophecies, Beep was destined to defeat Lucifer, which would explain his desire to destroy her and our desire to keep her safe.

A knock sounded at the window. I jumped, then looked over at a homeless woman named Cookie Kowalski Davidson and tried not to giggle. She stood enshrouded in rags that I was pretty sure were actually rags. She even had a shopping cart.

I rolled down the window. "Where the hell did you get that cart?"

"I borrowed it from Saratoga Sally."

"You know Saratoga Sally?" I asked, impressed. The woman didn't talk much.

"Not really."

"She just let you borrow her shopping cart? That's like her castle."

"Actually, I should have said I *rented* it from Saratoga Sally. She's a shrewd business woman, let me tell you."

"How much."

"Twenty. And I have to have it back to her in ten or she starts charging interest."

"I knew I liked her."

"Even after she threw peanut butter in your hair?"

"She said it was a great conditioner. She was only looking out for me."

Cookie nodded then winked at me. "Get ready."

I gave her a thumbs up and watched as she strolled to do her stuff, not sure what to expect. If she could just distract one of the cars, I could turn the opposite direction of the other so the building would be between us.

But what would she do? Would she bang on their car and demand they move? Would she pound on the glass and insist on money for Buffalo wings? Would she fall to the ground and feign injury, forcing them to leave their car to see to her, giving me a window of opportunity to hightail it outta there?

What she decided on had me both perplexed and in agony. She pushed her cart to the other side of the car, the side opposite me, and took out her phone. She pushed a few buttons as the G-men looked on, then she put it on top of the pile in the cart, turned to the lamppost and proceeded to use it as a stripper pole to preform a striptease.

When she flashed them a quick glimpse of a bra-clad Pico, I doubled over so fast I slammed my forehead into the steering wheel. It didn't matter. I was dying.

I clung to the steering wheel but could barely watch her through the tears. She was going to kill me for not leaving immediately, but how could I? I would never forgive myself for missing the show.

She ripped a ragged scarf off her shoulders and spun it in a circle, then lifted the hem of her housecoat to reveal a shapely ankle and calf seconds before she wrapped it around the pole and blew the boys a kiss.

The men were transfixed. As was I.

I scrambled to find the video setting on my phone through the blur of my tear-filled vision when another knock sounded on the window. I sobered and rolled it down.

Uncle Bob stood beside the car, his expression grave and slightly horrified. “What the fuck is my wife doing?”

Before I could explain, Cookie jutted out a hip and slapped a hand onto it. I doubled over again and fell across the console in helplessness. “You have to record her,” I said between gasps and laughter.

I crawled back up again just as she did a sexy spin, taking the opportunity to glare at me from over her shoulder. That was when she saw her husband. She stilled and I knew if I didn’t get out of there, I wasn’t going to.

Without explanation, I turned over the car engine and sped down the alley to Silver, leaving a confused and slightly disturbed uncle Bob in my wake.

I hauled ass to the Chuck E. Cheese on Wyoming, giggling like a maniac, and scoured every nook and cranny of the establishment. No departed, save one. Unfortunately, I wasn’t looking for a middle-aged woman in a tube top and biker chaps. So, I got back into Cookie’s bat mobile and headed to the west side.

To my great joy, most of the rush-hour traffic had dissipated, so the drive only took about twenty minutes. I threw Peanut—I’d named her on the way over—into park and rushed inside. It didn’t take me long to spot them. Just like Strawberry said, Rocket stood hovering over the Whac-A-Mole. At the moment, however, no one was playing the game. With a heavy sigh, he turned and sat on the edge, his posture downtrodden, the poor thing sad and despondent.

The moment he saw me, however, he brightened. "Miss Charlotte!" He ran toward me, and there was nothing to be done about it. He threw his arms around me and lifted me off the ground.

Thankfully, only a couple of children saw me floating in midair. And if they told their parents, they'd never believe them, poor things.

As I was being hefted off the ground, I looked over and saw the girls. Blue and Strawberry, bless their hearts, were riding a carousel in the back corner, laughing and having the best time. Had I known all it would take was a carousel for Blue to come out of her shell, I would've bought one eons ago.

"Miss Charlotte," Rocket said, putting me back on solid ground at last. "Did you come to play Whac-A-Mole?"

I laughed softly. "No, sweetheart. I need a name."

"But it's really fun."

"I need a priest's name. He just entered this plane."

He frowned and lowered his head. "That's breaking rules, Miss Charlotte. No breaking rules."

"Rocket," I said, putting my hand on his arm, partly for reassurance and partly because I couldn't have him disappearing on me. "The priest lived a long time ago and just reentered this plane from another one. I need his name."

He tried to step away from me. I didn't let him.

"No breaking rules, Miss Charlotte. You know that."

I stepped very close to him, ignoring the kids with gaping mouths who watched me talk to invisible people. "I am ordering you to break the rules, Rocket. Just this once."

He looked to the side, his expression full of worry. Blue stood beside him. She took his hand and nodded, her short, dark bob swaying with the movement.

She beckoned him with a tiny index finger, and he knelt down to her. I knelt, too, unwilling to miss this chance. If I lost Rocket, it could take days to find him again. Summoning him only upset his already addled brain, and getting information out of the Rocket Man when he was upset was never easy.

Rocket leaned toward Blue, and she whispered in his ear. He looked up at me and said, "Father Arneo de Piedrayta."

"What? That's his name?" Stunned, I took out my phone and typed the name in phonetically, no clue how to spell it. "How did you . . . ?"

Blue smiled and popped back on the carousel with Strawberry.

Rocket stood and grinned down at me. "Blue said just this once."

"Rocket, does Blue always help you keep track of the names?"

"No," he said with a laugh. "I don't know the names. Only Blue does. She whispers them to me, and I write them down. That's my job. I write the names on the walls for her."

I stood so taken aback, Rocket grew bored and went back to the Whac-A-Mole. But I couldn't drop it. I walked over to him, annoying a kid who was finally playing the game to Rocket's delight.

"I've seen you get the names. I've seen you search for them in your head."

He laughed again. "I don't search for them in my head. I search for them in Blue's. Only she knows the names."

I'd been communicating with the wrong departed savant the whole time? I glanced over at her. She grinned and pointed to her temple, to her mind, letting me know exactly where all the names were stored.

"But I've never seen her tell you a name I've asked for," I argued. "It's always just been you."

The look on Rocket's face almost doubled me over. He pressed his lips together, shook his head, and tsked as though I were a pitiful creature. "Miss Charlotte, just because you can't see someone doesn't mean they aren't there."

He had a point.

"Thank you, Rocket." I rolled onto my tiptoes and kissed his cheek, gaining a glare from the kid I bumped into. The kid Rocket was standing in.

I left the gang to their fun. Outside, I found an older kid, a blond skater with dreads, and offered him a twenty if he'd go inside and use the whole thing playing Whac-A-Mole.

"Sure," he said with a shrug.

If I was lucky, I'd get at least ten bucks out of it. He'd use the rest on other games or pizza, but that was cool, too.

19

I try to just take one day at a time,
but lately several days have attacked me at once.
—MEME

With no time to waste, I rushed to Peanut. I needed a place away from other people, just in case anyone in the vicinity was sensitive to the supernatural realm. If someone ended up hurt because of me, because of my summoning the priest, I'd never forgive myself.

I drove to the old rail yard that housed a series of abandoned warehouses. I'd used them before. Funny how useful abandoned warehouses could be in my line of work.

If I summoned the priest here, there'd be no one else around. No risk, if it were him. I had to resign myself to the fact that it very well may not be. I'd pretty much run out of suspects unless something else came out of the hell dimension I didn't know about, but that didn't mean it actually was the priest. Hopefully, all would be revealed soon.

After trying for twenty minutes to pick the lock on the gate—I was sorely out of practice—I ended up breaking it with a crowbar instead.

I drove inside the yard and cruised around to a familiar warehouse, one I'd recently used to help save a woman's life. I parked Peanut, busted yet another lock to get inside the warehouse, then strode to the middle of the massive building using the flashlight on my phone.

Moonlight shone across broken shards of glass on the floor and in the high-set windows overhead. It helped me get a feeling for the expanse that lay before me. Debris and the odd remnant of machinery lay here and there. Homeless people had used the building in the past, but the city had amped up security, so that rarely happened anymore.

Without further ado, I opened the notes on my phone and summoned the priest by saying his name aloud. "Père Arneo de Piedrayta, *se prèsenter.* Come forward."

When nothing happened, I shifted onto the celestial realm to get a better feel of what was hiding there. The sepia tones laid out a vast desert of harsh winds and violent storms. My hair whipped around my face as I turned in a circle, trying to find the priest.

Then I spotted something—someone—in the distance. A robed figure, stumbling blindly, trying to shield his face from the winds. I shifted back and demanded he come forward.

"Père, *se prèsenter immédiatement.*" Come forward, now.

He finally began to materialize in front of me. The astonishing fact that I was summoning a priest from the 1400s was not lost on me. If he ended up being cool and not a raging madman murdering people, I was totally taking him for a drive in Peanut. He would freak.

Parts of the celestial plane came through with him, the wind tossing him about until he settled onto this plane fully. He lay on the ground in a fetal position, spouting prayers in an old version of French, his accent so thick I could barely understand him.

"Père," I said to get his attention.

Once he realized he was no longer in the storms, he raised his head. His robe, tattered and burned around his sandaled feet, lay in tangles around him. His hair, a short bowl cut, was mussed and unkempt. Judging by his features, he was no more than forty. I hadn't expected someone so young.

His gaze, wide and wild, darted about in terror. I almost felt sorry for him, but if he truly was the malevolent priest who'd locked all those innocent souls inside the god glass, he didn't deserve my sympathy.

I grabbed a handful of his robes so he couldn't disappear on me, and I knelt to speak to him. Once he realized I was there and he focused on me, he winced and tried to scramble back. I kept a firm hold, but he started to panic.

"Père," I said, trying to calm him. I told him as much in his native tongue. "Calm down. I won't hurt you."

I didn't know what he saw when he looked at me, but he was scared shitless. He shook his head and kicked and clawed at me, managing to land a few punches. Then I realized he wasn't really looking at me.

I turned around to see Reyes, or Rey'azikeen, leaning against a beamed pillar, watching the goings-on with mild interest. He glanced down to focus on his manicure, as though bored with our interaction.

"Père," I said, trying to draw him back to me. "I need to know if you sent those people into the glass pendant. Was that you?"

"Good luck with that," Reyes said, still examining his nails.

But he glanced at me from underneath his lashes, an exquisite smile playing about his mouth before he pointed and said softly, "Careful. Hot."

I turned back just as the priest started screaming. He grabbed at me, clawing and scratching, begging for help as the ground opened up beneath him.

I fell backwards, stunned, as the father did his best to crawl out of the pit and on top of me. Then I felt the heat rising from it.

The priest, half on top of me, began hammering at my face and chest, begging me to help him, pleading with me to stop the burning. The fire beneath us became unbearable, but I couldn't seem to get away from him. He was all over me, digging his fingers into my skin, using me as an anchor to stay in this world when hell clearly wanted him in theirs.

I fought and kicked to get him off to no avail until Artemis rose from the ground beside us. She leaped forward and ripped into the priest with a ferocious growl, tearing him off me at last. I scrambled back and watched as the pit surrounding the priest grew larger and the fires grew higher. His screams echoed off the walls, and I clutched my throat, wanting to help but unable.

It all made sense, though. The scratches and bruises on the victims. The burns. In an attempt to get its man, hell had crossed onto this plane. It had burned innocent people, but the other wounds were caused by the priest. He'd tried to anchor himself to this plane, and the only people he could see were those who could see him. He clutched onto them to keep from going to hell. A place he clearly deserved to be.

The priest got a firm hold on Artemis, clasping his arms around her as hell tried to pull him under. Syrupy black tentacles twisted around him. Smoke rose in tendrils.

Artemis yelped. I lunged forward and grabbed hold, but something a few feet away caught my attention. The priest let go of Artemis and was almost sucked under, his arms flailing like a drowning swimmer.

But my gaze darted to a figure standing a few feet away. Then another.

I scanned the area and found no fewer than twenty figures shrouded in tattered gray gauze. Their hands folded at their chests. Their faces not faces at all. They had no eyes. No noses. Only mouths sitting where mouths would normally be, the rest of their faces a total blank. Bone protruded from their heads, encircling them like a crown.

But their mouths were the scariest thing about them. Their lips, if one could call the cracked lines around their teeth lips, were pulled back from their teeth in an eternal smile. Their teeth blended in with their complete grayness. They were square and blunt and twice the size they should have been.

Somehow, they watched the priest, their faces focused on the screaming man. And he'd noticed them. His terror multiplied when they came into view.

And then, so fast I didn't see them move, they were on him.

Reyes grabbed hold of my arms and jerked me out of the way as they descended on the priest like savage animals. Tearing into his flesh. Ripping parts of him off to eat.

The priest's screams subsided as what was left of him sank into the pit of hell, the gate closing behind him.

The wraiths ate with vigor, the sounds of them gnawing on flesh and crunching bone sickening me.

When they were finished, they stood in one liquid movement, as though the move were choreographed. Artemis whimpered beside me, then growled, readying for a fight.

They turned, pivoting in space, their feet never touching the ground, until they all faced us. I swallowed as their heads bent and tilted slightly, focused on yours truly.

My lungs seized. Some things I could fight. These things I'd prefer to run from, but I couldn't move. I had no idea what they were. I'd never seen anything like them. They couldn't be demons. My light did nothing to them. Then again, if I'd learned anything, it was that there were as many species of demons as there were stars in the universe.

But these were wraithlike, disembodied gray entities, their robes drifting like gauze in a light breeze.

Still on the ground, I lay afraid to move, terror seizing my muscles and locking my joints.

Facing the horde, Reyes straddled me, stepping on either side of my waist, smoke billowing off him as he lowered his head and growled at the wraiths. They looked from Reyes, to me, to Artemis and must've decided to save the fight for another day. They inclined their heads, again in one liquid movement, then dissipated and drifted away.

The warehouse sat empty save for us. Completely normal, as though nothing'd happened. A breeze whispered through the broken panes of glass overhead, causing me to gasp and glance around in fear.

Reyes switched positions. He turned around and straddled me again. I thought he'd been unaffected by the wraiths. I was wrong. His chest fought to push air in and out of his lungs. His fists clenched at his sides. His biceps bunched into rock hard mounds.

"Where is it?" he asked for the ten thousandth time.

I shook my head, astonished. "Reyes, what were those things?"

He shifted his weight and lowered a booted foot onto my chest, pinning me to the ground. "Where is it?" he asked, his voice low and deadly serious.

I spoke as calmly as I could. "Get off me."

"Where is the ash?" He squeezed his eyes shut, as though trying to remember, then refocused on me. "The ember? Where is it?"

"I told you, I don't know what you're talking about."

"You do!" he yelled. He jerked me off the ground and thrust me against a metal beam. "It's yours. You must know."

"What's mine?"

He closed his eyes again as though racking his brain, frustration welding his teeth together. "The ember. No." He opened his eyes at last, as though it were coming to him in bits and pieces, and the world fell out from under me with his next words. The barest hint of triumph widened his mouth when he said, "The Stardust."

I blinked in surprise, then denial, then horror. The book. When two stars collide, they create stardust. It was the author's way of writing about Beep.

He was after Beep.

Artemis growled beside him. He glanced down at her, and in that heartbeat of opportunity, I dematerialized out of his arms and into Garrett's house.

He'd been watching Pari and brought her home. She sat in his living room, curled up on his sofa, reading. I heard him in the kitchen and hurried to it.

"Beep," I said, suddenly terrified beyond clear thought. "He's after Beep."

Garrett, who'd been standing at his stove scrambling eggs, turned to me in alarm. "What do you mean?"

Pari walked into the room as well, confused.

"Rey'azikeen. He's after Beep, only he called her Stardust, like in the third book. But Reyes knows where she is." My voice rose as I began to panic. "He knows where the Loehrs are."

Garrett stepped to me and put his arms on my shoulders. "No, he doesn't."

I fought for air. Fought the darkening edges of my vision. Fought for coherent thought.

"Charley," Garrett said, rustling me with a slight shake. "I moved them the moment you told me what happened."

He let that sink in and everything that it entailed. He knew. He'd been prepared. When I realized what he'd done, I threw my arms around him.

"Oh, my God. Thank you, Garrett," I said into his T-shirt.

He wrapped me up and held me tight.

"Thank you," I said, tears stinging the backs of my eyes.

In the next instant, he thrust me away from him. Or at least I thought he did. Instead, Reyes had wrenched him off me. He threw Garrett against a wall, then looked back at me.

"Your Rey'aziel. He's hidden the ember away from me. Always so clever. He doesn't trust me any more than you do. But now I know how to find it."

He strode toward Garrett, his steps full of purpose.

"Reyes," Garrett said, backing away. He turned and searched for a weapon, anything he could use against him. Spotting a knife on the kitchen counter, he dove for it, but before he even got close, Reyes was on him. He threw him against a wall and pinned him to it, the force shaking the house off its foundation.

"Where is it?" he asked, forcing his forearm into Garrett's larynx.

Struggling for air, Garrett tried to shove him away, but Reyes was simply unmovable. When fighting a human, anyway.

But as he'd told me repeatedly, I was not human.

I ran to them, wrapped my arms around Reyes from behind, and shifted us onto the celestial plane. Reyes shifted us right back, but it was enough time for Garrett to scramble out of his hold.

As triumphant as that moment was, I'd forgotten about the incredible speed, the astounding agility, my husband possessed. He shoved me into Pari and went after Garrett again. Faster than my mind could comprehend. My only hope would be to slow time, but before I could even form the thought in my head, Reyes reached Garrett, wrapped his hands around his head and twisted, snapping Garrett's neck.

The loud crack that followed immobilized me. I had fallen to the floor with Pari and watched in stunned disbelief as Garrett Swopes, one of my closest friends, slumped to the ground, dead.

20

The Devil whispered in my ear,
"You're not strong enough to withstand the storm."
Today I whispered back, "I am the storm."
—MEME

My hands flew over my mouth, and I cried out in horror. Then, without thought, I scrambled to catch Garrett before his head hit the floor, but Reyes knocked me back, the air whooshing out of my lungs.

Then he stood over Garrett, waiting.

His actions confused me at first before I realized what he was doing.

We had two different agendas, Reyes and I. He stood like a sentinel, waiting for Garrett's soul to leave his body, a soul he could coerce and threaten, while I had to act fast to make sure his soul stayed in his body so I could heal him without breaking my one rule. Without being cast from this plane.

A few months prior, Reyes had sent Garrett to hell on an unwitting reconnaissance mission. He would do it again. Or at least threaten to. I couldn't let that happen, because if there was one absolute in this entire scenario, it was the fact that Garrett Swopes would burn in hell before giving up Beep's location.

But there was still time. I dove forward, ducked under Reyes's swing, and grazed my fingertips along Garrett's arm.

He jolted awake and clambered to his feet only to face Rey'azikeen's wrath again. And again, before Garrett could even think about dodging him, the angry god snapped his neck.

I slowed time, healing Garrett before Rey'azikeen could match my temporal speed. I dragged Garrett, who was now frozen in time, to the side, then turned to face my husband.

He matched my speed almost instantly, and we squared off, as they say, preparing for battle.

"At last," he said, a knowing smile on his face. "The god eater emerges. Will you devour my heart as you have so many before me? Will you feast on my soul?"

"I'm seriously considering it," I said, only half lying. To keep him away from Beep, I might have no choice.

But now I had a new problem. Rey'azikeen was painfully aware that Garrett knew where to find Beep. Where could I put Garrett so that Rey'azikeen couldn't find him? And how would I do that without my bloodthirsty husband knowing?

He seemed to have the uncanny ability to read my mind. He would know where I'd stashed Garrett. And if I involved anyone else, that person would be in just as much danger.

No, I didn't need to stash Garrett Swopes. I needed to stash the god Rey'azikeen. Even for just a few moments.

I charged forward and shifted. He was ready, but the moment I started toward him, another thought hit me. If I could slow time, who's to say I couldn't speed it up as well?

I reversed my hold on time, sped it up to roughly the speed of light, and slammed into him. He had no defense ready against a guided missile. I disintegrated his molecules along with mine, and I took him to the one place I feared. The place of my nightmares.

I dragged him to the center of the sun.

We crossed through the void of space in seconds, splashed into the corona, and careened through the layers of gas until we stopped at the core of the burning ball of gas. Then I did the unthinkable. I shifted us, body and soul, back onto the earthly plane, forcing us both to materialize into the center of a fireball with temperatures reaching twenty-seven million degrees.

I'd surprised him. He gazed at me with utter shock on his face a microsecond before I dematerialized and left Reyes in my dust. Or, well, my solar gases.

In the seconds it took me to get back, I came up with a plan to get Garrett to safety and was working on finding a way to get Reyes back when it hit me. I'd done it. I'd faced my nightmare.

Then again, maybe it wasn't a nightmare at all. Maybe it was a message, but from whom? Had someone planted that idea—the one where I accidently materialized in the center of the sun—in my head via my dreams?

Stranger things had happened. Perhaps not to me. My life was completely and perfectly and incandescently normal. Gawd, I loved *Pride and Prejudice.*

I materialized back in Garrett's apartment, completely naked once again, smoke drifting off me.

"Chuck!" Pari rushed forward and patted my hair, hopefully because she liked me. My hair could not afford to be on fire. It had been through so much this week already.

"Again?" Garrett asked, incredulous.

"I left him in the center of the sun, but I don't think he'll stay there long."

They stood speechless for a solid minute.

"Is that a metaphor for something?" Garrett asked.

I gaped at them. "Seriously, guys, we don't have much time. We have to get you out of here and have them move Beep, this time without your knowing where."

He rushed to get me a T-shirt and a pair of lounge pants with a drawstring. I dragged them on in record time. They still hung off me, but at least they wouldn't fall down.

"Shoes?" he asked.

"No, I'm fine. Let's go."

"Charles, you need to go to the Loehrs. You need to move them somewhere I don't know about."

"He can read my thoughts. I've caught him doing it more than once."

Garrett sank onto the arm of his sofa. "Then we've lost. He'll find her."

"No. We just need to keep you hidden until I can get Reyes back. He's in there, Garrett. He's keeping Beep a secret. He wouldn't even let Rey'azikeen see her. It's like he's blocking the memory of her. I have no idea how, but he's in there. I just need to find him and bring him out."

He nodded. "I'll get word to the others. Just to be safe. We'll move the Loehrs again tonight. They're not far."

He stood and headed for the door, only to find Rey'azikeen blocking his path. Completely naked, engulfed in fire with smoke billowing around him and lightning crackling along his skin, Rey'azikeen grabbed hold of Garrett's throat and looked into his eyes.

But he'd caught Garrett off guard. And he got what he'd come for.

"There," he said softly, a microsecond before he snapped Garrett's neck again and disappeared.

I ran and caught Garrett as he crumbled to the floor, healing him for a third time, when I realized he did it for a reason. Rey'azikeen. He broke Garrett's neck again for a reason. To slow me down. He knew where to find our daughter, and he didn't want me interfering.

Garrett had been thinking of the location at the exact moment Rey'azikeen looked into his eyes. He saw it. He saw where Garrett had hidden her. And he wanted to get to her first.

"Garrett," I said, my voice breathy with fear, "where is she? Where did you hide her?"

He shook his head, trying to clear it. "Did he break my neck again?"

"Yes, and he knows. He saw her location in your eyes. Where is she?"

His lids rounded. "She's in Santa Fe. She's at the Loretto Chapel."

"The church? The one with the staircase?" The Loretto Chapel in Santa Fe was famous mostly due to a staircase that was built there in the 1870s. Because of several anomalies surrounding the staircase, many believe the carpenter who built it was Saint Joseph, or even Jesus himself.

He nodded. "They're keeping her in a back room. I thought, you know, sacred ground."

I saw the famous church in my mind's eye and materialized there in an instant. I showed up just in time to see Rey'azikeen lift Beep from her crib and cradle her in his arms. I showed up just in time to see a dozen hellhounds rise from the ground and emerge through walls, snarling and gnashing their teeth. I showed up just in time to see a hundred angels materialize around the vengeful god, Michael leading them, swords drawn, wings outstretched.

Then I realized I was still straddling the earthly plane and the celestial one, because the room we were in was tiny. There weren't a hundred angels surrounding us but a hundred thousand. They spread as far into the celestial realm as the eye could see.

God had sent His army.

The angels nearest to Rey'azikeen closed in, swords at the ready. The hellhounds, Beep's guardians for life, crept forward, heads down, teeth bared. And Rey'azikeen stood in the middle of the mêlée, so impossibly beautiful with our daughter in his sinewy arms.

The smoke that billowed around him covered his more carnal parts, but only to me. If another human walked in, they'd get an eyeful. They would no more see the smoke than the advancing hellhounds or the avenging angels.

I lowered my hand to the ground, palm down, and lifted Artemis into it. She rose growling, bearing back on her haunches, readying to launch herself into the fray.

In the next instant, time slowed as the forces charged. Swords arced from every direction with the sole purpose of shredding my husband.

Three hellhounds had made it close enough to rip him apart. They lunged forward, their teeth centimeters away from tearing into his flesh.

The whole thing played out like a dream. A nightmare. Partly because he was still my husband and partly because he was holding our daughter.

I held up my hands and slowed time even more. Brought everything to a full stop. It was all going too fast. The world was spinning out of control. And a vengeful god was holding my daughter.

Artemis awaited my command. My own general, a celestial being I'd named Mr. Wong, materialized by my side, sword in hand, head bowed awaiting my command as well. But I stood stunned. The picture frozen before me was the most surreal I'd ever seen.

A dozen swords were suspended in midair, the razor-sharp tips a hairsbreadth from Rey'azikeen's skin. His major arteries. His heart. One sword was even above him pointed down to sever Reyes's spine at the neck in what I was certain would have been one skilled thrust.

But the angels surrounding him had obeyed my command. I couldn't imagine why. They stood suspended in time awaiting further instruction.

The same held true for the hellhounds. Their jaws open wide, ready to rip into flesh and bone. But their teeth stayed steady, the needle-like tips pressed impatiently against his skin. One hound stood on a cabinet overhead, his massive jaw spanning the circumference of Rey'azikeen's skull, salivating for the chance to bite down.

I inched forward, glancing at the bundle in his arms. At the soft cheeks and large, dark eyes. So like her father's.

"Rey'azikeen, please," I said softly. "Please don't do this."

He tore his gaze away from her and planted it on me. "And what is it you think I'm doing?"

"Reyes kept her location a secret from you. That tells me you mean her harm."

"Does it?"

"Val-Eeth," Mr. Wong, my most trusted advisor, said at my side, calling me by my celestial title: god. "He could vanish at any second. We must take him now or risk losing Elwyn Alexandra."

I nodded, knowing he was right. But I couldn't give the order that would see my husband ripped apart. The order that would risk my daughter's life. So I did something else instead. I summoned the one Being I hoped could get through to him. I summoned his Brother.

He appeared on the opposite side of me, His power startling. The form He'd chosen was so startlingly similar to Reyes's, I had to think that perhaps it was His true form. Perhaps He looked stunningly similar to His brother. Not quite as beautiful, but similar nevertheless.

Rey'azikeen scoffed and scolded me with a glare. "Siccing the puritan on me? I thought you had better taste than that."

I ignored him and spoke to Jehovah, more than a tad annoyed with Him myself. "You sent Your army. You swore You wouldn't."

The barest hint of a smile lifted one corner of his mouth. "I did not send My army, Elle-Ryn-Ahleethia. You did, just as I said you would."

I furrowed my brows in confusion.

Rey'azikeen narrowed his lids on me, then focused his attention on his Brother.

"You tricked me. You imprisoned me. You allowed the traitor

Lucifer to use my energy to create his son." Disgust lined Reyes's face. Disappointment.

"You took life, Rey'azikeen. Your temper could not be controlled."

He lowered his head and scowled from beneath thick lashes. "You're wrong. I had perfect control."

Beep made a squeak and kicked out against the restraints of her blanket, but her face, so painfully perfect, turned up to look at the being holding her. And she seemed fascinated. Happy even.

Jehovah drew in a deep breath. "I'd hoped through these trials you would learn all life is precious."

"You think I don't know?" He glanced at me, his anger palpable.

Then I remembered what he told me in the Jeep on the way to El Paso. Would I trust him when the time came? When he found the object he'd been searching for?

Beep's fascination sank in. She wasn't scared in the least. In fact, she was the only one in the room perfectly content.

She squeaked again, and I began to relax, realizing if he were to trust me, I had to trust him, just as our daughter obviously did.

I stepped closer and called his bluff. "I have loved you since the first time I saw you."

He cast a suspicious scowl. "You've loved Reyes. Rey'aziel even. Not me."

"You're wrong," easing even closer. "Why do you think I begged Jehovah not to send you into that prison?"

"The same prison you sent me into?"

I grinned. "You did insist."

He ground his teeth, his long lashes trapping the glistening wetness between them.

"You stole Lucifer's fire to release me from the hell you created for me. You. Not Reyes. Not Rey'aziel."

He closed his eyes and bent his head, relief flooding every cell in his body as a slow, gratified smile widened his mouth.

"You knew I'd call Him," I said, surprised. "Your Brother."

One corner of his exquisite mouth rose to transform his smile into a lopsided grin.

He'd wanted his Brother here to witness. He'd brought all this on to confront Him, to prove to Him what he'd become.

But his Brother wasn't finished with him yet. "This is how you control your temper? Your actions?" God asked him. "By ravaging? By pillaging?"

I offered Rey'azikeen a conspiratorial smirk, encouraged him to reveal the real reason we were all there.

"No, Brother. By this."

He took his right hand and sliced his palm open on Michael's sword. Rich, dark blood rushed out, and he placed his palm on Beep's forehead, then lowered his own and whispered a protection prayer in an ancient celestial language. A spell. An incantation.

When he was finished, he lifted his palm. Beep's skin absorbed the blood in a shimmer of light. It faded into her, and her only acknowledgment that her father had just cast a powerful protection spell over her was another soft squeak and a loveable wiggle, as though nestling against him.

His face brightened and he beamed down at her.

"What did you do?" I asked him, fascinated myself.

"I have made her invisible to all who would cause her harm. Our enemies will not be able to find her until she wants to be found." He looked at his Brother. "I will protect her with my life. And with that, I will prove who I am. I will prove that I'm worthy of—"

"Forgiveness," Jehovah said, His expression a mixture of surprise and knowing. "It was always there, Rey'azikeen, waiting. I knew you'd take it when you were ready."

He glanced back at me, the grin on his face turning playful. "Call me Reyes."

Jehovah nodded and disappeared without another word.

I just wanted to be closer to my husband and daughter, so I picked my way through angel wings and hellhounds and swords, scooting the latter to the side as I walked through the statues, still at the ready.

"Careful," Reyes said. "An angel's sword is very powerful."

I grinned. "So is my husband."

Humor shone brightly in his dark irises. "Perhaps you could call them off?"

With hardly a thought, they vanished. A split second before they disappeared, Michael turned to me and nodded, confirming that we were good. Then he was gone. They were all gone, except Mr. Wong.

I turned to him. "Thank you."

He performed a deep, reverent bow, then disappeared into a sea of shimmering light. Dude was so cool.

I turned back and wrapped my arms around my husband and daughter.

"I needed you to trust me," Reyes said. "In all my incarnations. And I needed her safe."

I looked down at the bundle in his hands. At her rosy cheeks and pink mouth.

"For what is to come," he added.

"And what is that?"

"A demon horde."

I lifted a brow. "Yours?"

He lowered his head in shame. "Yes. When I created the god glass and the hell within, I created hundreds of thousands of guards. Wraith demons. Depraved. Bloodthirsty."

"Because what's a hell without a few thousand goblins?" I asked, teasing him.

"They felt me awaken. I had to find her to keep her safe, but a part of me couldn't let that happen. Couldn't let me find her, just in case."

"Reyes."

He nodded. "It's an odd feeling, not trusting oneself."

"I'm certain it is. The way I see it, if we can get through the last few days as unscathed as we have, we can get through anything as long as we're together."

"I apologize for the deception."

I looked at our beautiful daughter. "You could have told me earlier."

"I had to prove this to you. To prove I could be trusted."

"Maybe you needed to prove it to yourself even more."

"Perhaps. We'll need that when the time comes. That bond. That unconditional trust."

"Which will be when?"

He glanced at an imaginary watch on his wrist. "Any second now." He looked down at me, his expression grave. "I fear the end is nigh."

I sighed aloud. "If it's not one nigh, it's another."

"So," he said, playing with a tiny dark curl on the top of Beep's head, "the center of the sun?"

"Right. About that—"

Before I could explain where that little nugget had originated from and ask him if Reyes had placed it in my dreams, Mrs. Loehr walked into the room. "Charley?"

"Oops. Hold up, Mrs. Loehr." I slipped off the loungers Garrett had given me, the T-shirt plenty long enough to cover my most valuable assets, and bent at Reyes's feet. He stepped in the legs and I slid them up and tied them at his waist.

We gazed at our daughter a good while longer, then handed her back to Mrs. Loehr, who was confused but thankful.

When we showed up at Garrett's, he was ready for us. Or, ready for Rey'azikeen. Kind of. He raised a gun the moment we appeared, aiming the barrel at Reyes's heart. Not that it would have done any good, but it's the thought that counts.

"It's okay, Swopes," I said, raising my hands in surrender. "He's Reyes again. And Rey'aziel, and Rey'azikeen. But he's just going by Reyes for now."

Reyes, who was standing in Garrett's loungers, cleared his throat and had the presence of mind to look repentant.

"Reyes," I said, "is there anything you want to say to Garrett?"

Reyes lifted a shoulder. "Sorry I killed you. Repeatedly."

"Garrett," I said, turning my admonishing attention to the most understanding guy on planet Earth, "is there anything you want to say to Reyes?"

Before I could stop him, Garrett dropped the gun into his left hand and swung, his large fist making contact with Reyes's jaw. The sound was awful, a hard, crunchy sound, and I didn't know what was hurt worse, Reyes's jaw or Garrett's fist.

But, being manly men, neither of them gave up the game. Neither showed weakness. They stood for an hour, give or take fifty-five minutes, glaring at each other nose to nose, before Garrett asked, "Beer?"

Reyes gave a single, solitary nod, then all was right with the world. In an instant, the plane had righted itself.

I sat in Reyes's lap at the table as we explained everything that happened at the chapel, including how Reyes ended up with Garrett's pajama bottoms.

Pari sat enthralled, and Garrett took it remarkably well, mostly because he was astounded by the whole center-of-the-sun thing. I had to repeat that story three times, a little astounded myself.

But our regaling had to be cut short when Garrett's date, the one he forgot to cancel, showed up with lasagna and breadsticks. Zoe from Hope Christian Academy. Garrett made the introductions all around, but when he got to Pari, the look that passed between the two women could only be described as thunderstruck.

With an arm wrapped around my husband's neck, I looked into his eyes and said, "So, the dark, whooshy things in our apartment, that wasn't you swooshing around, was it?"

He shook his head. "The wraith demons. Our apartment is ground zero. The hell dimension is expanding exponentially, and it'll take over this world if we don't stop it. This entire dimension."

"You didn't think of that before you shattered the god glass inside our humble abode?"

A sexy grin lifted one corner of his mouth. "Sorry."

"Don't ever leave me like that again." I wrapped my hands around his throat and pretended to choke him. "Promise."

His gaze dropped to my mouth and lingered there as he said, "You first."

Just as I was about to kiss the man I'd loved, quite literally, for millennia, my phone rang in my bag. I dug it out as Pari insisted on helping Zoe with plates and flatware. Poor Garrett. Still, served him right. He needed to set things straight with the mother of his child.

I checked the phone. It was Cookie, and I silently chastised myself for not calling her sooner.

"Hey, Cook. We're all alive. I meant to call—"

"Ch-Charley?"

The sound of Cookie's voice straightened my shoulders. "Cook, what's wrong?"

"Charley, something . . . something happened. She . . ." The phone went silent for a moment before Cookie broke down, sobbing into the phone.

I shot out of Reyes's lap. Dread dumped adrenaline into my system by the bucketsful. "Cookie, what happened? Where are you?"

"What's going on?" Garrett asked.

"The school," Cookie said, her voice cracking. "She's here. I thought she was at her school in Albuquerque."

Reyes stood and listened beside me.

"Which school? Is it Amber? Cookie, did something happen to Amber?"

"The—the School for the Deaf."

With hardly a thought about Zoe and what this would do to her, I dematerialized instantly and rematerialized at the New Mexico School for the Deaf in Santa Fe. Emergency vehicles of all shapes and sizes swam around me. Lights glared into the darkness. Kids and adults stood around a border the emergency crews had set up. I followed the flashing lights to the parking lot beside the gym.

I walked forward, the world not quite moving right. Everything was too harsh. Too acrid. Voices were muffled as though they were all underwater, and yet they were too loud, assaulting my senses and making me dizzy.

Glancing to the side, I saw Uncle Bob holding Cookie in his arms as she sobbed. She fought him a moment, trying to wrench free, and I got the impression she'd been doing that off and on for a while now. His expression grave, he tightened his hold, then nodded at an EMT.

The young technician administered a shot as Cookie wailed into Uncle Bob's chest.

Another crowd, smaller, was huddled around a kid on the ground. A blond boy about sixteen sat on his knees, doubled over with his arms wrapped around his head.

Quentin.

A couple of girls sat beside him, rubbing his back as a cop tried to talk to him through an interpreter. But he was beyond talking. He rocked back and forth from his knees to his arms, cradling his head, so distraught he'd vomited onto the pavement.

Then he saw me. No, he felt me. He looked up and watched as I walked toward a tarp-covered body on the ground, his expression full of remorse. And anguish. And grief.

Normally, I wouldn't have been able to get close to the body lying in the center of the parking lot, but I'd shifted and straddled both planes. If anyone tried to stop me, and they did try to stop me, their arms went right through my only half-corporeal body. They would gape at me, too shocked to try it again, until the next officer rushed forward and gave it a shot.

I felt Reyes at my back as I walked, not quite sure my feet were on the ground. I felt his emotions. As astonished and grief-stricken as my own.

"Charley?"

I turned to Cookie. She'd spotted me and tried, once again, to wrench free from her husband.

Uncle Bob's expression crushed my heart. While Cookie's blossomed into one of hope, his was far less optimistic. He lowered his gaze in resignation.

I knelt beside the body and pulled back the tarp to see Amber's precious face, her mouth bruised and swollen, her huge blue eyes open, looking toward heaven like she now knew what so many others did not.

Then I caught sight of her from the corner of my eye. The assistant coach who'd threatened the kids. She stood in a group of teachers talking softly in the distance.

I started to stand, to walk over and snap her neck, but Quentin had somehow gotten past the perimeter guards as well. He stood over me, his chest heaving with emotion.

I sank back down and looked up at him, waiting for an explanation, but his eyes were locked onto the girl he loved, his face wet with tears and blood. After an eternity, he spoke.

"I tried to stop him," he said, his signs listless, barely readable. He was in shock. "A man. A priest. I tried to stop him. He grabbed her, seemed to beg her for help, but she couldn't understand him. So he hit her. Again and again as fire came up out of the ground. It tried to pull him under. I kicked him and hit him to get him off her, but he just—" He sank to his knees beside me. "He just disappeared."

No. I shook my head. I'd stopped him. I summoned him and—

"Two hours," Cookie said, sobbing on my other side. I blinked at her. Uncle Bob had flashed his badge and escorted her past the perimeter. "She'd been gone for two hours before we got here. Beaten and burned. Same as the others." She broke down again.

The priest must have been in the middle of attacking her when I'd summoned him.

"Five minutes earlier," I said, my voice soft with disbelief. "If I'd been five minutes earlier. If I hadn't gone to the warehouses. If I'd summoned him the second I learned his name."

I hadn't even thought of Amber when compiling my list of potential victims. She'd showed signs of clairvoyance, but I'd never even considered her a candidate. She didn't see the departed like Quentin or even Pari. She had never been a part of that world. Not in that way.

"Why were they here so late?" I asked Cookie.

"Basketball game," Uncle Bob answered for her. "Playoffs."

My lungs filled with cement and I could barely see past the wetness in my eyes. But it was Cookie's anguish that broke me. Her excruciating agony that made my decision.

Michael appeared as though the archangel monitored my every thought. He pinned me with a warning glower.

I turned back to Reyes, to my beautiful husband whom I'd fought so hard for these past days, and whispered, "I'll find a way back. I promise."

Instantly registering where my thoughts had landed, he lunged forward, but before he could grab me, before he could stop me, I laid my fingers across Amber's pale cheek. Her lids fluttered, and a soft pink hue blossomed across her face. She filled her lungs with air a microsecond before the world fell away from me.

The last thing I felt before completely disappearing into the ether was the heat, the blinding heat, of Reyes's incomprehensible fury as I was cast into a lightless realm.

piatkus